WOLF CREEK HOMECOMING

This Large Print Book carries the
Seal of Approval of N.A.V.H.

WOLF CREEK HOMECOMING

PENNY RICHARDS

THORNDIKE PRESS
A part of Gale, Cengage Learning

GALE
CENGAGE Learning

Farmington Hills, Mich • San Francisco • New York • Waterville, Maine
Meriden, Conn • Mason, Ohio • Chicago

LIBRARY OF CONGRESS CATALOGING-IN-PUBLICATION DATA

Richards, Penny.
    Wolf creek homecoming / Penny Richards.
      pages cm-(Thorndike press large print gentle romance)
    ISBN 978-1-4104-7170-3 (hardcover) — ISBN 1-4104-7170-5 (hardcover)
    1. Men—Conduct of life—Fiction. 2. Forgiveness—Fiction. 3. Arkansas—Social life and Customs—19th century—Fiction. 4. Large type books. I. Title.
    PS3618.I3437W65 2014
    813'.6—dc23   2014015753

Published in 2014 by arrangement with Harlequin Books S.A.

Printed in Mexico
1 2 3 4 5 6 7 18 17 16 15 14

For all have sinned and fall short of the glory of God, and are justified freely by his grace through the redemption that came by Christ Jesus.

— *Romans* 3:23–24

For LaRee and Sandy —
friends, confidantes, mentors,
brainstorming partners, critique group
and travelin' buds who listen, help,
inspire, set me straight and pick me up,
dust me off and tell me I can. Whoever
would have thought we'd be here when
we met at a writer's conference almost
thirty years ago?

PROLOGUE

St. Louis, 1877

"Hey there, Rachel Stone!"

Weighted down with loneliness and bone tired, Rachel was mounting the steps of her boardinghouse when she heard the greeting. The familiar, husky voice stopped her in her tracks and caused her heart to stumble. There was no way it could be who it sounded like, she thought, turning. But it was. Her mouth fell open in surprise.

Gabe Gentry, the handsome, younger Gentry son, was standing there. The same son who, if the rumors could be believed, had asked for his inheritance prior to his father's death and left their hometown of Wolf Creek two years ago. If the gossipmongers were correct, he was busily running through the funds, chasing every good time he could find.

But Rachel believed that gossip was just bits and pieces of the truth often distorted

9

and exaggerated as the tattletales passed the story around. She had a hard time believing he was as bad as everyone claimed, since her own experiences with him had been good ones.

He was attractive, friendly, fun loving and always pleasant, and she'd liked being around him. Of course, that might be because she had always had a bit of a "thing" for him, even though she was the elder by two years. Guilty or not, his reputation made him the kind of male who inhabited a young woman's daydreams, and the kind parents prayed would give their daughters a wide berth.

While she was woolgathering, he stopped less than two feet from her and reached out to tap her chin with a gentle finger. Her mouth snapped shut.

"Cat got your tongue?" he asked, favoring her with a mischievous half smile.

Rachel stared into his dark blue eyes, willing steadiness to her trembling voice. "Gabe?" she said at last. "What are you doing here, and how did you find me?" she asked, still trying to come to terms with the fact that the man who had been the subject of too many of her youthful fantasies was standing on her doorstep.

He laughed, thrusting his hands into the

pockets of his stylish trousers. "It really is a small world. Would you believe I ran into Buck Hargrove coming out of a restaurant last night? He's here on some sort of railroad business, and while we were catching up on what's been going on back home, he mentioned you were here studying to be a doctor. Since I don't see too many folks from home traveling around the way I do, I thought I'd look you up." He smiled, a rueful twist of his lips. "Never thought I'd admit it, but I'm a little homesick for Wolf Creek."

"You could go back for a visit sometime, you know."

Was it her imagination, or did a shadow cross his attractive face? "Yeah," he said with a bright smile. "Maybe I'll do that."

He seemed uncomfortable for a moment then rallied. "So are you really going to be a doctor?"

"That's the plan."

"That's unbelievable."

"Why is it unbelievable? I thought everyone knew I wanted to follow in my father's footsteps."

"Yeah, but saying something like that and actually doing it . . . Maybe it's so incredible because everyone thinks of medicine as a man's line of work."

She loved talking about her chosen field but felt strange trying to justify her decision standing in front of her rented rooms. "Would you like to come inside? Mrs. Abernathy usually has lemonade made, and I don't think she'll object if we sit in the parlor awhile."

He looked indecisive for just a second, but then smiled and said, "I'd like that very much."

Inside, Rachel fetched the beverage and some cookies, and they sat in the shabby parlor. Gabe looked out of place in his fine, tailor-made clothing, sitting among her landlady's simple, worn furnishings.

Settled in a threadbare armchair, a glass of lemonade in hand, she asked, "Where were we?"

"You were about to tell me the woes of women entering medicine."

"Oh, yes. The annoying part is the arrogance of the male students and even some of the professors. They make no secret that they think it's utter folly for a woman to even think of entering their elite ranks."

Her face took on a pompous expression. "Women are not mentally equipped to grasp the intricacies of the circulatory, lymphatic and muscular systems and they are *far* too delicate to deal with the sight of blood and

12

innards," she intoned.

Gabe threw back his head and roared with laughter. "They actually said that?" he asked when he'd regained his composure.

"Among other things."

"And how are you doing with the blood and guts?"

"Actually very well. I have yet to faint at anything we've dealt with in the lab, which not all of them can say."

"They don't know you grew up around that sort of thing. I remember that you rescued every injured critter you came across."

He remembered that? So did she. One time in particular came to mind. She'd been around fourteen and Gabe had helped carry home a dog that Luther Thomerson had beaten with his buggy whip.

"So tell me your plans," he urged, leaning forward and resting his elbows on his knees. All of his attention was focused on her. "Will you set up practice here in St. Louis?"

"Oh, no! I'd never be happy in a place so big and impersonal. I intend to help my father."

"And waste your skills on folks who probably can't pay for them?" he scoffed. "You could make a lot of money in a big city."

"There's more to life than money," she

told him, her expression earnest. "Those people need medical attention, too. My father gets a great deal of satisfaction helping those who need it."

"You can't live on satisfaction."

Her passionate gaze sought his. "Perhaps not, but if we put God first, He'll see to it we have what we need. I know it's a cliché, but money really can't buy happiness." She placed a palm against her chest. "That comes from inside us. From knowing who we are, and what we stand for."

"You really believe that, don't you?" he said, his eyes filled with wonder.

"I know it's true."

He laughed again. "Well, money may not buy happiness," he quipped, clearly uncomfortable, "but it certainly does a fine job of mimicking it." He pulled the gold watch from his pocket. "I should be going. I don't want to wear out my welcome."

"Of course." She stood, clasping her hands together, both sorry and relieved that he was going. As wonderful as it was to see him, he made her very uncomfortable. Rising, he set his glass on a nearby table. She followed him to the door and opened it, realizing that when he left he wouldn't be back.

They stepped out onto the stoop, and Rachel extended her hand. His fingers curled warmly, excitingly around hers. Urging a smile, she said, "Thank you for stopping by. Like you, I miss seeing people from home."

"I've enjoyed it, too." He turned to go, but at the top of the steps, he came back, his eyes filled with indecision. "Would you like to have dinner tomorrow evening?"

For a heartbeat, Rachel wasn't certain she'd heard correctly. She knew she should say no, but for the life of her could not bring to mind a good reason why. It was doubtless that she would see him after tomorrow, and she would at least have one brilliant memory to see her through the lonely months ahead. "I'd love to."

He looked pleased, relieved. "About seven?"

"Fine."

Before she realized what he meant to do, he brushed a kiss to her cheek and then ran lightly down the steps. Stunned by the unexpected gesture, she reached up and touched the place with her fingertips, wondering what it would be like to feel his lips touch hers.

CHAPTER ONE

Wolf Creek, Arkansas, 1886

Rachel stepped inside the medical office that was situated in the rear of the house she'd shared with her father and son since receiving her medical degree.

The rush of warm air from the fireplace was welcome after a cold drive in from the country. In a capricious mood, Mother Nature had dumped more than a foot of snow the night before, something rare in the southwestern part of the state.

She'd just come from the Gentry farm, where she had given Abby Gentry and her newborn son, Eli, a thorough examination. Baby Eli had been so eager to enter the world, there had been no time for his father to fetch help, forcing Caleb to help birth his son. Thankfully, mother and baby had come through the delivery with flying colors. Father was fine, too, but still a little shaky.

Breathing a weary sigh of satisfaction, Rachel set her medical bag on a nearby table and placed the quilt she'd used for added warmth on the seat of a straight-backed chair. She unwound the scarf from around her head and neck and shrugged out of her coat. Tossing them both over the back of the chair, she headed for the kitchen, where her son, Danny, and her father sat at the table near a rip-roaring fire, playing Chinese checkers.

"How are Abby and the baby?" Edward asked, with a smile of welcome.

"Just dandy," Rachel assured him as she leaned down to give her son a welcoming hug. She was about to launch into the story of Caleb delivering the baby when a loud pounding came from the direction of her office. She gave a little groan. "I should have known better than to think I could spend the rest of the day baking cookies for Santa."

"It's part of the job," Edward called as she retraced her steps to the office.

Danny, who followed her out of curiosity, pushed aside the lace curtains and peered out the window. "It's Mr. Teasdale!" he cried, recognizing the peddler's wagon. He brushed past Rachel to the door.

No doubt Simon was making a final tour of customers before Christmas to make sure they had everything they needed for the holiday. She wondered why he had come to the office entrance instead of the front and stood back while Danny flung open the door. Simon, whose fist was raised for another round of pounding, jumped.

"Simon," she said, seeing the panic in his eyes, "what is it?"

"Oh, Doc," he squeaked, his high-pitched voice quavering with emotion, "I was coming in from Antoine when I come upon this fella by the side of the road. His wallet was a few feet away, and it was empty. Looked like he'd been beat within an inch of his life. I was afraid to move him, but I wasn't sure how long he'd been there, and I was more scared he'd freeze to death if I came to town for help, so I loaded him up." The words tripped over themselves in their hurry to get out.

With no knowledge of how badly the victim was hurt, Rachel could only hope that Simon hadn't done any additional damage by moving him.

"You did right, Simon," she said, putting on her coat and following him to the back of the cart.

"Run get Roland," she told Danny, who lost no time hurrying toward a small house down the way.

"I like to have never got him in the

wagon," Simon was saying. "And it took me more than two hours to get here. My Addie Sue is plumb wore down slogging through all that snow." He unlatched the rear door and threw it open.

The man lay in the makeshift bed where Simon slept when it was impossible to make the next town at day's end. The shadowy interior made it difficult to tell anything about the stranger except that he was big and tall.

"I'll get the stretcher while we're waiting for Danny," she said.

In a matter of moments, Danny was back with Roland, the brawny teen who helped Rachel whenever and however she needed. "Let's see if we can get him inside, so I can take a look at him."

Working together, they carefully transferred the injured man onto the gurney and into the morning sunlight, where Rachel gave the stranger a quick once-over. Young. Strong. Bloody knuckles. He'd fought back. Good.

Her gaze moved to his face, and it suddenly became impossible to draw in a decent lungful of air. Every molecule of oxygen seemed to have been sucked into a vast void somewhere. Her head began to spin, and her heart began to race.

Despite the multiple bruises and the swelling and the blood still seeping from the jagged cut angling from his forehead through his left eyebrow and across his temple to just below his ear, and despite the fact that she had not seen him in more than nine years, she had no problem recognizing him.

It was none other than Gabe Gentry. Simon squeaked out his name in a shocked voice.

Gabe. As handsome as ever. She had traced those heavy brows and the bow of his top lip with her fingertips. She had felt the rasp of his whiskers against her cheek. Had . . .

Stop it!

Common sense returned, and a rush of fury and self-loathing banished the beguiling memories that jeopardized her hard-won detachment. Rachel's jaw tightened and she felt the bite of her fingernails into her palms. She would have liked nothing more than to load Gabriel Gentry back into Simon's wagon and order him to take the blackguard elsewhere, but she had taken an oath to heal, and as wretched as this man was, she was bound by her promise as a physician to do her best by him.

More to the point, and her consternation,

it was her God-given duty as a Christian to do so.

Once she and Roland had transferred Gabe to the examination table, Simon said his goodbyes and went to see that his horse got a generous ration of oats while he went to Ellie's café to see about getting some hot food in his belly. Roland stayed to help move Gabe to a proper bed after Rachel finished tending him.

She was alone with her patient when her father rolled his wheelchair into the room. The fact that he was using it, instead of the two canes he used to get around since the stroke, told her he'd done too much during the day.

"Good grief!" Edward murmured, rolling closer. "Unless I'm mistaken, that's Gabe Gentry."

"It is," she said, pleased that her anger was manifested by nothing but the brusque reply.

"Do you need any help?" Edward asked.

"I will in a moment," she told him.

Wielding the scissors with a rough carelessness, she cut away Gabe's expensive coat and shirt. Deep purple bruises covered his chest. Her fingers began a gentle probing.

"Ouch!" Edward said, leaning in for a better look. "That's going to be painful when

22

he wakes up. Any broken ribs?"

"Two, at least," she said, finishing her careful examination of his torso. "And his left arm, obviously." Both of Gabe's eyes were black. His perfect, straight nose was broken. When the dirt and blood were washed away, she straightened his nose and taped it into place.

"Who would do something like this to another human?"

"From what I've heard about his escapades since he left here, I imagine he's made his share of enemies," Rachel observed, as she began to cut away his trousers to check his lower body for injuries. They were minimal, just several nasty bruises.

"Boots?" Edward asked.

"I'd say so," she concurred, thoughtfully. "That's probably how the ribs were broken. He'll spend a miserable few weeks," she stated and felt a sudden rush of shame for the jolt of satisfaction that accompanied the thought. Her father's puzzled expression told her that he, too, was wondering at the root of her animosity. Well, let him wonder. She had no intention of enlightening him. Not now. Not ever.

"Was he robbed?" Edward asked.

"Apparently. Simon said his empty wallet was lying a few feet from him."

"Wasn't there another robbery near Antoine a couple of months ago?"

"Yes," she said, pulling a sheet over his lower body. "Can you reach the bandages?"

"Sure."

"I'll lift him upright if you can stand long enough to wrap him up."

"I can," Edward said, and they proceeded to bind the broken ribs.

"Do you think it was the same bunch, since Sheriff Garrett never caught the culprits?" he asked, as he tied off the ends of the bandage.

"Probably."

"Do you need any help with the arm?"

"I can get it, thanks." She splinted the arm and then poured a basin of water and began to wash the congealed blood from the gash on his face. It would leave an ugly scar.

"He's going to need stitches," she noted, staring dispassionately at the jagged wound, possibly made with a knife.

And how will your lady friends like that? I wonder.

Her teeth clamped down on her lower lip, and shame again swept through her at her uncharacteristic spitefulness. She felt angry and sick to her stomach and oddly depleted.

"Too bad," Edward said. "He's always been such a good-looking guy."

Gabe was starting to move around by the time she finished stitching him up, so she gave him a draft of laudanum to help him sleep. Once she finished treating him, she and Roland settled Gabe in the downstairs bedroom she reserved for the occasional overnight patient.

"Do you know him?" Roland asked.

"It's Gabe Gentry," she said, pulling the quilts up to his chin.

"I sort of remember him from when I was a little kid. Didn't he take off to see the world several years ago?"

"Yes."

"I heard he made a name for himself with the ladies," Roland said with a sly smile.

"So they say."

Not really wanting to talk about Gabe's past, whatever it might or might not include, she thanked Roland, paid him for his time and wished him a merry Christmas.

She was cleaning up the examination room when her father rolled to the doorway, where he sat watching her with an unreadable expression in his eyes. "Did I miss anything?"

"You did a splendid job, Rachel. You should know by now that you're a fine doctor, and I'm very proud of you."

Proud of her. She turned away so he

25

wouldn't see the tears that sprang into her eyes. How could he be proud of her after the humiliation and disgrace she'd brought to him and to the family name?

"Thank you," she murmured, knowing she had to reply. With her emotions and her features under control, she said, "He should sleep for a while. If you don't mind keeping an eye on him for an hour or so, I think I'll try to do the same."

Edward nodded. "If he needs you, I'll call."

"He won't," she retorted. "People like him don't need anyone."

Lying in her tousled bed, her forearm covering her eyes in a futile attempt to block the memories sweeping over her, Rachel gave a soft groan of anguish. She hadn't expected to see Gabe in Simon's wagon.

Indeed, since he hadn't been back to Wolf Creek since leaving, she'd begun to think she'd never again set eyes on him. Being confronted with his very real presence had rekindled the feelings she'd experienced when he'd walked away from her without a second thought.

Shame suffused her. Because she'd been fool enough to discount the stories she'd heard about him, because he'd been sweet

26

and made her laugh, and *listened* to her, she had made the biggest mistake of her life.

She was a self-sufficient woman who had gone alone to a big city and challenged tradition by daring to go into in a field dominated by men. She came from a loving home and had a solid Christian background. She should have known better than to let him into her heart, but she had been so lonely and homesick, and he brought back memories of easier, happier times. He made her feel smart and special and important.

She'd fallen in love with him. Believing that he loved her in return, she had indulged in her forbidden longings and given him everything his kisses demanded.

Three weeks later, he'd left her with nothing but a note for goodbye, a bleeding, aching heart and three weeks of memories that seemed sordid in light of his defection. She had faced the truth: Gabe Gentry was everything the gossips said he was and more. A liar, a cheat and a womanizer. Oh, certainly he was fun, friendly and he *listened.* And he used each and every one of those traits she'd been so enamored of against her. Sheltered and innocent, she hadn't stood a chance. He'd worked at breaching her defenses until she'd given up and given in.

Like Eve, she'd been lured from the straight path. Overnight, Gabe went from being funny and charming to a handsome rogue endowed with more skill and cunning than any man she'd ever met.

She'd found out the hard way the lessons her parents had tried to instill in her. Sin was so tempting because it came wrapped in such an attractive, alluring package, all tied up with the subtle lie that it was not wrong, that it was all right . . . really.

Realizing how easily he'd deceived her set her to crying so hard and heavily she'd feared the tears would never stop. Eventually anger replaced her sorrow, anger that burned so hotly that it dried her tears. Anger at Gabe. Anger at herself.

She'd moved through the days, more alone and miserable than before, barely able to concentrate on her schooling. Unable to eat, she'd grown so thin and hollow-eyed that Mrs. Abernathy had urged her to see a physician.

"I regret to inform you that you're expecting a child, Miss Stone," the doctor had said, peering at her over the tops of his spectacles. He didn't bother hiding his disapproval.

Rachel felt her heart plummet. Her already queasy stomach churned. Having a baby? Impossible! Having a baby was supposed to be a joyous occasion, not something that just . . . happened. And not to unmarried women. Babies were supposed to be the result of . . . of love.

She must have spoken, because the doctor stood.

"All I can tell you, Miss Stone, is that you are not the first young lady foolish enough to believe a man's lies. I can just hope that you are not so imprudent as to make the mistake a second time."

"B-but what am I going to do? My family . . ." She paused and swallowed hard.

"Will be devastated, I'm sure," he'd told her, offering her not one iota of help or comfort. "Now, you should try to get as much rest as possible, and eat three healthy meals a day."

She thought she might upchuck at the idea of eating three meals a day. "But I'm so sick, I can't hold anything down."

"Tut-tut!" he'd said, looking at her as if she were a strange organism under a microscope's lens. "My wife was never sick a day during her confinements. I can assure you that you will not rid yourself of this child by vomiting it up. I strongly suggest that you accept your situation and start preparing

29

for some significant changes to your life."

She'd left his office vacillating between despair and fury. The man's bedside manner was nonexistent! He was so uncaring he had no right to hang out his shingle. He was right about one thing, though. She had been very foolish. She'd thrown away her good name, turned her back on a lifetime of teaching and jeopardized her soul. All for three weeks of feeling cherished and loved by a man who'd lied to her about his feelings. Lied to her about everything.

A baby was to be her punishment for loving him.

Ever practical, she supposed it was no more than she deserved. Well, so be it. She pushed aside the panic nibbling at the edges of her composure. Despite her lapses in judgment, she was smart and possessed plenty of grit. She was handling medical school, and she could handle this, too — somehow.

She sat down with pen and paper and considered her options. The doctor had been right when he'd said her parents would be devastated and ashamed of her actions if they found out what she'd done, so she would take measures to see that they didn't find out. That meant returning to Wolf Creek or asking for help from them was out of the question. She couldn't afford to bring up a child and continue with her studies. The small allowance her father sent for her upkeep barely stretched from one month to the next.

Her only recourse was to have the child and put it up for adoption. Only then could she go home and try to put the whole thing behind her. The next months would be torture as she faced the stares and snide smirks she knew she'd receive from her fellow classmates, but it still seemed her best option.

She soon learned that life seldom went as planned. She was in the final month of her pregnancy when Sarah VanSickle, the biggest gossip in Pike County, happened to be visiting her sister in St. Louis and decided to pay Rachel an impromptu visit.

Rachel could still picture the jubilation in Sarah's eyes as she'd swept her up and down with a knowing eye. The loathsome woman had wasted no time scurrying home to recount the news to not only Rachel's parents, but everyone else in town.

It was little wonder that she gave birth to a baby boy the very day her father arrived to confront her about the rumors. Seeing the anguish in his eyes, knowing how deeply she'd disappointed him, she vowed that no amount of persuasion could tempt her to tell him who had fathered her child.

Though he was heartbroken over her actions, Edward Stone was as stubborn as his daughter. From the moment the baby was born, he began to campaign for her to keep him.

After two days of reasoning that sometimes bordered on outright coercion, she'd agreed. She and the son she named Daniel had stayed in St. Louis until she received her medical degree, something made possible when Edward upped his monthly stipend and arranged for Mrs. Abernathy to keep Danny while Rachel was in class. Only then was she forced to summon the courage to go back home and face the music.

Since Sarah had blabbed the news all over town, there was no way Rachel could pretend she'd married while she was away, and even if that had been an option, she wouldn't have added lying to her sins. Instead, with her well-respected father at her side, she'd brazened out the whispers and cold shoulders with the same determination and dedication that had seen her through her schooling.

A week after arriving home, her mother died, and Rachel always felt at fault. A short time later, she'd found the courage to go back to church and seek God's forgiveness.

Since then, she had worked alongside her father trying to earn back the respect and goodwill of the towns-folk. When Edward suffered a stroke two years ago, she'd taken on the bulk of his practice. Though there were a few who still regarded her as a fallen woman, for the most part she'd been restored into the town's good graces.

To this day no one — not even her father — knew the identity of Danny's father.

Now that man lay in her downstairs bedroom and there was nowhere to run from her past. She'd always believed God had a plan, that things happened for a reason and that He was in control. When Gabe had walked out on her after taking her innocence, she'd wondered what the Lord could possibly have been thinking by bringing them together. Now she wondered what on earth He could possibly have in mind by doing it again.

That afternoon, still weary and upset, Rachel decided that since sickness and accidents seemed to be taking a holiday, she would take her mind off of what she'd begun to think of as the *situation* and bake oatmeal cookies with Danny.

She knew she should drive out and tell

Caleb his brother was back and seriously injured, but she didn't want to talk about Gabe Gentry, didn't want to waste one single moment even thinking about him. Therein lay the problem. All she'd done since she'd recognized him on the gurney was think about him.

She was reaching for a tea towel to take a batch of cookies from the oven when Danny asked, "Do you know that man, Mama?"

Rachel paused, halfway to the stove. *Take a deep breath and answer him.* After all, he was only exhibiting the natural curiosity of an eight-year-old.

"I knew him a long time ago," she said, choosing her words with care. "But not very well, it seems." It was the truth, after all.

"Pops said he's Mr. Gentry's younger brother."

"That's right." One by one she lifted the hot cookies onto a stoneware platter with the egg turner. Mercifully, before Danny could ask another question, she heard someone knocking. Her father was dozing in his favorite chair, so there was no need to stop. He'd answer the door.

She heard the rumble of masculine voices, and in a matter of minutes Caleb entered the kitchen. "Caleb!" she said, surprised to see him.

"Edward told me it's true," he said, twisting his hat in his big work-roughened hands. His unusual silvery eyes were a dark, stormy gray.

"Yes." Rachel gestured toward a chair at the table. "Have a seat. I'm sorry I didn't come out and tell you, but it was a long morning, and I took a little rest."

"No need," Caleb said, stepping farther into the room but refusing to sit down. "Between Simon and Roland, the Wolf Creek grapevine is in prime working order. Sarah drove out about noon on the pretext of wanting to be the first to see Eli. Of course, she couldn't wait to tell me the news."

"After the way she slandered you and Abby, I can't believe that woman would have the gall to even look you in the eye," Rachel said with a bitter twist of her lips.

Caleb's smile mimicked hers. "I warned her last year not to ever step foot on the place again, but I guess she decided facing my anger was a fair trade for the pleasure of being the first to tell me about Gabe. How bad is he?"

"Bad enough." Rachel listed his injuries and Caleb winced.

"Can I see him?"

"Of course. I should check on him anyway.

35

I've given him some laudanum, so he's unconscious. It's best if I keep him that way for a day or two, until he's past the worst of the pain," she said, preceding Caleb into the bedroom.

As he approached the bed, Rachel heard him draw in a sharp breath. He swallowed hard and looked up at her with an expression of horror. "His face . . ."

She nodded. "Whoever did this to him intended for him to remember it."

Never one to show emotion, Caleb's response was to turn and walk out of the room. In the hall, he hesitated, almost as if he wanted to say something and didn't know how . . . or what.

"Would you like a cup of coffee and some cookies?" Rachel asked in a gentle voice. "They're straight from the oven."

"That would be nice," he said. He followed her into the kitchen, where Edward was plopping out spoons full of dough, and pulled out a chair.

Rachel sent her father a silent message and Edward said, "Come on, Danny. It's warmed up some, so let's go outside awhile. I'll sit on the porch while you make a snowman."

Since he'd been begging to go out all day, Danny gave a shout of joy and bounded from the room.

"Bundle up!" Edward shouted to his retreating back, turning his chair and following.

When they were gone, Caleb said simply, "Thank you."

Rachel sat down across from him. "You wanted to tell me something?"

He took a swallow of coffee. "I don't know what I want. When I first heard Gabe was back, I intended to come here and give him a piece of my mind for walking out all those years ago and never once contacting us. That was before I saw how bad he is."

He swallowed hard. A smart, self-educated man known for his toughness and an unyielding attitude, Caleb had softened a lot since marrying Abby Carter.

"Now I don't know how I feel or what to say to him," he confessed, rubbing a hand down his cheek. "Seeing him like that caught me off guard." He gave another half-hearted smile. "It's hard to summon up a lot of anger when someone is lying there battered and bleeding and can't defend himself."

She gave a half shrug. "True, I suppose, but there's absolutely no excuse for him to not contact you all these years," Rachel said before she could temper her tongue.

Caleb frowned at her animosity.

Realizing she'd let too much of her antagonism show, she took a calming breath. "You never really got along, did you?"

"No." He ran his hand through his shaggy hair. "Well, that's not exactly true. Actually, we never had much to do with each other. He was four years younger than me, and I was always expected to toe the line, get the work done. Lucas mostly let Gabe go his own way, so he never did much of anything that resembled work. When he asked for his inheritance, Lucas just up and gave it to him, and I was left to deal with everything here."

"It must have seemed very unfair."

Caleb's short bark of laughter lacked true mirth. "In more ways than you can imagine. I guess it's pretty obvious that Gabe was always the handsome one, the charming one, the one who could make everyone laugh. I was the drudge, the sensible one, the serious brother. Right or wrong, I always resented him for it."

Caleb pinned her with a hard look. "Maybe I still do. It will be interesting to hear what kind of story he spins when he wakes up. I can't imagine anything he could possibly say to make me feel different toward him, so he needn't expect me to welcome him with open arms. In fact, once he gets better, I won't mind seeing him leave town."

It was quite a speech for the taciturn farmer. Knowing the feelings of her own heart, Rachel kept quiet.

Caleb lifted his gaze to hers. "I know the Bible says I should forgive him and let go of the past, but I don't mind telling you I'm having a real hard time with this."

Rachel offered him a wan smile. "Believe me," she said. "I understand better than you think."

That night, after checking on the patient, Rachel went into Danny's room and sat on the side of the bed. Sweet, innocent little man, she thought, brushing the dark, wavy, too-long hair away from his forehead. Until today, she'd never realized just how much he looked like Gabe, probably because she had taken such pains to bury her memories of him.

With him now beneath her roof, that was impossible. She could only hope and pray that he mended soon so that he could be on his way, preferably, as Caleb suggested, out of town. She didn't want Danny around Gabe any more than necessary.

Brushing her lips against her son's forehead, she rose and went to join her father in the parlor.

"Everyone okay?" he asked, looking up from his book and peering at her over the tops of the glasses that lent his attractively lined face a professorial look.

"Everyone's fine."

Edward laid aside his book, and Rachel sat on the end of the sofa. "What about you?" he asked.

"What do you mean?"

"Are you fine? You don't seem so," he said, tapping into his uncanny ability to see things beyond the surface. "You've been jumpy all day, and angry and . . . oh, I don't know, maybe even sad. Would you like to tell me why?"

She crossed her arms across her chest. "No."

"Well, then," he said, "do you mind if I hazard a guess?"

Rachel gave him a narrow-eyed look. "Guess away," she said with a nonchalance that did a reasonable job of masking her apprehension.

Edward tented his fingertips and regarded her for a few long seconds. She felt as if he could see into her very heart and soul, and that all the secrets she'd held so close were about to be exposed. He was no fool.

Perception and spot-on intuition were two of Edward Stone's greatest assets.

"In all your thirty-one years, I've never seen you the way you've been today. I've tried and tried to figure out what's behind this hostility you have toward Gabe, especially since you never had much truck with him before he left town."

"And have you come up with a reason?" she asked in a voice that, like her hands, trembled the slightest bit.

"I have."

"And?" she asked, regarding him with a steady expression.

"The only thing that makes a woman act the way you have today is rejection. You know, the old 'Hell hath no fury like a woman scorned.' " He looked her squarely in the eye. "I believe Gabe Gentry looked you up when you were in St. Louis. I believe he's Danny's father."

An anguished cry escaped Rachel. How could he have figured it out just from her attitude? She felt a sob claw its way up her throat and pressed a fist to her mouth to hold it back.

"Oh, my dear!" Edward said in a tortured voice, rolling his chair over to her and putting a consoling hand on her shoulder. "How hard it must have been for you to keep that secret all this time."

"I would never have told you," she said as tears slipped down her cheeks. "Never."

"I know that, you hard-headed, silly girl. Would you like to tell me about it? The abridged version, of course," he asked with an awkward attempt at a smile.

Why not? Rachel thought. Perhaps if she told him how it had happened and how she'd felt, it would release some of the guilt and misery that had made her prickly and skeptical and robbed her of so much joy through the years.

"There isn't much to tell," she said almost thoughtfully. She told him how she'd come home from school and found Gabe at her boardinghouse. "I was so lonely and homesick, and it was so good to see a familiar face . . ." Her voice trailed away. "I invited him in and we had lemonade.

"As he was leaving, he asked me to dinner the next night and we spent every day together after I got home from school," she said, allowing long-suppressed memories their freedom. "He brought me flowers from a street vendor, took me out to eat at fancy restaurants, bought me trinkets and told me all sorts of wonderful, fantastic stories of the places he'd been and hoped to go."

Her tears ran freely as the memories

continued to tumble out. "He teased me, and it was —" she gave a huge hiccuping sob "— so nice to laugh. Every evening, he insisted I tell him about what I'd done and what I'd learned. He was just so encouraging, both about my studies and . . . just everything. I told him all about my dearest hopes and dreams."

She took the handkerchief Edward offered, mopped at her eyes and blew her running nose.

"He made me believe that all of those hopes and dreams could come true. I fell in love with him," she said, summing everything up in those few words. "I'm sure you can figure out the rest."

"I think I understand," Edward said when she ran out of words. "Your upbringing gave you little or no defense. You had no idea how to guard your heart. So tell me why he left. Did you quarrel?"

Rachel shook her head. "Nothing like that. I thought things were going along just fine. And then I came home from school one day, and he'd left a note with Mrs. Abernathy that said a friend had caught up with him and talked him into taking a paddle wheeler to New Orleans. It was supposed to be great fun, and he'd always wanted to go there. He said the next time he was in town, he'd look me up and we'd go to dinner."

"That's it?" Edward said, with a look of disbelief.

"Oh, no. He said it had been a fun few weeks and that he'd never forget me."

She laughed, but there was no joy in the sound. "I was so ashamed," she said in an anguished whisper. "I'd ruined my whole life. That was bad enough, but when I found out I was going to have a baby, I was terrified. I thought I'd figured out a way that no one would ever find out. Then Sarah showed up and sent all my plans tumbling down."

Tears spilled down Rachel's cheeks. "I know bearing my shame was hard for you and Mother, especially after I came home, and I know my actions are what brought on her death, but I want to thank you for never once throwing it back in my face and for . . . for making me . . . k-keep Danny." She choked on another sob.

Edward gave her hand an awkward pat. "Your mother had a heart condition, Rachel. Her health had been going downhill for more than a year. Her passing so soon after you came back was just an unfortunate coincidence. She loved you and she adored Danny."

He smiled. "And as for that young scamp, I hope I didn't *make* you do anything. I

44

hope I just encouraged you to do what you really wanted. I know you well, my precious girl, and I don't believe you'd have been able to live with yourself if you'd given him up. And selfishly, I couldn't bear the thought of strangers bringing up my flesh and blood — or worse, him being put into an orphanage and never knowing the joys of real family. He's a delight, Rachel. I can't imagine life without him."

"Neither can I."

"Besides," he added, "I've never been one to think that two wrongs make a right."

For long moments, the fire popped and crackled while Rachel worked at regaining her composure.

"What do you plan to do now?" Edward asked, at last.

"Do? About what?"

"Gabe. How do you feel about him after all this time?"

"Nothing," she snapped. "I plan to *do* nothing and I *feel* nothing but anger toward him. I hope and pray that he'll leave town again as soon as he's able, which will suit me just fine."

"And if he doesn't? It will certainly be a test, won't it? How long do you think it will take before he figures things out?"

Rachel's face drained of color. "What are

you saying?"

There was no compromise in Edward's eyes. "You need to tell Gabe the truth. Danny, too."

Her horrified gaze met his. "I can't!"

"Listen to me, Rachel. You need to tell Danny before someone else sees the resemblance and starts spreading it around town. Believe me, as hard as it may be, he'll be much better off hearing the truth from you than someone else. They both will."

CHAPTER TWO

Christmas Eve morning dawned crisp and cold. Just as dawn was breaking, Rachel rose from the cot beside Gabe's bed and lit the lamp.

He had rested well in his laudanum-induced sleep, but she had not been so blessed. Sleep had eluded her, as thoughts and recollections tumbled round and round in her mind like colorful fragments in a kaleidoscope. Besides a jumble of troubling memories, her mind replayed the conversation with her father again and again.

She couldn't believe how light her heart felt since sharing the secret she'd carried alone for so long. Who would have thought that something that seemed so small could weigh so heavily on a heart? She would be eternally grateful that her father's love and support had not wavered, even after learning the truth.

She knew Edward was right about telling

Danny about Gabe, yet the very thought of doing so filled her with dread. How would she find the words? What would Danny say . . . and think?

She stoked the dying fire and went to see how Gabe was doing, busying herself with changing his bandages and checking his temperature. Her ministering seemed to agitate him, and he began to move about. When she tried to restrain him, he cried out and opened his eyes. Thankfully she saw no recollection there, no wicked, teasing gleam, nothing but agony. The doctor in her wanted him to be pain free and improve under her care; the woman in her shrank from the moment he would open his eyes and look up at her with recognition.

What would he see when he awakened? What would he think when he saw her for the first time in nine years? She turned toward the mirror hanging above the washstand, drawn to it like a June bug to the light. Her reflection wavered in the flickering light of the oil lamp.

She stared at herself for long moments and then, womanlike, rubbed at her forehead with her fingertips as if she could massage away the few slight creases she saw there, lines etched by her deep concern for her patients.

Exposure to the elements in all sorts of weather had tanned her face and hands despite the bonnet she wore, and squinting against the sun had left tiny lines at the corners of her eyes. Despite regular treatments of lemon juice, a faint spattering of freckles dotted her nose.

Age and Danny's birth had added a few pounds, but according to her father, it was weight she needed. Strangely, her face was thinner than it had been nine years ago, refined by age and life.

She had no illusions. She no longer looked twenty-two. Shouldering the responsibilities that went hand in hand with the demands of her father's practice had taken its toll on her in many ways.

Mirror, mirror on the wall, would Gabe still think her fair at all?

Would he even recognize her? What would he say? What would she? Would he be the shocking flirt she recalled, or would he be filled with contrition?

Telling herself she was a fool for wasting so much as a thought on him, she went back to the bed and dabbed some antiseptic to the cut on Gabe's face.

As she tended to his needs, her mind turned to Caleb's ambivalent feelings about his brother's return. She could relate to them only too well. Like Caleb, and even though she knew that not to pardon Gabe jeopardized her own forgiveness, she couldn't imagine any scenario that would make her feel differently about the man who had taken everything she had to give and walked away as if it meant nothing to him.

Then why are you having such contradictory thoughts about him?

She had no answer for that.

Satisfied that he was fine for the moment, she went to the kitchen, rekindled the fire in the stove and filled the coffeepot. While she waited for the stove to get hot enough to start breakfast, she opened her Bible. Instead of reading, she flipped the pages until she found the pressed petunia she'd placed there. A gift from Gabe, plucked from Mrs. Abernathy's flower bed and tucked behind Rachel's ear when they'd returned from a walk. *"A memento of this evening."*

She could picture the half-light of dusk, could almost hear the sounds of children playing and smell the sweet scent of the petunias dancing in the breeze. Felt again the light brush of his lips against hers. A small, impromptu gesture was so like him. She planned. Gabe lived for the moment.

Impatient with her unruly thoughts, she

slammed her Bible shut and began to slice the bacon, placing the strips into the cold cast-iron skillet. Gathering the ingredients for buttermilk biscuits, she measured and mixed flour, salt and leavening and started working the lard into the flour with her fingertips, finding comfort in the simplicity of the everyday task.

Seeing that the stove was hot, she set the skillet of bacon over the heat. After adding just the right amount of buttermilk, she pinched off a biscuit-size piece of dough and deftly rolled the edges under to make it reasonably smooth and round. Placing it into the greased pan, she made a dimple in the center with her knuckle.

Danny, his dark hair standing on end and covering a yawn, came into the kitchen as she was filling the slight indentations with a small dollop of extra lard, just the way her mama had done.

"Good morning," she said, sliding the pan into the oven.

"Morning."

She wiped her hands on a wet cloth and sighed as she watched him pour a splash of coffee into a tin cup and fill it to the brim with milk and two spoons full of sugar. He'd started having morning "coffee milk," as he called it, when Edward had started sharing his own sweetened brew. When she'd questioned the wisdom of the action, Edward had assured her that it was more milk than anything else and maintained it was fine; it hadn't hurt her, had it?

Grandparents! she thought, lifting the crispy strips of bacon onto a platter. If she didn't remain vigilant, no telling how Edward would spoil Danny. But how could she deny him his little indulgences when he had taken on a very special role in Danny's life? Not only was he the child's grandfather, he'd been the closest thing to a father as he was ever likely to know.

Until now.

With her father's words ringing through her mind, Rachel searched her son's face for anything that might give away his paternity. He definitely had Gabe's long, lush eyelashes, as well as the slant of his eyebrows. The dimple in Danny's chin would be a dead giveaway as he grew closer to manhood and his jawline firmed the way his father's had.

His father. Rachel stifled a groan. How could she not think of him when he lay just down the hall? Resolutely, she opened a jar of red plum jam one of her patients had given her in lieu of payment for stitching up a nasty cut.

"Are you excited about going to the Gentrys' tomorrow?" she asked Danny as she smoothed down the recalcitrant "rooster tail" sticking up from the crown of his dark head.

He nodded, his eyes bright. "I made a present for baby Eli."

"Really? What did you make?"

"Roland gave me some old cedar shingles and helped me drill some holes on one edge so I could put some leather laces through them. I painted Ben's, Betsy's and Laura's names on them with different colors. I made one for Eli yesterday. I thought Miss Abby could hang it on the end of his cradle."

"That was very sweet of you, Danny."

"I made some for the Carruthers kids, too," he said. "I thought they could hang them on the wall above their beds."

"I'm sure everyone will love them," she said, marveling as she often did at what a thoughtful child he was.

Feeling blessed to have him, she peeked at the biscuits. "Almost done," she announced. "How many eggs do you want?"

"Two," he said promptly. "Soft."

"I'll have two, myself," Edward said from the doorway.

"Coming right up," Rachel said, reaching for the brown crockery bowl that held the eggs she bought from a lady in town.

"I've been thinking about tomorrow," she said, cracking the first egg into the sizzling bacon grease.

As they had the previous year, the Stones had planned to have their Christmas meal with the Gentrys and Caleb's former in-laws, the Emersons. "Why don't I stay here with Gabe and you and Danny go to Abby and Caleb's?"

"Absolutely not!" Edward told her. "You and Danny go, and I'll stay here with Gabe. You can bring me back a plate."

"It will be stone cold in this weather," she argued.

"Then we'll warm it up in the oven. Really, Rachel, you go. It's a special day for Danny, and it's seldom you get much uninterrupted time with him. Besides, it will give you the opportunity to check on Abby and the baby."

He had a point. Rachel put the first two eggs onto a plate and set it in front of him. The hot biscuits and a bowl of fresh-churned butter were placed on the table next to a platter of bacon. She looked from the determination in her father's eyes to the hopeful expression in Danny's. "If you're sure . . ." she said. "We'll be gone most of the day."

"I'm sure. Gabe is stable, and I think I can handle anything that comes up during that short time. Besides —" he shot a smile toward Danny "— I can read that new book on Italy you're giving me for Christmas."

"Edward Stone!" Rachel cried, her eyes widening in disbelief. "How do you know you got a book about Italy?"

Edward's eyes twinkled. "Never tell an eight-year-old anything you don't want repeated."

Rachel pinned her son with a familiar, narrow-eyed look. "You little rascal!" she said. "Christmas presents are supposed to be a secret."

"I didn't exactly *tell* him," Danny hedged, slathering a biscuit with butter. "He just asked me a buncha questions and sorta guessed."

"Mmm-hmm," Rachel said, trying to fix her father with that same stern look and failing as her mouth began to twitch with the beginnings of a smile. It was no secret that when it came to Christmas and secrecy, Edward Stone was a total failure.

"You're as bad as he is," she charged. "Worse. At least he's just a child."

Stifling a smile, Edward said, "It's settled, then. You and Danny are going. Now don't you need to see to those eggs?"

With the cookies all baked, Rachel spent the day stirring up pumpkin pies and an apple cake liberally laced with raisins and the black walnuts she and Edward had cracked and painstakingly picked out.

Finished with the baking, she and Danny loaded up their goodies and made deliveries to the Carruthers family and a widow or two who had a hard time making ends meet.

By the time their visits were over and they'd finished the evening meal, she was pleasantly weary. The day had been so busy that at times she was able to forget the man lying in the bedroom down the way. Danny helped with the dishes, and they were getting ready to begin their yearly Christmas Eve ritual when an agonized cry came from Gabe's room.

Tossing her dish towel onto the table, Rachel ran toward the sound, throwing the door open against the wall in her haste.

Gabe lay on his back, just as he had been, but as she neared the bed she realized that he was fully awake. His eyes were shadowed with pain that became stunned disbelief as he struggled to raise himself up to his uninjured elbow.

"Rachel?" His voice was deep and husky, as if he were getting over a bad sore throat. Looking to blame him for everything, she'd often thought that his voice was the first weapon he'd used in his insidious assault on her senses. Now, even in her concern, she imagined she heard a hint of wonder in his voice.

"Lie still," she commanded, placing a restraining hand against his shoulder. Offering him no time to formulate a reply, she continued, "What on earth were you thinking trying to get up? You might have injured yourself worse than you already are."

Ever professional even in her irritation, she placed gentle, questing fingers against his bound ribs. "Does it hurt?" she asked, unaware that the question was somewhat silly under the circumstances. She just wanted to get him easy again and steer clear of the feelings churning inside her now that they were face-to-face.

Despite the pain and grogginess reflected in his eyes, he attempted a smile that more resembled a grimace. "Only when I breathe."

Nothing had changed, she thought. Still quick with a smile and a glib reply.

"Do you remember what happened?"

A spasm of pain crossed his features. "A

couple of guys jumped me between here and Antoine. How did I get *here*?"

All business, she leaned over him to check the bandage on his head. "Simon Teasdale found you and brought you to me."

She stepped back and allowed her gaze to roam his face. As she had, he'd aged and looked older than the twenty-nine she knew him to be. But, as it seemed with most men, he'd done it better. Maturity had firmed the boyish softness of his jaw and chin as she knew it would Danny's, making it more sharply defined and making his resemblance to Caleb more pronounced, though Gabe would always be the handsomer of the two.

He, too, had a tanned face with crinkly lines at the corners of his eyes, but she knew from past experience that these lines would not have come from worry or the elements but laughter as he pursued countless pleasures. He was still disturbingly handsome and she suspected the inevitable scar he would carry would only add to his aura of mystery and danger. That thought awakened her slumbering anger.

"Did you know them?"

He gave a slight shake of his head. "They had bandannas. I won a lotta . . . money from a couple guys in a poker game . . . Little Rock." He made another pitiful attempt to smile. "Guess they wanted it back."

She dabbed at the still-seeping gash on his head with a piece of cotton wool saturated with peroxide. His hiss of pain gave her far more satisfaction than it should have.

"Simon did find your wallet nearby, and it was empty, but if it was someone from Little Rock, why would they wait so long to attack you?"

His eyes looked troubled. "Guess I'm not . . . thinking straight. Feel like . . . death warmed over."

"As well you should. You have broken ribs and a dislocated shoulder, which will be pretty painful while it heals. You have a possible concussion. There's a cut on your scalp and another on your cheek that will probably leave a nasty scar."

He attempted a shrug that elicited another grunt of pain.

"You need to go back to sleep," she told him, feeling a sudden, unexpected and annoying rush of sympathy.

"How long have I been here?" he asked, once more speaking through clenched teeth.

"Since yesterday morning."

She could almost see his fuzzy mind trying to calculate what day it was. "So it's . . ."

"Christmas Eve."

"I'd hoped to be home for Christmas."

The confession surprised her. Home? He'd meant to come back to Wolf Creek?

Of course he was coming home. Why else would he have been between Wolf Creek and Antoine?

"Why? Why now, after all this time?"

Without thinking, she blurted out the question that leaped into her mind, even though she knew that he was in no condition for the battle she felt brewing.

"To try to . . . fix things . . . with Caleb."

No wish to try to make amends with her. "Caleb knows you're here, and frankly, he wasn't exactly overjoyed about it." She started to turn away, and his good hand reached out and grabbed hers.

"And you, Rachel?" he asked, as she stared down at the fingers that manacled her wrist. "I know how I left was . . . wrong. I'm sorry."

So he *did* want to make things right with her. The knowledge gave her no satisfaction; it only stoked her anger. "Why should I believe your contrition is genuine, Gabe? You once told me a lot of things, all of them lies. Why should I believe this sudden change of heart is any different? And your behavior wasn't just wrong. It was contemptible!"

She knew that her tirade was inappropriate and unprofessional, and that the fury consuming her was no doubt reflected in her face and in her voice, which shook as badly as her hands. He was in pain from numerous injuries. It was neither the time nor the place to confront him, but the dam that had held back her pain for so many years had burst, and she could not seem to stop the words that spewed from her like lava from a volcano.

"Did you really think you could just waltz into town and expect everyone to welcome you with open arms? Did you think that maybe Caleb would be so overjoyed by the prodigal's return that he would trot out the fatted calf? Guess what, Gabe, this is real life, not a Bible story, and I don't see any happy endings in sight!"

He looked stricken by her outburst. She didn't care. She *wanted* him to know he had behaved despicably. Wanted him to know the pain *she'd* suffered. She even hoped the knowledge of what he'd done added to his own pain.

His grip relaxed and he allowed her to pull free. She stared at him, but his eyes gave away nothing of what he was feeling.

"Mama?" Danny spoke from the doorway.

Trembling as if she had the ague, she turned. "What is it, Danny?" she asked in a far harsher tone than she'd intended and he was accustomed to.

The child looked from her to the man in the bed, his eyes wide with uncertainty. "Pops wanted me to see if everything is all right."

"Tell him everything's fine," she said in a softer voice.

She kept her gaze studiously on her son, who looked shocked by the side of his mother he'd never seen. She wished she could call back her heated words. No. Gabe Gentry deserved her anger. She only wished Danny hadn't heard. "Mr. Gentry is just in a lot of pain at the moment."

"But you were mad at him," Danny said, sensing there was more than she was saying. Like his grandfather, he was prone to probe until his curiosity was satisfied.

"Only because he tried to get out of bed," she fibbed, casting a quick glance at Gabe, whose eyes were now shut. "He might have hurt himself worse."

"Oh."

Once more, Danny looked from one adult to the other before backing out the door, leaving Rachel alone with her patient, who stared at her with no visible expression. Why didn't that surprise her? The celebrated Gabriel Gentry would never see his actions as despicable.

"I'll get you some medication," she told him, wanting nothing more than to escape him.

"I don't want it," he said, his jaw set in a stubborn line. "I want . . . to get up . . . awhile."

"There's no way you can —"

"It's Christmas Eve," he interrupted, his voice rough with his own anger and something she couldn't put a name to. "Help me to . . . a chair. I'll be . . . okay for a while."

"Fine," she snapped. "I'll let you sit up, but only if you let me give you a little something."

He looked as if he would like to argue further, but nodded. She turned toward the door. "Where are you going?"

"To get Pops's wheelchair."

"Rachel," he said, the sound of his voice stopping her. She turned.

"I had no idea you had a son."

She stiffened but managed a twisted smile. "What did you expect, Gabe? That I would carry a torch for you forever?"

For once in his life, Gabe had no witty comeback.

After a lot of moaning and groaning, Rachel got Gabe into one of her father's robes

63

and settled into the wheelchair with a quilt over his legs. Then she rolled him to the kitchen, where he picked at a bowl of beef stew he didn't want while trying — without much success and despite the small dose of laudanum she'd forced on him — to ignore the various excruciating pains throbbing throughout his body. It irritated him that she'd been right. He should have stayed in bed.

When the simple meal was finished, he was rolled into the parlor, where he sat watching as the Stones went through their Christmas Eve celebration. His muddled thoughts bounced around from one topic to the next.

When he'd awakened, he remembered how he'd come to be in so much agony but had no idea where he was. He'd chosen not to call for help, instead enduring long pain-filled moments as he struggled to sit up with a shoulder that felt on fire and a rib cage that felt as if someone had taken a club to it. No. Not a club. Boots.

When he'd seen Rachel standing beside the bed, he'd thought she was an illusion, and his reaction had been profound pleasure. It hadn't taken long to realize that she was very real and that she did not share his happiness at being reunited.

She was right, he thought as he watched her with her family. He'd treated her worse than terribly. He remembered their short few weeks together as good ones even though she was nothing like the women he usually spent time with.

She was very smart, which was a little intimidating, as was her desire to become a doctor and settle down in Wolf Creek. His greatest goal was to see as much as he could while his money held out. There was plenty of time to worry about what he would do with his life after he finished seeing the world.

It was years before he'd come to grips with the reality that the lifestyle he'd chosen when he left home had lost its luster and that his interest in aimless pursuits had declined dramatically. He'd begun to feel as if he were living in a world of make-believe, while somewhere out there people led real and meaningful lives.

Comprehension led to months of reflection and careful examination of his upbringing and the life he'd tried so hard to leave behind. He'd realized that the void he'd felt in his heart since the day his mother abandoned him and his brother could not be filled with laughter and joking, senseless reveling or meaningless relationships. All attempts to do so had been futile, masking, but never filling, the emptiness.

He'd been left with the sobering realization that his entire life was nothing but an effort to escape the pain that gnawed at him every moment of every day and could not be assuaged by any thrill, pleasure or sinful indulgence known to man. He'd accepted the truth that there was no escaping the past or how it shaped the person you became. At some point you had to come to terms with that, both the good and the bad.

Then one day in Atlanta almost a year ago, he'd been strolling through a park and heard a woman laugh, laughter filled with such undiluted joy that it triggered an unexpected, long-forgotten memory of Rachel. The moment was sharply poignant. In those few out-of-time seconds, he'd been struck with the sudden conviction that he'd had something rare within his grasp and thrown it away.

Over the next few weeks, memories of their time together drifted through his mind with the sweetness of springtime scents on a subtle breeze: Her affirmation that money was not the important thing for happiness, which he'd scoffed at and now knew was true. Her serious, unwavering dedication when mocked for daring to brave entrance

66

to a profession dominated by men. Her willingness to dedicate herself to a life that was not necessarily conducive to her own well-being, but to the well-being of others.

Longing for something he couldn't put into words, he'd begun to wonder if there was redemption for him out there somewhere. If so, he knew he'd have to start in Wolf Creek, the place where his life had first begun to unravel. There, he'd hoped to find new direction and a new purpose for his life, though he had no idea what that might be or how to go about finding it.

Now, sitting in the Stones' parlor while Edward read the story of baby Jesus from the Bible, he wanted to ask Rachel if he could sit in the parlor the next morning and watch the gift opening. Thanks to his mother's leaving and his father's indifference, he and Caleb had never known what these three people shared. Christmas was just another day. Lucas's only concession to the holiday had been a traditional meal because he liked showing off to some of his friends.

Gabe longed just once to experience what a real Christmas should be, but Rachel had made it clear that the less she had to do with him the better, and he had no wish to disrupt their day. The solemn sounds of their prayer, and their happy, laughing voices as they joked and teased each other, brought about a pang of regret so painful that his heart hurt almost as badly as his physical injuries.

The desire to have that kind of love and the knowledge that he had willfully ruined any chance of experiencing it with Rachel was overwhelming in its intensity. The woman he now knew was the most important person to come into his life had made it clear that she had not forgiven him and was not likely to.

He couldn't blame her. She was right. He had used her — not deliberately, perhaps — but she'd been there and they'd both been willing. In his mind she was no different from other girls he'd spent time with. Except, of course, she was very different.

Filled with an incredible sorrow for what he'd tossed away, Gabe blinked back the unmanly sting of tears. Tears were a luxury he had not allowed himself since the day he'd come home and been told that his mother had left for a new life in Boston . . . a life that was more important to her than her husband or her sons.

Funny how history repeated itself. For all intents and purposes, he'd done to Rachel exactly what his mother had done to him and his brother.

■ ■ ■ ■

Christmas morning dawned bright and cold. Rachel slipped into Gabe's room to stoke the fire in his fireplace, stunned to find him sitting on the edge of the bed, as upright as possible. A blanket covered his legs. He clutched a shirt in his fists. He was trembling and sweat dripped down his face despite the chill of the room. A basin of soapy water sat on the stand next to the bed. He'd given himself a sponge bath and was trying to get dressed. He looked near to passing out from the effort.

"What do you think you're doing?" She shook her head. Stubborn, stubborn man.

"Getting dressed," he told her in a terse tone. Knowing how she felt about him, he couldn't bear being near her any longer than was absolutely necessary, so he'd forced himself to the limit to make her believe he was feeling better than he really was.

"Why didn't you ring for help?"

"It wasn't necessary." Despite the medicine still dulling his senses and the pain racking his body, he made his voice as crisp and no-nonsense as hers.

"How do you feel?"

His blue eyes roamed over her, as restless

69

as the wind tossing the tree branches outside the window. "I'll live."

"I certainly hope so," she said, going to the fireplace. She removed the screen and placed a couple of slivers of pine knot and a couple of logs on the bed of coals. He needed to get warm.

"Do you?"

The simple question fell into the silence of the room. Moving with extreme care, she set the screen back in place.

"Of course I do." She went to the bed and set about changing the bandages on his head and face, probing his swollen shoulder and making a swift examination of his bruised chest.

"Can you bring me some hot water?" he asked. "My sponge bath was a bit chilly, and I'd like to shave and clean my teeth. Maybe I'll feel a bit more human."

She pressed her lips together to keep from saying something to antagonize him. It was too soon for him to be doing so much. "I'm not sure you can —"

"I'll manage."

The determined angle of his chin brooked no argument.

When she returned twenty minutes later, Gabe stood at the shaving stand, his mouth set in a grim line of agony. She didn't know how he'd managed to do all he'd done or why he wasn't passed out on the floor. He was dressed in the clean clothes she'd brought him and had somehow buttoned the shirt over the arm that was held against his chest by the sling. The unused sleeve hung loose. He'd shaved what he could of the stubble shadowing his face, but not without leaving a few oozing nicks here and there. He made no comment about the ugly wound that marred his lean cheek.

Placing the straight-edge razor on the stand, he met her gaze in the mirror. "You don't know how badly I hate to ask this of you, but would you mind washing my feet? I couldn't get below the knees."

Her eyes widened. The simple request, one she'd done countless times for other patients, caught her off guard. Taking care of their needs was her duty as a physician and caretaker, but she didn't want to do any more for Gabe Gentry than was absolutely necessary.

As soon as the thought entered her mind, she felt a familiar wave of shame wash over her. Where was her compassion for this man who might well have died if Simon hadn't found him when he had? Where was her Christian charity? She was a good doctor who had never backed away from a challenge or shirked her responsibilities.

Without a word, she picked up the basin of cooling water, placed it on the floor and knelt beside it, going about her task with quick efficiency and reminding herself that serving his needs while he was injured was not only her duty as a physician; it was her duty as a Christian.

As she worked, the story of Jesus, sinless, perfect, washing His apostles' feet slipped into her mind. She concentrated on her task so that Gabe wouldn't see how near she was to tears.

By nature she was a caring person. She knew she couldn't continue to harbor this soul-destroying resentment, but she seemed unable to free herself from it. Could she find a way to set aside the hostility that had taken hold of her the day he'd destroyed her love with his callous dismissal?

She sighed as she pulled a heavy pair of woolen socks onto his feet. She didn't know. But she knew that if she was ever to be the person the Lord expected her to be she had to try a lot harder.

Gabe heard the sigh and watched as she stood and picked up the basin of water to set it on the shaving stand.

"I'll bring you some breakfast a bit later," she told him, gathering the soiled laundry. "Danny will want to open his gifts first."

"That's fine. I'll just rest until then."

He started to lower himself in gradual increments, using his workable arm and clenching his teeth against the pain. Rachel was beside him in an instant, her arms around his shoulders to help ease him to the pillows. She was strong, he thought, as she lifted his legs to the bed and spread a double layer of quilts over him. Stronger than she looked. He didn't know why that should be such a surprise, but it was.

Gabe waited for the screaming pain in his ribs to subside to a dull, throbbing ache. Many things about Rachel surprised him. She was older, but no less beautiful than he remembered. She'd gained some much-needed weight, which only added to the femininity she tried to hide beneath her tailored, no-nonsense wardrobe. The intriguing scent of magnolia blossoms still clung to her.

What surprised him most was that she was no longer the shy woman who'd had trouble carrying on a conversation unless it was a topic she felt passionately about. Her worshipful eyes no longer followed his every move and she certainly didn't hang on to every word he spoke, as she once had.

She was a woman, not a girl. She was a devoted daughter. She was a mother. She was a professional with long-standing ties to the community, successfully crossing the threshold of a field most women were afraid to enter. That alone made her exceptional.

"You must be in terrible pain after moving around so much. Would you like a bit of medication now?"

Was that actual compassion he heard in her voice? He clenched his teeth together and met her gaze steadily. "No, thank you. I've seen too many people get addicted to it. I'll just tough it out."

"I'm only giving you small doses, and I don't think you're in jeopardy of addiction at this point. Toughing it out isn't really a good idea."

Somehow he managed a derisive smile. "A lot of things I've done haven't been good ideas, but that never stopped me, did it?"

Rachel stared at him for several seconds then scooped up the laundry and left him without another word. Let him hurt. It wasn't her problem. Except, of course, that it was. The very thought of the pain he must be suffering went against everything she stood for and left her feeling undeserving of her calling. Unfortunately, some people had to learn the hard way.

As planned, Rachel and Danny went to Caleb and Abby's at midmorning so that Danny could play with the Gentry children and Rachel could help Mary, Caleb's former mother-in-law, with the last-minute meal preparations, since Abby was still confined to bed.

Rachel made the visit double duty, examining mother and baby and concluding they were both fine, at which Abby declared she was able to get up long enough to eat her Christmas meal with the family. Like Gabe, she would not be deterred.

Abby loved the little signs Danny had made. Caleb tied the leather cords to the end of the crib while Danny watched with pride. The other children, too, were happy with their name signs, and Caleb promised to hang them at the heads of their beds before nightfall. Though he had no talent for building things from wood, he did dabble with whittling and had fashioned a stunning replica of a Colt pistol for his children to give to Danny. Each of them had taken turns putting a coat of shellac on it.

When the dishes were done, Rachel and Mary Emerson put the little ones down for naps. The men went to the parlor, where Rachel suspected there might be as much afternoon dozing as dominoes and conversation. The older children played with their new toys while Mary Emerson supervised, giving Rachel and Abby time for some uninterrupted "woman talk."

Rachel cut two pieces of pumpkin pie, poured two mugs of coffee and went to Abby's bedroom, to find her once again propped up in bed.

"Thank you," she said, as Rachel handed her the pie and set the mug of coffee on a bedside table. "It's been a lovely day, hasn't it?"

"It has," Rachel agreed. "And you got the best Christmas present of all, albeit a couple of days early."

"I did, didn't I?" Abby said with a smile, glancing at the baby all snug in his cradle. She took a bite of pie and washed it down with a sip of coffee.

"What does Caleb think of Eli now that he's here and you're both well?" Rachel asked.

Since Caleb's first wife had died in childbirth the previous winter, Caleb had been terrified when Abby told him she was expecting his child.

"He's beside himself with happiness —

and pride," she said with a satisfied grin.

"Well, his fear was certainly understandable," Rachel said.

"I agree."

"You're happy, aren't you, Abby?" Rachel asked, unaware of the wistful note in her voice.

"I am." There was no denying her contentment. "I loved William, but what I felt for him pales in comparison to what I feel for Caleb."

"I'm really happy for you."

Abby reached out a hand to her friend. "Don't look so sad. There's someone out there for you. Don't ever doubt that."

"Do you really think so?"

"I know so." Abby's eyes brightened at a sudden thought. "What about Gabe?"

"What about Gabe?" she asked with a lift of her dark eyebrows.

"As a potential husband, goose! If you married him we'd be sisters-in-law."

Rachel felt the color drain from her face, felt the stiffness in her cheeks as she forced a smile. "Thank you but no thank you," she said. "Gabriel Gentry is not the marrying type."

"You sound very sure of that."

"Haven't you heard the gossip?"

Abby nodded. "Caleb's told me everything

about Gabe, but people do change. Caleb is proof of that."

Not everything.

"It must have been hard for both of them growing up," Abby mused. "Caleb told me that until he married Emily, Christmas was just another day."

Rachel registered her friend's comment with a bit of a shock. With the Gentry money, she would have thought Lucas would have seen to it his boys had anything they wanted. What kind of man would deprive children of a bit of happiness once a year?

"Well, Lucas didn't pretend to be anything but who he was," she said. "I don't imagine he was too interested in conforming to society's expectations. Dad says that for all his unreasonableness, Lucas had a reputation for being hardworking. At least he passed that on to Caleb."

"But not Gabe, from what I hear."

"No. Not Gabe."

"Did you know him?" Abby queried, taking another forkful of pie.

"Yes," Rachel said, concentrating on the steam rising from her mug. "Gabe was two years younger than I, though, and we didn't share the same circle of friends."

"Caleb said he was . . . spoiled." Abby

said the word almost apologetically.

"To put it mildly," Rachel said, struggling to suppress the sarcasm in her voice.

"I've heard he's very handsome."

"He's also wild, dangerous and has no sense of decency . . . from what I hear," Rachel tacked on.

Abby wondered why her friend was so irritated by the topic of Gabriel Gentry. "So I've heard from Caleb. As I said, people do change. I suppose only time will tell if Gabe has."

Rachel took a sip of coffee before answering. "He did tell me he came back to try to make amends."

"That's promising, but I'm here to say that Caleb is struggling with the idea that Gabe is even back after so long. There's been a lot of bad blood between them."

Rachel nodded. "I certainly understand how he feels." Perhaps more than Caleb.

That conversation stayed with Rachel as she drove the buggy back to town. Like Caleb, she was having a hard time accepting Gabe's return. *Because he broke your heart and trampled your woman's pride beneath his fancy handmade boots.*

True enough. That aside, surely she was mature enough to put the past into perspective. As terrible as it had been, she *had* learned from the experience. She was a better person. Stronger and more tolerant of others' mistakes. So why not Gabe's?

No doubt about it, she thought, giving her head a shake. She was a terrible, terrible person! Not forgiving wasn't an option to a Christian, but like Caleb's, her forgiveness of Gabe would come hard.

She prayed he would heal and move on soon. If he chose to stay, she wasn't sure how she would deal with seeing him on a regular basis. *Stop borrowing trouble, Rachel Stone.* No one had any idea what he would do once his injuries healed. Still, there was the remote possibility that he would stay in the area, which meant her father had a point. She had to tell Danny and pray he understood.

But not today.

To her dismay, she and Danny found Edward and Gabe sitting at the kitchen table playing a game of chess. Gabe sat ramrod straight in the chair. He looked awful. He was far too pale, and there was no masking the pain shadowing his sapphire-hued eyes or the challenge in them as he looked at her. He expected her to rail at him for being out of bed, but she was too weary for another battle and kept silent.

"Can I play, Pops?" Danny wheedled, shoving his small body beneath Edward's arm so he could get a better look at the board.

Intent on the game pieces, Edward gave the boy a distracted hug. "Not this game, Danny."

"No one ever wants to play with me," he said, his shoulders slumping.

"That isn't true," Rachel told him, hanging her coat by the door. She turned and took two plates out of the basket she'd carried in. "Pops plays with you all the time."

"Supper?" Edward asked, spying the plates.

"Turkey and all the trimmings," she replied. "I'll stick them in the oven for a bit," she said, doing just that. "They'll be hot in no time."

Finally reaching a decision, Edward moved a piece and then gave his attention to his daughter. "Makes my mouth water just thinking about Mary's dressing."

"I wasn't sure if you liked turkey or not, so I brought ham, too," she said to Gabe. Even as she spoke the words, she regretted showing any concern for his likes or dislikes.

"Either is fine, thank you. And I'll play a game with you sometime, Danny, but I think I'd best get back to bed after I eat."

The unexpected thanks and offer to Danny took Rachel by surprise, though it shouldn't have. Gabe Gentry epitomized charm and grace and friendliness.

What he lacked was integrity and common decency.

CHAPTER THREE

By the time a new year rolled around, the snow was nothing but a pleasant memory, leaving behind a dingy mush that froze at night and thawed during the day. The old year had ended with a rash of croup that kept Rachel running all over town. She had treated no less than seven people on New Year's Eve.

Gabe was still in considerable pain if he moved the wrong way, but his injuries and his strength were improving in slow increments. Despite the sometimes excruciating agony, he was determined to leave the Stone house — and the intolerable tension between him and Rachel — as soon as humanly possible. For both their sakes, he had no desire to prolong the misery.

When he finished shaving shortly after breakfast on New Year's Day, he saw that the gash on his face was healing nicely, though it would leave an ugly scar. He thought about that for a moment and shrugged. There wasn't much he could do about it. Thanks to Simon and Rachel, he was alive.

His once dislocated shoulder was not so tender and his hand was much steadier; he'd only nicked himself in two places. He was congratulating himself on the progress when a knock sounded on his door.

"Come in," he called, glancing up and seeing Danny's reflection in the mirror. He stood in the doorway, staring at Gabe with unconcealed curiosity. "Not too pretty to look at, is it?" Gabe said.

"Must hurt."

"Not much, but the ribs . . . that's another thing."

When the boy continued to watch him and made no move to say anything, Gabe prompted, "What can I do for you, Danny?"

"Pops said to tell you that Mr. Gentry — Caleb — is here to see you."

Gabe smiled, the action pulling at the stitches closing the wound on his cheek. "Thanks, son."

Danny's eyes widened. He smiled, a smile so bright and wide that Gabe resisted the urge to chuckle.

"Do you need anything?" Danny asked, a look of hope in his eyes. "I can get whatever you want. I'm not doing anything."

"I'm fine, thanks. You can send Caleb in."

"Would you like to play a game of Chinese checkers after he goes?"

The past week, they'd fallen into a habit of playing a game or two in the afternoons. Though Gabe would have preferred to play chess with Edward, he got a lot of satisfaction at how much Danny seemed to enjoy the time they spent together. He also recalled how he'd wished his father was the kind of man who wanted to play with his boys.

"We'll see. I'll probably be ready for a good rest by the time Caleb leaves. Why don't you go get him?"

"Oh. Okay."

Gabe wondered if Danny was as disappointed as he looked. He'd be sure to try to play a game or two with him sometime during the afternoon.

When Caleb came into the bedroom, it was the first time the two brothers had faced each other on a more or less equal footing since Gabe left. Caleb had stopped by on other occasions, but knowing Gabe was still in a lot of pain, they'd postponed any serious discussions.

Though Gabe had wanted this chance to try to make things right and had mentally rehearsed their meeting dozens of times, now that the opportunity was here, he had no idea where to begin.

"How are you feeling?" Caleb asked, taking a chair next to the fireplace. The question was his usual conversational opening. Gabe wiped the shaving soap from his face and eased down into the chair's mate.

"Far from well, but better."

"That's good."

An uncomfortable silence stretched between them. "Rachel mentioned that you got married again last year," Gabe said, hoping to fill the growing silence left by his habitually reticent brother. That hadn't changed.

Caleb nodded. "My first wife, Emily, died during childbirth. I married Abby Carter, a newly widowed woman Rachel suggested I hire for my daughter's wet nurse."

Gabe raised his eyebrows. "That's a bit unconventional, isn't it? Not to mention extreme."

"More than a bit," Caleb agreed. "But we didn't have much choice when Sarah Van-Sickle started spreading rumors about us, even though I was staying in the bunkhouse with Frank and Leo."

"So Sarah's still doling out misery, is she?" Gabe asked, recalling more than one occasion when she'd caused unnecessary suffering.

"Yep. I keep thinking she'll get her comeuppance, but so far, she just goes along, giving everyone a hard time along the way." There was more silence.

"So tell me about your . . . Abby. How are things working out?" Gabe asked, in an attempt to keep the struggling conversation going.

"Very well. She's a wonderful person and a great mother."

Gabe saw a gleam in his brother's eyes he'd never seen before. Happiness.

"I love her very much," Caleb added, almost, Gabe thought, as if his brother expected him to make some sort of snide comment about the situation. "We had a son born two days before Christmas."

"A son! You have a son and a daughter?" Caleb nodded and Gabe smiled, unexpectedly pleased for the brother who had borne the brunt of their father's domineering personality. "I envy you."

Caleb looked up to meet Gabe's smiling gaze. "You do?"

"Even I had to grow up eventually, Caleb," Gabe said, poking a bit of fun at himself. He knew what most people thought of him.

"Why have you come back, Gabriel?" Caleb asked, done with idle chitchat.

He shrugged. "I'm not sure I can explain. A while back, I realized that I'd done just about everything and seen all the places I wanted to see, and Lucas Gentry's shadow was still hanging over me. I was as miserable away from Wolf Creek as I had been here.

"Believe it or not, I've given our childhood a lot of thought the past several months, and I came up with some reasons why I felt that way. A few months back, I got the notion to come and see if there was any way for us to make sense of our past. I even hoped that maybe I could make up for the things I've done."

Caleb's eyes reflected his impatience. "Words are fine, Gabe. You were always good with them, but actions speak a lot louder. It's easy to come home when you're down-and-out. It's easy to claim regret and say you're sorry and then saddle up and leave again, convinced you did all you could or should to fix things."

For the first time, Gabe realized just how deep the chasm was between him and his brother. "I know what you're saying is true, and that I've given you plenty of reason to feel the way you do, but I have no intention of leaving."

"What!"

Gabe met his brother's astonished gaze. "I'm staying in Wolf Creek. I'm twenty-nine years old. Wouldn't you say it's time I found a good woman and settled down?"

"What will you do? How will you live with no money?" Caleb asked, unable to hide his shock.

"You're the one who said I was down-and-out, not me. I have a bit stuck by. As for what I'll do, I have no idea." He managed a wry smile. "It'll be a while before I'm able to do much of anything, but when the time is right, something will come along."

Another silence ensued. Finally, Gabe gave a heavy sigh, grimaced in pain and curved his arm around his battered ribs as if to protect them.

"Look, Caleb. I'm truly sorry for the way I acted when we were kids. I think I was trying to get Lucas to notice me, to acknowledge I was alive. If it took acting up to do it, so be it. I'm sorry my behavior left most of the work and responsibility on you. In a strange sort of way, though, I think you actually benefited."

"How do you figure that?" Caleb snapped. "I was the slave who worked and you were the spoiled brat who got by with everything and did next to nothing." His lips tightened with the stubbornness he was known for. "I've hated you for that."

"I can't say that I blame you," Gabe said. He understood Caleb's feelings, but just as Rachel's disgust had been hard to swallow, Caleb's words hurt, far more than Gabe had expected.

"Just think about it a minute. You were the one learning how to work, how to become a productive citizen, while I learned nothing except how to goof off and finagle others into doing my chores. I thought it was funny then, but not now. I cheated myself out of a lot of lessons."

Caleb stared at Gabe as if he'd never seen him before.

"I know it's a lot to ask, and I'll understand if you say no, but I'd like to ask your forgiveness. I'd like the opportunity to get to know you and your family. Believe it or not, I want to be an uncle, and I'd really like it if you and I could find some common ground to build a relationship on."

Rachel returned from a visit with one of her patients just before noon. She found her father sitting at the kitchen table in his wheelchair, slicing a skillet of corn bread into wedges.

"Hey, Pops!" she said, pressing a kiss to the top of his head. "How is everything?"

"Just dandy. How is little Jimmy doing?"

"As well as can be expected."

"Good. Food's ready," he said, indicating a pot of pinto beans and salt pork Rachel had set on the back of the woodstove before she left earlier in that morning. "Will you get Danny and Gabe while I finish up here?"

"Of course."

"Rachel," he said, his voice stopping her.

"Yes?" she said, turning.

"Caleb came to see Gabe this morning. I have no idea what they talked about, but I thought you'd like to know."

"Yes," she said, nodding. "Thank you."

Thoughts of what might have transpired between the brothers filled her mind as she went to fetch Danny. She found him reading one of the books he'd received for Christmas and more than ready to eat, since there were cookies to be had afterward.

Rachel went to Gabe's room, knocked on the door and opened it at his summons.

"Pops has dinner ready," she said, noticing that he was dressed in the extra clothes she'd found in his carpetbag instead of Edward's castoffs. She couldn't help noticing how well they fit his lean, broad-shouldered body. No doubt they'd been

91

tailor-made for him.

"Thank you," he said. "I've been waiting to talk to you."

"Oh?"

He nodded. "I wanted to tell you that I'll be leaving after we eat."

"Leaving?" she echoed, disbelief in her voice. "You're in no condition to be on a horse."

"I don't plan to be. I'm not leaving town, just checking into the boardinghouse. I think I'm well enough to take care of myself if I don't do anything stupid."

Though she'd wished him gone a hundred times, now that he planned to go she was filled with something that felt far too much like disappointment for her peace of mind.

"And how do you propose to pay for it?" she said, her voice sharper than she'd intended as the nebulous distress vanished in the face of her irritation.

"I had some money stuck in my boot the thieves didn't find," he explained. "It will see me through for a while. Besides, I think you'd agree that I've disrupted your life enough."

Indeed he had, she thought, though she would never admit it. "You have not disrupted my life."

His smile mocked. "Could've fooled me."

Embarrassment flushed her cheeks. "Caring for people is what I do."

"And I'll be the first one to attest to the fact that you're a fine doctor," he said in a gentle voice. "But let's be honest here."

"By all means. If that's possible," she said, unable to mask the sarcasm in her voice.

"Touché." Meeting her irate gaze was one of the hardest things he'd ever done. "Again, I know I treated you badly in St. Louis, and I should have said goodbye in person instead of leaving you that note."

Rachel began to laugh, a terrible parody of the sound. "You think I'm angry at you because you left me a *note*?" she cried.

"Weren't you?"

"Angry?" She shook her head. "No. Try furious. Or hurt. Or better yet, *devastated.*" She took a deep breath, and feelings and words that had festered far too long erupted from her lips.

"Silly, naive me! I was bound to fall for your smooth-talking ways. I believed everything you told me, and it was all lies. Every single word of it! So tell me, Gabe, where was your honesty back then?"

The vitriol in her voice caused all the color to drain from his face. "I have no excuse, except . . ."

She made a slashing movement through

the air to silence him. "You're right. You have no excuse. Lucky, lucky me! Handsome, worldly Gabe Gentry, the boy every girl in Wolf Creek longed to snare, looked me up."

She gave a bitter laugh. "I can't believe I was so gullible. I actually scoffed at the tales I'd heard about you, because you seemed so kind, and my memories of you were good. So I listened to your lies and fell for your pretty words. I gave you everything I had, Gabe. *Everything.* My love, my —" her voice faltered "— my entire being. You played me for a fool, and when you got what you wanted, you left without a backward glance, off to the next place of interest, the next easy mark."

"I never thought you were an easy —" He tried to interrupt, but again she held up her palm for silence and drew in several deep, steadying breaths. As quickly as it had come, her anger disappeared. He almost wished it hadn't. The anguish in her eyes was almost his undoing.

"Do you have any idea what you did to me?" she said, her voice breaking. "Do you have any idea how ugly and discarded and *used* I felt?"

Truthfully, he'd never considered that. For the first time he realized how badly his casual treatment had wounded her. There had been other girls, other times, and never once had he considered how his cavalier dismissal might have made them feel. He'd always assumed that they expected no more or less than he was willing to offer. He'd used his God-given looks and charm with utter disregard for anyone's feelings but his own. All his life it had been about him. About what he felt, what he wanted.

The knowledge shamed him.

A glib apology couldn't begin to cover his faults, but still he searched his mind for words to ease her pain, knowing deep in his gut that there were none.

"I think I understand what you felt and why you still feel the way you do."

The harsh laughter was back. "You understand nothing!" she said in a tone of deadly quiet. "Nothing. But you're a man, and men get to walk away. Women are the ones who pay, and I'll pay for my folly the rest of my life."

She swiped at her tears with her fingertips. "Thanks to you, I learned never to trust anything a man says." Empty of words, she felt the heat of anger drain away and turned to leave the room.

Gabe's voice followed her. "You must have trusted at least one man."

She turned back to him with a blank expression.

"You must have trusted one other man," he repeated. "You must have trusted Danny's father."

She paled, and turning left him standing near the fire.

He closed his eyes against the pain.

She'd loved him.

Was it possible that he'd loved her but had been too immature and wrapped up in himself to realize it? He didn't know. All he knew was that staying would have meant putting an end to his roaming ways, and he hadn't been ready to do that. So he had moved on. He had walked away from the one bit of goodness in his sordid past, possibly the best thing to ever happen to him, and, he suspected, the one person who might have saved him from himself.

She'd moved on, too. She'd found someone who wasn't afraid to settle down. Someone who would cherish her enough to make her his wife.

Someone who had fathered her son.

That indisputable fact, more than anything she'd said to him, brought the most grief. The love he'd tossed away so carelessly, another had gained. Staying in Wolf Creek wouldn't be easy, for a lot of reasons.

■ ■ ■ ■

When Rachel entered the kitchen, she was greeted by two pairs of questioning eyes. She wondered if either of them had heard the actual words of the argument, or if they'd just heard her voice raised in anger.

"He insists on moving to the boarding-house after lunch," she offered, hoping the statement would be enough of an answer to assuage their curiosity, at least for now.

"Ah," Edward said, but the look in his eyes told her that he knew there was more than she was letting on.

"He isn't well yet," Danny said.

Rachel stifled a sigh. Danny was becoming far too attached to Gabe. Another reason he needed to move on.

"That's what I told him, but he's a grown man and can do as he wishes."

Though he would rather have walked over hot coals barefoot, Gabe went into the kitchen for lunch. The time for running away from his mistakes had passed. Rachel's color was still high, and her full lips were compressed into a tight line of disapproval. From Edward's forced smile and Danny's wary expression, Gabe knew they'd overheard the argument. Just another reason to be gone, he thought, easing himself into the straight-backed chair.

After Edward prayed, and everyone's plate was full, he broke the deafening silence.

"Rachel says you're planning to move to Hattie's this afternoon."

"Yes."

"Of course, it's up to you, but I'm not sure that's wise," Edward told him. "You still have a long way to go to be really out of the woods. Why don't you stay until the weekend — three more days — so that we can monitor your progress a bit longer?"

"I'm not sure that's wise, either," Gabe said cryptically.

"But you can't leave today." Danny's voice was as near a whine as Gabe had ever heard. "You promised to play Chinese checkers with me this afternoon."

Despite telling himself that he wouldn't, Gabe looked at Rachel. It was very possible that she was recalling — as he was — her scathing commentary about his lies, but she was concentrating on buttering a wedge of corn bread and didn't look up except to shoot her son a brief, grim look.

Drat it, he *had* promised! Though he would feel better if he left, was his peace of mind worth breaking a vow to a child?

98

Hadn't he and Rachel just argued about how little his word meant? Hadn't he done enough hedging and misleading? Gabe's fingers tightened around his fork. Making atonement required much more and was far harder than he'd expected, but he wouldn't give her the satisfaction of saying "I told you so."

He forced a tight smile. "That's right," he said. "I did. I'll stay at least tonight, and then we'll see."

After lunch, Danny took Gabe into the parlor and set up the Chinese checkers while Rachel began to clear the table.

"You may as well sit down and tell me what happened," her father said. "You know I won't let up until you do."

Rachel cast him a woebegone look. Edward's persistence in getting to the bottom of things was legend. "I thought it was pretty obvious that Gabe and I had words."

"Indeed. But if I were a wagering man I'd bet it wasn't about his leaving."

"And you would win that wager," she said, turning her back on him.

Edward waited while she washed the glassware and then the flatware. Finally, she turned with a sigh and her signature, narrow-eyed look. "You are the most exasperating man I've ever known."

"That's what your mother used to say," Edward said, holding out his coffee cup for her to refill. "But I would have thought Gabe held that honor."

"You're right. He does. He is." She gave a reluctant, halfhearted smile. "Which makes you the second most irritating man I've ever known."

"So what were the fireworks all about?"

"He said he knew he'd behaved badly and apologized."

"And you yelled at him?"

Rachel's eyes widened. "What was I supposed to do? Tell him all was forgiven?"

"Yes."

Rachel sucked in a shocked breath and stared at him for a few seconds more. Then, with an angry shake of her head, she turned back to her dishes. "You expect too much."

"You've had years to come to terms with what happened, Rachel. Not forgiving isn't like you. You're one of the least judgmental, compassionate people I know, except evidently when it comes to Gabe, and maybe yourself."

"How can I forgive myself?" she asked, scrubbing at a fork with excessive force.

"How can you not when you asked God for His forgiveness and He's given it,"

Edward countered, his voice gentle.

"I'd like to think so," she said with a sigh. "But how can He?"

"It's what He does."

Again, Rachel stared at her father for long considering moments and went back to her dishes once more.

"Danny is very taken with Gabe," Edward offered.

"I know. It's . . . concerning."

"He's looking for a father figure."

She whirled to face him. "You're his father figure."

"I'm his grandfather. I do what I can, but it isn't enough. You have to tell him, Rachel."

"I know!" she cried, turning back to her dishes. After a while, she asked without turning to face him, "Does Danny talk to you about Gabe?"

"Sometimes."

"What does he say?" Though she couldn't find the courage to tell Danny the truth about Gabe, she still wanted to know what her son thought about the man who had fathered him.

Then again, maybe she didn't.

Edward smiled. "He wanted to know if I knew Gabe when he was a boy, and what he was like back then. I told him he was full of himself. Actually, he's asked me that about every unattached man in town."

"He has?" Rachel couldn't hide her surprise. She'd never realized just how much Danny wanted a man — a father — in his life. She'd certainly had no idea he was gathering information about the town's bachelors, no doubt looking for one that fit his own personal criteria for a husband and father.

She would have to have that talk with Danny. Soon. Bringing her thoughts back to the present, she said, "Gabe was rowdy, wasn't he?" Her voice was almost wistful. "But I remember he was always friendly and nice to me."

"Being rowdy doesn't begin to cover it and doesn't mean a person can't be nice as well as rambunctious," Edward said. "Suffice it to say that I told Danny he reminds me a lot of Gabe. It seemed to please him."

"He's nothing like Gabe!" Rachel said, appalled at the very idea.

Edward shrugged. "As I said, Danny is looking for someone he can look up to. He needs that, Rachel."

"And you think he can look up to Gabriel Gentry?" she asked.

"I think that you aren't giving the man enough credit. Whatever he's been and done in the past does not mean he will say or do anything to taint your son, especially while he's living under our roof. And the very fact that he's come back to try to set things straight says a lot."

"I suppose you're right."

"Aren't I always?" Edward deadpanned.

"Right *and* conceited," Rachel said, but she was smiling when she said it. "What about later? When he leaves here? What then?"

"He isn't physically able to leave town for a while, and it's the dead of winter. Once he goes to Hattie's, Danny won't see much of him, and I imagine Gabe will be gone by spring."

Rachel shook her head.

"What?"

"He told me he isn't leaving. He's staying in Wolf Creek."

Edward's gaze met hers over the rim of his coffee cup, his expression thoughtful. "Won't that be interesting?"

Hattie's Hotel and Boardinghouse looked a mile away from Rachel's front porch, where Gabe stood, his carpetbag clutched in his "good" hand. It held nothing but a change of clothes and his shaving gear, but it already felt as if it weighed a hundred pounds. He wished he'd listened to Edward, who had offered to have Roland drive him over.

It was spitting sleet, and the hotel, which sat on the corner just beyond the railroad track, was a blur in the distance. Not that far, really. Getting there shouldn't be too taxing, even with his injuries. He made his way carefully down the steps and the path.

He had given in to Edward's persuasion and stayed the three extra days, spending as much time as possible with Danny, since the boy seemed so needy for a friend. His obvious yearning for male companionship brought back painful memories of that same need. Gabe knew what it was to ache for approval, and how it felt to crave a smile or even a word of scolding that would prove that Lucas realized he existed.

Lucas had never been there for Gabe or Caleb in any meaningful way. The closest anyone came to fulfilling the role he'd abdicated had been Frank, their hired hand.

Edward Stone was a good grandfather, but his stroke had left him unable to share many activities with the boy — especially outdoor activities. Edward had mentioned that Danny liked fishing, and before he realized his intent to do so, Gabe had offered to take him to the creek when the weather grew warmer. The suggestion had brought a wide smile to Danny's face.

He'd seen little of Rachel the past three days except when she came to check his injuries. Strangely, the animosity had all but disappeared, and she now treated him in a far different way. Not friendly, exactly. Civil. It was an improvement.

He found himself longing to have a normal conversation with her, like those they'd shared in St. Louis. He wanted to hear if her hopes and dreams had changed and if her work in Wolf Creek was as fulfilling as she'd expected, but he figured a heart-to-heart talk was way out of the realm of possibility, at least for the time being.

She might be unwilling to forgive him just yet, but clearly she'd forgotten how single-minded he could be when he decided he wanted something. He would do everything in his power to gain her pardon. It was something he had to have if he was to ever move on with his life in any meaningful way.

A frigid wind blew the icy particles against his face, stinging like hundreds of tiny needles. The ground was already covered with a thin layer of the wintry precipitation that made every step treacherous, especially for an injured man.

He turned and looked back at the house.

It would be so easy to go back, but something told him it would be easier to gain Rachel's forgiveness, and far easier on both of them if he wasn't around to remind her of the past.

He'd made the break, and nothing but a terrible setback would make him return to Rachel's home.

With her brow furrowed with worry, Rachel stood at the window, the fingertips of her right hand pressed against her mouth, the lace curtain pushed aside so that she could better see Gabe's progress along the treacherous road. He slipped a little. She gasped, and her heart flew to her throat. Ridiculous, irritating man! Exasperation nudged aside her concern. He'd had no business leaving, and he certainly should not be walking in this icy downpour. He'd catch his death of a cold, and then he'd be right back here.

Well, leaving was what he wanted, and she'd never held a patient hostage before. Good riddance to him! She wouldn't have to cook and do laundry for another person and wouldn't have to wait on him hand and foot. No more arguments. No more frustration and anger. Maybe her life could get back to normal now.

She let the curtain fall back into place and

turned away, her gaze roaming the empty room. The problem with normal was that it was terribly dreary sometimes.

CHAPTER FOUR

Rachel carried an armload of fresh linens into the bedroom Gabe had used. He had been gone a week and thus far she had refused to admit she missed him. All she would admit was that she missed doing things for him. She'd become accustomed to checking on him before she made her daily calls and again when she came in. She missed seeing him at meals, and it seemed that without his clothes, even the laundry seemed lacking somehow.

She placed the sheets and towels into the linen press, closed the doors and turned to lean against them, letting her bleak gaze roam the room. There was no sign he'd ever been there beyond the memory of his dark head against the pillows and the way he watched her with that intense blue gaze as she treated his injuries — a look that, despite all attempts to not respond, made her heart pound, as aware of him as she'd ever been.

Tears burned her eyes. That was the problem. She might tell herself she was over him. She might claim to despise him, but what she really despised was the fact that she wasn't over him and couldn't rout him from her mind or her heart.

Heaven help her, despite everything, she still loved him.

It made her furious and at the same time miserable. Had she learned nothing nine years ago? Was she deficient of even one ounce of intelligence or self-respect? Was she so weak and lonely that she was willing to ignore the pain and shame of the past and fall willy-nilly into his arms again?

No. She had determined that, no matter what, she would not fall for his flattery and lies a second time. In her orderly, play-by-the-book mind, the fact that she missed him was tantamount to a character flaw. She was no longer the innocent she'd been when she first went to St. Louis.

She'd learned a lot of important lessons through the years. Feelings could be suppressed, ignored and even manipulated if you tried hard enough, and she intended to try very hard to rid herself of the renegade emotions she felt for Gabe.

She would fight them with work and common sense, and if that wasn't enough to keep her from entrusting him with her heart, she would play her trump card: Danny.

Her heart was one thing — Danny's was quite another.

Edward claimed Danny craved a father, so maybe she'd consider trying to give him one. That would drive Gabe Gentry from her mind. She had always expected to marry someday; how could she hope to find love and a father for Danny if she didn't give the single men in town a chance? Maybe it was time for her to start accepting some of the offers of courtship that came her way. Unfortunately, single men were few and far between. She'd had high hopes for Colt Garrett when he'd first come to town as the new sheriff, but there had been no romantic spark between them. Still, she had not abandoned the dream. There was always the off chance of a miracle happening.

She heard Danny's voice in the kitchen. He was more or less himself since Gabe had moved to the hotel, but there were times she caught him staring off into space as if he were miles away, and she knew he was suffering the loss of his new "friend." In retrospect, she was glad she hadn't caved to her father's wishes and her own guilt and told Danny that Gabe was his father. If she had, chances were that he would be even deeper in the doldrums.

Shaking off her dark mood, she pushed away from the linen press and turned toward the door. The Bible promised that these troubled, unsettled feelings Gabe's return had stirred would pass. She wished they would hurry.

As the weeks passed and his body healed, cabin fever almost drove Gabe to insanity. Caleb, his well-read, book-educated brother, had brought him a stack of books and periodicals from his extensive library and Gabe had read until he thought his eyes must surely cross.

Inevitably, his thoughts turned to how he was going to spend the rest of his life. Though he claimed he'd come home to stay, he had no idea how he might make a living. The time he spent recuperating gave him ample time to think about his future, but thoughts and dreams could only fill so much of a day, and boredom had not just staked a claim, it had homesteaded.

At the end of January, on one of the unexpected balmy winter days not uncommon to southwest Arkansas, Caleb picked up Gabe for Sunday dinner after the morning church service. Though neither of them would claim they were friends, they were trying to put the past behind them and see if there could be more to their relationship than enmity and hard feelings.

Wearing a wide smile, Abby met them at the front door and gave Gabe a hug of welcome. Something close to embarrassment flooded him. Friendly hugs were not something he'd experienced often. The unexpected gesture left him feeling a bit self-conscious.

"None for me?" Caleb asked when Abby turned to hang up Gabe's coat.

A becoming blush crept into her cheeks. "Oh, you!" she said, but grabbed his coat front, pulled him close and pressed a quick kiss to his lips. Gabe noticed how her hands lingered on Caleb's chest and was stunned when his brother dropped another kiss to her mouth.

Gabe was amazed by the obvious love between his brother and Abby. The grave, exacting Caleb whom Gabe recalled from their youth was gone, and in his place was a man satisfied with his lot in life. His brother was happy. Content. Though Gabe was genuinely delighted for him, he admitted to being a tad jealous.

Like forgiveness, he wondered if he would

ever experience the love and happiness surrounding his brother or know the kind of satisfaction reflected in his eyes. He knew there were young women around town who thought he was handsome despite the scar on his cheek, but he had no interest in giggling, blushing girls. There was even a widow or two who cast doe eyes at him whenever he passed them on the sidewalk, but no one so far had prompted a smidgen of interest.

Knowing it was foolishness on his part, yet unable to stop, he measured every female against Rachel, and they all came up lacking. Since it was pretty clear that she was unlikely to ever forgive him, he saw his life stretching out into a long, endless expanse of regrets. He was left with the distasteful possibility that if he were to marry, he would be forced to settle for less than his heart's desire.

Abby lost no time introducing "Uncle Gabe" to the children. There was her son, Ben, who was obviously as fond of Caleb as he was the boy, and two-year-old Laura, who vied with her brother for Caleb's attention. Then there was one-year-old Betsy — whose mother had died at her birth, bringing Abby into their lives — and baby Eli, barely a month old.

Frank and Leo showed up to share the meal, and there was much laughter and many reminiscences as they ate. Frank had no compunction about trotting out Gabe's misdemeanors one by one, and Gabe was surprised when everyone, including Caleb, laughed at the reminders of some of his most memorable antics.

He finally begged Frank to be quiet so his less-than-sterling past would not tempt young Ben to follow in his uncle's footsteps. Frank agreed with a throaty laugh, and Gabe was struck by how different this meal was compared to meals when Lucas had presided over the dinner table.

"Just in case things get chaotic later and I forget, I want to ask you to join us at Wolf Creek Church next week," Abby said. "Well, join Caleb, anyway. It's still too cold to get Eli out, so the little ones and I will be staying at home for a bit yet."

Church? Gabe knew from several conversations with Ellie at the café that Abby was a devout Christian and that his brother had rededicated his life the past summer, just one more change Abby Gentry had brought about. But church for himself? Gabe wasn't so sure about that, and he was less sure how the membership would accept him, considering his past.

"I'll think about it."

"See that you do," Abby said in her best schoolmarm voice, but she tempered the comment with a smile.

When they finished eating, Frank and Leo headed for the bunkhouse, and Caleb started to help with the dishes, another in a growing list of mind-boggling changes time had wrought in his brother.

Abby refused his help, shooing him toward the door. "I'll give you time off since Gabe is here. Why don't you two take your coffee into the parlor and catch up?"

As the two headed for the doorway, she called Caleb's name. When he turned, she smiled and said, "Just so you know, you needn't think I'll make a habit of it."

"No ma'am," Caleb said with a smile. He led the way to the parlor.

The brothers settled into their preferred chairs and spent several minutes talking about the books Gabe had read.

"I know reading can get tiresome," Caleb told him, "but I have plenty more titles I think would interest you. I don't think you'll be ready to look for a job just yet," Caleb said.

"Probably not," Gabe agreed, "and even if I were, I have no idea what I'd be good at or what I might like. How did you know

115

what you wanted to do with your life, and why on earth did you stay with farming after having it crammed down your throat?"

There was little humor in Caleb's laughter. "If you'll recall, I wasn't given a choice," he said. "You took off and Lucas made it very clear that he expected me to 'step up,' as he put it."

Gabe felt another surge of the guilt that had often beset him since returning to Wolf Creek. No acts of contrition or request for forgiveness would ever be enough to make up for how he'd wronged the people in his past.

"Besides," Caleb continued, "as you pointed out, I knew farming inside and out, and I was pretty good at it. Then one day I realized I actually liked it."

"Thank goodness for that," Gabe said. "I can't say that anything in my background has given me any credentials. Gambling and carousing aren't much as job experience goes."

"I've been thinking about that," Caleb said, after a slight pause. "Abby and I have talked about it."

Gabe waited, uncertain if he liked being the topic of dinnertime conversation, yet knowing that it was inevitable, not just with Caleb and Abby but the whole town.

"You know that when Lucas died, he left everything to me, since you'd already received your inheritance."

Gabe nodded and shrugged. "As was only right and fair."

Caleb took a deep breath. "Maybe so, but nevertheless, I want to offer you a half interest in the farm, if you're willing to do half the work."

Gabe's startled gaze searched his brother's. In his wildest imaginings he would never have expected such a generous offer. "You aren't serious?"

"I am," Caleb said, reaching for the cup of coffee he'd brought from the kitchen.

"But why?"

"It was Abby's idea," Caleb confessed. "And I'd be less than honest if I didn't tell you that it didn't sit well at first." He drew in another breath. "Then I started thinking about it, and she's right. You're as much Lucas's son as I am, and there's more than enough for the two of us."

Gabe stared at his brother. Just as there was no doubting the sincerity of his confession, there was no doubting the sincerity of the offer. Gabe had to blink back tears. He heard the trembling in his voice as he said, "I can't thank you enough, Caleb. It's a more-than-generous offer, and I realize you're giving me a wonderful opportunity, but it isn't fair to you. I got my part, and I threw it away. This farm is yours, so if it's all the same to you, I'll pass."

Caleb sat up straighter. "Why? I thought you were planning on staying around here."

"I am."

"Well, if you're worried about the cost, let me be clear. I'm not offering to *sell* you part of the farm. I'm *giving* it to you."

"Again, I thank you, but the answer is no."

"Then —"

Gabe held up a silencing hand. "What you've done means more to me than you'll ever know, considering the way things have always been between us, but I won't take you up on your offer because I know in my heart that, unlike you, farming isn't for me. Besides, it's your farm, Caleb. Always will be. You've given it your blood, sweat and tears your whole life. Lucas didn't *give* you anything. You paid for it. Every acre. Every fence post. Every head of livestock."

"But what will you do?" Caleb's expression was troubled.

"I'm not sure, but something will come along," Gabe said. "It always does."

By the end of February, spring was making promises everyone knew she would not

118

keep. Gabe smoothed his shirt collar as a loud rapping sounded at his door. Caleb, no doubt. Abby had been unrelenting in her pleas for Gabe to attend church. Until today, he'd managed to put her off with the excuse that his ribs just weren't up to sitting so long in the hard pews. But with the thrashing he'd received two months past, he was feeling much better, and Abby had declared that his excuse was getting old.

So here he was, dressed up in his Sunday best and waiting to come face-to-face with people who'd known him since birth. People who knew about his many youthful escapades . . . and indiscretions.

Though the room was a bit chilly, Gabe broke out into a sweat just thinking of the gauntlet he was about to run. He took a steadying breath and flung open the door. If he intended to make a life here, the time for hiding was past.

It was time to face the music.

Time to pay the fiddler.

Gabe followed his brother and Abby into the small church, certain he'd never been more uncomfortable in his life. Expecting censure, he was surprised when a tall, heavy-set man with salt-and-pepper hair and matching beard covering his fleshy cheeks spoke to Caleb and Abby then grabbed Gabe's hand and began to pump it up and down.

"Gabriel Gentry! It's good to have you."

Taken aback by the man's enthusiastic welcome, Gabe barely managed a weak smile. "Thank you."

"You remember me, don't you? Earl Pickens?"

Earl Pickens. Gabe did remember him. "Do you still have the newspaper?"

"I still keep my hand in, but my son, Charles, does most of the work these days."

They talked for a few more minutes, and Abby introduced him to some other couples, people near his and Caleb's age. A few greetings were warmer than others, but no one snubbed him outright. That in itself was gratifying and humbling. Of course, he hadn't seen Sarah VanSickle yet.

"Gabe!"

He turned at the sound of the childish voice. Danny, Rachel and Edward, who was using his canes to get around this morning, were entering the double doors. The boy headed toward Gabe, a wide smile on his face. Rachel reached out to stop him with a hand on his shoulder.

He glanced up at his mother with a questioning look.

"We need to get Pops settled. The service is about to start." Her expression was carefully neutral, and her halfhearted smile did not quite reach her brown eyes when she turned to Gabe. "I didn't expect to see you here."

"You can thank Abby for that," he said, the simple reply challenging her to say anything to her friend. For a moment, she seemed to be searching for a comeback.

Apparently unable to come up with anything pithy, she murmured, "I hope you enjoy the service," and then she followed her father down the aisle.

Gabe could add Rachel's name to the column of folks who were not particularly happy to see him there.

By the time the song leader began the first hymn, voices raised in the a cappella rendition of "The Old Rugged Cross," Gabe had managed to push her cool disapproval from his mind and was able to concentrate on the service.

The minister's sermon was about God's divine providence and how there were lessons to be learned from life's difficulties and bad experiences. He went on to say that problems often enabled us to grow not only as individuals, but in our faith. Always, His goal was for ultimate good, even though many were unable to recognize His plan in the midst of pain and turmoil. People either grew closer to God or turned away when trouble struck.

Gabe wondered what the Lord's plan was for him. He was truly sorry for his past behavior, but he failed to see how Lucas's treatment of him and his brother, his mother's abandonment and his own youthful transgressions could be part of a plan to bring about his betterment or his happiness — or anyone else's, for that matter.

He cast a surreptitious glance at Rachel, who chose that moment to look his way. Her mouth was set in an uncompromising line, and her eyes reflected coolness. It didn't look as if she saw the wisdom of God's providence in his return, either.

CHAPTER FIVE

By mid-March, Gabe began to wander to the Emersons' mercantile several times a week in an effort to thwart his boredom. He spent hours talking to Bart and Mary Emerson, catching up on the town's happenings.

He found out who had died, who had married and that there was a growing interest in timber and gravel. He gained insights into his brother's character and details about Caleb's marriage to the Emersons' daughter. He was a bit surprised that they had so wholeheartedly accepted Abby as a mother for their little granddaughter so soon after Emily's death, but then the Emersons were exceptional people.

When he tried to bring the conversation around to Rachel, hoping to learn more about her missing husband, the Emersons, like Caleb, claimed to know nothing. They were not ones to gossip. Since Abby was reasonably new to town, the only thing she knew about Rachel was that she was a good person and a fantastic doctor. Gabe didn't miss the considering expression in his sister-in-law's eyes and wondered if what he thought were casual questions had tipped his hand about his growing feelings for the lady physician.

Some days, he helped unpack new merchandise and rearrange other stock, hoping that the reshuffling would bring attention to product that was slow to sell. Other times, he joined the men whose sole occupation was passing the day by striking up conversations with whoever came through the doors and playing chess or checkers until one of them pulled out a pocket watch and announced that it was "time to get home before Sally/Bessie/Mable/Annie threw out their supper."

At the end of the month, Gabe was surprised when Bart said he wanted to have a talk with him.

"Sure, Bart," Gabe said. "What can I do for you?"

"Mary and I have discussed this, and we decided to talk to you before we do anything else."

"Okay," Gabe said, uncertain where the conversation was headed. There was almost

124

a feeling of déjà vu, as he recalled his talk with Caleb.

"We've decided to sell the store and move to St. Louis."

"Why?" Gabe asked, unable to hide his surprise. "I thought you were happy in Wolf Creek?"

"We are," Bart said, "but we have another daughter and five grandchildren we seldom get to see. We've been so tied down here that we seldom get away."

"Joanna's children are growing up without us knowing them at all," Mary chimed in. "We've decided that we want to spend more time with them now that Emily is gone."

"What will you do there?"

"Our son-in-law's factory is doing well, and he could use some part-time help in the office. I'd help him a couple of days a week. With our savings and the sale of the store, we should be able to live comfortably enough," Bart told him.

"What about Betsy?" Gabe asked, still trying to take everything in. "You'll miss out on her growing up, too."

"We adore her," Mary said. "Please don't think we don't. We've even talked about taking her with us, if Caleb would let us . . ."

". . . which we both doubt," Bart said.

"But Joanna's hands are full, and we're

too old to bring up another child."

"We know that Caleb and Abby will take good care of her," Bart chimed in. "And Caleb *is* her father. Once we move, and I just work part time, we can come back for a visit whenever we want. And we would always welcome Caleb and Abby if they wanted to come visit us."

Gabe saw that they'd given the notion a lot of thought. "Why are you telling me about this?"

"We'd like you to buy the store."

Gabe was sure his mouth fell open. He looked from one to the other. "Me? Why?"

"It was Mary's idea," Bart said. "I know you're trying to decide what to do if you stay here, and this is a good business if it's handled correctly."

"I don't know the first thing about the mercantile business," Gabe said, though the offer had definitely piqued his interest and his mind was already whirling with possibilities.

"Nonsense! You've been a great help to us the past few weeks, and you have some fantastic ideas for new products and promoting sales. Besides, we won't be leaving until early May," Bart said. "It will take that long to make arrangements. If you buy, we could come in every day and work with you . . . show you the ropes until you get the hang of things."

Gabe's head was spinning. "What about the price?" he asked. "I have a little money stuck back, but I'm sure it isn't enough, and I doubt Mr. Haversham would give me a loan, since I haven't been here long to establish any credit."

"Oh, I figure he might, if I have a talk with him," Bart said. "If not, I'll finance the balance myself."

"You'd do that?" Gabe asked, stunned at the unexpected generosity of the offer. "Why?"

"Because I see you trying to change your life, son," Bart said, clamping a hand on Gabe's shoulder, "and I'm a firm believer that we all deserve a second chance. Nobody gets it right all the time."

Gabe thought it over for a week before deciding to become a retail merchant. Arrangements for the purchase were less trouble than he'd expected. Nathan Haversham might not have agreed with Gabe's previous lifestyle, but like Bart, he liked the idea of a young man who'd seen what was happening in other parts of the country bringing some of those fresh ideas to their town. He was also counting on the fact that

Lucas Gentry's blood flowed in Gabe's veins. That alone meant he had a pretty good chance of making the enterprise a success.

While awaiting the arrival of May, Bart and Mary showed him how to take inventory; how many, what kind, how much and when to order; and to whom he should extend credit — as well as to whom he should not. Somewhat surprisingly, he enjoyed the learning process. He liked that no two days were alike. Always gregarious, he liked visiting with the customers, liked hearing their problems and offering his commiseration, even though he had no idea how to fix his own problems.

He'd made a start, though. He'd realized that Rachel might not pardon him, but God could and would, if only Gabe made things right with Him and turned his life around. Feeling the weight of his unworthiness, and humbled by the depth of God's grace, he had become a Christian two weeks earlier. As he'd come up from the still-cold waters of Wolf Creek, he'd felt a sense of peace and responsibility he'd never known before.

Lucas Gentry had not been a God-fearing man in any respect, and the idea of a life built with Christ at its center was an alien one to Gabe; nevertheless, he was committed to doing his best. Since then, he'd worked even harder at trying to be everything he should be, but there were times he knew he failed miserably. That, Abby had assured him with a confident smile, was where grace continued to cleanse.

The morning in late April after he'd signed the papers, he got up before daybreak, dressed and unlocked the front doors before the town was stirring — though he did see a light at the café. Ellie was up making pies and setting her bread to rise. He lit a couple of lamps and walked around the store, looking around, making plans, running his hand over the counter, unable to stop the heady pride of possession that swept through him.

He'd done it! For better or worse, he'd found a way to stay. Now he needed to make himself an accepted member of the community. Whether or not he would be a success was up to him. He *would* be successful. He was smart, willing and, like Nate Haversham, knew he'd inherited enough of Lucas Gentry's business savvy to make a go of things. With just over a week until Bart and Mary left, he needed to soak up every bit of knowledge he could from them.

Folding his arms across his chest, he surveyed the large area, thinking of ways to make his mark on the store. First thing today, he'd order a new sign: GENTRY MERCANTILE. He would choose a day and advertise a grand opening in the newspaper, like the one he'd seen in New York — or was that Boston? — with cookies or cake and punch. He would give away some merchandise as door prizes. People liked that.

He scrutinized the large plate-glass windows and pictured a raised display area built in front of each of them. He could purchase some dress forms to show off the new spring fashions and drape some of his new fabrics over . . . well, *something* to display their bright hues.

He contemplated the arrangements of the shelving and tables. The chess and checkerboards would be better moved nearer to the potbellied stove. He'd hang a lantern above the tables for better lighting. He could make a pot of coffee every day in one of the blue spatterware coffeepots he sold and keep it warming on the back of the stove. It would be a nice gesture to offer a free coffee to those who came to shop, especially in winter.

He was heading toward the curtain that separated the front of the store from the back room when he heard the bell at the door tinkle. Turning, he saw Rachel poised just inside the entryway.

"You actually did it."

There was no missing the disbelief lacing her voice.

"If you mean buying the Emersons out, then yes, I did it."

"Why?"

Weary of her resentment, Gabe tamped down his own temper. "I told you months ago that I planned on staying."

"So you did," she said with a hollow smile. "I just never thought you really would. How could you do this to me?"

"My staying has nothing to do with you, Rachel," he tried to explain. "It's a choice I made because I believe it's the best course for me. Believe it or not, I didn't set out to ruin your life or decide to stay to make you miserable."

"Well, that's what it feels like." Like him, she was carefully civil.

Feeling the familiar despair sweep through him, he struggled for calmness he was far from feeling. "I'm sorry for that," he said, "but I have tried to make amends."

"You have, but do you really think it's as simple as saying 'I'm sorry'?"

He stepped from behind the counter and advanced on her with a purposeful stride, not stopping until he was within touching distance. If he expected her to retreat as the old Rachel would have, he was disappointed. This Rachel stood her ground.

"Oh, I forgot," he mocked, forgetting that he was supposed to be the peacemaker. "Apologies, even sincere apologies, mean nothing to the upstanding Dr. Stone, epitome of all that is pure and proper."

"No longer pure, thanks to you."

Gabe clenched his fists at his sides, closed his eyes and counted to ten. Then he drew a deep breath, again struggling to find some measure of rationality before speaking. "You're right. Because of me you are no longer innocent, but I wonder if you've forgotten that what happened was by mutual agreement."

Her eyes widened in surprise, and the blood drained from her face, as if she'd just heard something she'd never thought of before. Her voice quavered with something that sounded like pain. "What I remember is that you left me when you found something that interested you more."

It was an accusation he couldn't deny. Gabe scrubbed a hand over his face. *Dear Lord, help me.*

"You're right. And I have asked for your forgiveness on more than one occasion, which you have denied." The frustration and sorrow inside him was etched on his face. "I can't undo the past, Rachel. So what more would you have me do? Go out on the street wearing sackcloth and ashes? Maybe I should take a cat-o'-nine and flog myself before the whole town. Would that make you happy?"

"I'm not sure I'll ever be truly happy, thanks to you."

"I find that incredibly sad," he said, with a shake of his head, "but I will not allow you to place all the blame for a lifetime of misery on me, when we were equally responsible for what happened.

"The first day I visited church, the preacher said we were given trials because we were expected to grow in faith and to learn from them. One thing I've learned the past nine years — and believe me, everything I've learned has been the hard way — is that we all make mistakes, even the blameless Dr. Stone.

"I've also learned that you were right about us making our own happiness. We can't rely on money or things or other people, because we'll never reach that state until we are satisfied with who and what we are."

"So wise," she said, with a shake of her

head. "Tell me, Gabe, are you happy?"

He hesitated no more than a fraction of a second. "I'm getting there." It came as a bit of a surprise to realize it was true.

Speechless, she turned to leave. He reached out and placed his hand on her shoulder. With a gasp, she whirled to face him. "Do you know what *I* remember about those three weeks?" he asked.

She stood mute, trembling beneath his touch.

"I remember a beautiful, shy, incredibly intelligent young woman with a core of determination that awed me." Unable to help himself, he trailed a whisper-soft touch along the curve of her jaw and saw the lingering misery in her eyes dim.

"I remember how delightful she was. . . ." His thumb brushed the fullness of her lower lip, and she sucked in a startled breath. "And I remember how her sweet kisses took away my breath."

He felt the starch go out of her. For perhaps the first time since returning, there was no reproach in the dark gaze that probed his.

"If you felt all that, why did you leave the way you did?"

"Because I was young and unbelievably stupid," he told her.

Their probing gazes clung for long expectant seconds. Then, shrugging free of his hold, she turned and opened the door.

Heaving a sigh of sorrow, he spoke to her back. "The supplies you ordered should be in by week's end. I'll let you know when they arrive."

Without answering, she shut the door behind her and hurried across the street. The bells tinkled merrily as he watched her go, wondering again if she would ever forgive him . . . wondering if he would ever forgive himself for the way his thoughtless treatment had changed her.

Rachel exited the mercantile, the image of Gabe's contrition, anger and frustration branded into her mind. Ellie was just flipping around the sign to announce she was open for business. Rachel thought about getting a cup of coffee to settle her nerves, but instead turned the other way, heading toward the house, her trembling hands clenched inside her coat pockets, faced with a new reality and an old guilt she could no longer deny.

Until the moment Gabe had brutally reminded her that what happened between them was as much her choice as his, it had been easy to cast herself in the role of the victim, place all the blame on him and take refuge in her anger. That was no longer possible. It was a hard pill to swallow, but he was right. They were both to blame. It was a notion she would have to get used to, just as she would have to get accustomed to the fact that he was not leaving Wolf Creek. She'd pinned all her hopes on his wanderlust, certain that when he was healed, he would take off again.

Since that wasn't to be, either, her immediate problem was what to do about Danny. His welfare was the most important thing in her life, and she was so afraid he was asking for heartbreak if he grew too close to the man who'd fathered him. If only he weren't so infatuated with Gabe!

She recalled the day Danny had come home with a wide smile on his face.

"He's staying, Mama!" he'd crowed, literally jumping up and down.

"Who's staying, Danny?" she'd asked, though she feared she already knew the answer.

"Gabe."

There was no missing the gleam of excitement in her son's eyes or the little leap of her own heart. Both irritated her to no end. How was she expected to keep her treacherous feelings for him from growing if she had to deal with him on a regular basis for the rest of her life?

Up until now, avoiding him had been fairly easy. A polite nod, a perfunctory hello, a pleasant expression when he was around so that no one would suspect what was really in her heart had not been too much of a strain. But there was no way she could ignore him now. She had to have medical supplies and household necessities, and there was nowhere else to get them.

To give Gabe his due, he had become a Christian, and it had not escaped her that he was faithful in his church attendance. For the most part, people around town seemed fine with his attempts to reestablish himself in the community. While both signs were encouraging, she told herself that a few months of good living could not wipe out a lifetime of debauchery.

Except in God's eyes.

The errant thought made her feel ashamed all over again, and she vowed to pray for His forgiveness more vigorously.

"Where did you get that idea?" she'd asked Danny as she locked the glass-front cabinet that held her medical supplies. "I told you he never stays in one place for very long."

"When I went to the mercantile to spend

the penny Pops gave me, there was a Sold sign in the window," he'd told her. "I asked Mr. Emerson who bought the store, and he said Gabe. He's going to live upstairs."

Rachel had found herself speechless.

Now, with her early-morning talk with Gabe sitting like curdled milk in her stomach, there was another truth to face. With the recent changes in his life, it was entirely possible that she was borrowing trouble. Maybe Gabe would not hurt Danny at all.

One thing was certain, though. There was no putting off telling Danny about Gabe. It would have to be done. Soon.

At the house, she found her son and father in the kitchen making breakfast. Edward was buttering toast, while Danny stood on a small stool, stirring scrambled eggs with a wooden spoon.

"Good morning," Rachel said, bending to press a kiss to the top of her father's head. Doing the same to Danny's cheek, she warned, "Be careful."

He cast a surprisingly accurate imitation of her famous "look" over his shoulder. "I am."

"How is Meg?" Edward asked.

Meg Thomerson was a young wife whose husband's main source of pleasure when he was liquored up seemed to be beating her

138

to within an inch of her life. "She's not nearly as bad as the last time, but that isn't saying much."

"Do you think she'll ever leave him?"

"Only in a casket, I'm afraid." Rachel poured herself a cup of coffee. "Elton has her convinced it's her fault he loses control."

"Luther was just like him," Edward said, thoughtfully. "It's a self-perpetuating evil." He shot a severe look at his grandson. "Are you listening, Danny? It's never okay to hit girls."

"I know," he said over his shoulder. "Boys are supposed to take care of girls and keep bad things from happening to them, like I do for Bethany."

Rachel smiled. Bethany was Ellie's eleven-year-old daughter, a Mongoloid who was often the brunt of teasing and practical jokes. "Exactly."

"Is the mercantile opening up today?" Edward asked, peering over the tops of his glasses.

By now, everyone in town knew of the Emersons' sale to Gabe the day before. Unfortunately, Rachel seemed to be the only person who'd felt the necessity to confront him about his reasons. "He's already open."

Danny glanced up from his stirring, eager

to hear news about the man he'd taken to so easily.

"I told you," he said.

"So you did. Are those eggs done?" she asked, deftly changing the subject.

"Think so. They aren't runny anymore."

"Good." She scooped the eggs from the skillet and added two sausage patties to each plate before setting them in front of Danny and her father.

They gave thanks for the food and the two guys dug in while Rachel nibbled at her sausage and pushed the eggs around on her plate.

"Anything wrong?" Edward asked.

"Only what you might imagine," she said, offering him a false, sweet smile.

Edward lifted his eyebrows in understanding. "Ah."

That night, Rachel knew she had put off the inevitable as long as possible. She knocked and let herself into Danny's room. He was propped up in bed reading, something he did almost every night before she made him blow out the lamp.

Dreading the next few moments, she sat down on the side of the bed and rested her hand against his soft cheek. "Danny, I have something to tell you." The unsteadiness she heard in her voice confirmed her anxiety.

"Yes, Mama?" The blue eyes so much like Gabe's regarded her solemnly.

Drawing a breath, she plunged. "Do you remember when you asked me about your father, and I told you that he'd gone away before you were born?"

Danny's dark head moved up and down against the pillow. "You said he was young and wasn't ready for the responsibility of a family."

Her mouth lifted in a sad smile. That much was true. But she'd omitted so much more in an effort to keep from telling him an out-and-out lie. "Well, he's come back."

Danny bolted upright. "He has? Can I see him?"

The joy in his eyes was almost her undoing. Tears burned beneath her eyelids and her heart seemed to stop for a beat. "You have seen him," she whispered.

"I have?" he asked with a puzzled frown.

"Danny, Gabe Gentry is your father."

For long moments, he didn't speak, only looked at her while his eight-year-old mind struggled to understand. Finally, he said, "Does he know about me?"

His previous enthusiasm was tempered somewhat by something she couldn't put her finger on. A touch of anxiety? She shook her head. "No. I never told him about you."

"Why not?"

Dear Lord, help me find the words . . . "There were reasons, Danny, reasons you're too young to understand. Your father and I . . . we made a mistake. We were a mistake."

"Because he wasn't ready for the responsibility of a family," he said, repeating by rote what she'd told him before.

"Yes."

"What about now?" he asked. "Will you tell him about me now? I'm eight, so he's older, too, and he's probably ready for a family now, don't you think?"

Rachel's heart turned to ice. How could she have forgotten the second half of the equation? Sooner or later Gabe would have to be told the truth.

"Preferably later," she muttered.

"What?"

"Later, Danny," she told him, forcing a smile. "Be patient for just a little longer. The time to tell someone something like this has to be just right."

And Lord help me, I have to find the courage.

"Do you think he'll be happy, Mama?" Danny asked, his face wreathed in a wide smile. "Do you think he'll be glad I'm his son?"

Rachel pressed her lips together to hold back her tears. How to answer? With Gabe, who could predict? "Oh, Danny!"

She reached out and pulled him into her arms, hugging him close. *Dear God, why does this have to be so hard?* She smoothed his dark hair away from his forehead.

"I know he will," she told him fervently, praying it would be so. "But I still think we should wait to say anything a bit longer."

"Why?" Danny demanded. "Because I'm a mistake?"

A little cry of distress escaped her. How quickly little minds were able to get to the crux of a matter. Regardless of how it had happened or whose fault it was, she did not regret him. Not for a second.

"Oh, no, Danny! Never believe that. I never thought *you* were a mistake. You're a blessing. The mistake was mine. The mistake was my loving Gabe more than he loved me and for not loving God more than I did Gabe."

"How could Gabe not love you, Mama?" Danny asked. "You're so pretty and so nice."

She smiled a watery smile at his gallant defense. "Thank you. It's sweet of you to say so. But that's the way it was." She paused. "As for telling Gabe about you, I believe it's best if this is our secret, at least for a while. Can you do that?"

Danny's face fell. He nodded. Uncertain if she could take any more of his disappointment, she stood to leave.

"Mama?"

"Yes, Danny?"

"Do you think if he gets to know me, he'd learn to love me enough to take on some responsibility?"

Rachel's heart broke just a little bit more as the uncertainty of the situation settled over her. It terrified her to imagine where the next few weeks might take them. She only hoped that Danny would survive with his happiness and his hope intact. She cradled his freckled face between her palms. "Everyone who knows you loves you."

He thought about that for a moment and asked, "Would you ever leave me?"

"Never! Not for any reason."

The words seemed to reassure him. Then he smiled and she saw a hint of mischief enter his eyes. "Except to go to heaven."

"Well, yes," she said, forcing a reciprocal smile. "Except that. And that would be okay, because one day you'd be right up there beside me."

Once again, she started to go; once again,

he stopped her.

"Mama, does Pops know about Gabe?"

"You must call him 'Mr. Gentry,' Danny, not 'Gabe.' And yes, Pops knows."

"Is it okay if I talk to him about it?"

Rachel hesitated and then nodded her approval. She wondered what kinds of questions Danny might come up with for her father and knew that Edward Stone could handle whatever came his way.

CHAPTER SIX

By the time the Emersons left, Gabe was physically back to normal. He worked from daylight until long after dark doing everything possible to improve the store and its contents. Keeping busy was a far better way to spend his time than thinking about Rachel, but even working, his thoughts turned to her as often as not.

He wished there was someone he could talk to about his past and his feelings for her, but no one in town knew about their past, so to say anything would be unthinkable. He couldn't even confide to Caleb, though they were making strides in their efforts at becoming closer.

Spending more time with Caleb showed just how much he had changed. His eyes held happiness based not only on his love for Abby, but on his love of the Lord. It was humbling to see his brother setting the example for his family.

As uplifting as it was to see the changes in Caleb, it was also a bit disheartening, since Gabe wasn't sure he would ever reach that point of commitment to God, and he despaired of ever finding happiness with Rachel. When he realized there was nothing he could do to change her mind and there was no one to talk to, he resorted to something he'd never done much of before — prayer. He didn't think he was very good at it, but sharing his thoughts and feelings felt so good that he unburdened himself completely, pouring out his sorrow and feelings and frustrations. After all, it wasn't as if God didn't already know what was on his heart. Now there was nothing to do but keep praying and wait for the answer. Yes. No. Or wait awhile.

He was stacking new bolts of fabric onto the table in the dry-goods section, while watching for a glimpse of Rachel through the front window, which now read Gentry Mercantile in bold red and black letters. Earlier, he'd been putting a dress of sunshine-yellow dotted Swiss on one of the dress forms there, hoping it might catch the eye of some lady who needed a new summer frock, when he just happened to catch a glimpse of Rachel and Abby heading toward Ellie's. Abby held Eli, and Rachel had Betsy on her hip, while Laura clung to her mother's skirts. The older boys were nowhere to be seen, since school was in session until the end of the month.

He had watched the two women enter the café, smiling and chatting, caught up in whatever things women talked about when they were together, not, Gabe supposed, unlike the way the old men who played checkers every day talked about their interests when they congregated. All too soon, the ladies had disappeared inside, and he was left staring at the restaurant's facade and wondering how long it might be before they emerged again. Shaking his head in disgust, he'd started putting out the remainder of the shipment.

Gabe saw Danny often. It seemed that no matter where he went, if school wasn't in session, the child appeared sooner or later. Gabe often caught Danny staring at him in a contemplative way, but whenever he asked what he was thinking about, he'd just smile and say "My father," which set Gabe off on another round of mental torture that left him miserable.

"What a lovely fabric, Gabriel."

The comment came from Sarah Van-Sickle, who had been back in the shoe section, trying to cram her size eight into a size

148

seven. Now he looked down at the bolt of sea-green seersucker in his hands.

"It is, isn't it?" He picked up a spool of delicate ivory lace. "I thought this might go well with it," he said, trying to make conversation, though everything the woman did grated on his nerves. "What do you think?"

Sarah gave him an arch look, and a smirk intended to pass for a smile lifted the corners of her mouth. "You know women and what they might like *very* well, is what I think."

There was no mistaking the meaning behind the words. Though Sarah had gone through all the outward motions of happiness the day Gabe became a Christian, there had been a disdainful gleam in her eyes that shouted of her insincerity.

Before he could stop himself, he said, "Perhaps all that riotous living wasn't entirely in vain, right, Mrs. VanSickle?"

Undeterred, Sarah asked, "Wasn't that your sister-in-law and Rachel Stone going into the restaurant a bit ago?"

"I believe it was."

"An interesting situation, that," Sarah said, pretending to sort through a box holding cards of buttons.

"What situation is that?"

"Why, your brother marrying Mrs. Car-

149

ter, who was a virtual stranger when she moved in with him."

The implication was clear, and the obnoxious woman had left out the important fact that Abby hadn't just *moved in.* She had been hired as Betsy's wet nurse. Caleb had explained how Sarah's vicious gossip had left him and Abby with no recourse but to marry. Control or not, Gabe refused to stand there and have the reputation of one of the most wonderful women he'd ever had the privilege of knowing undermined by the likes of this tacky person. Bestowing his most charming smile on her, he said, "I understand we can thank you for that."

Sarah gasped, and her dark eyes snapped in annoyance. "Whatever do you mean?"

He lifted his shoulders in a nonchalant shrug. "I understand from several people in town that you were the one to play matchmaker to Caleb and Abby."

The portly woman's face turned an unbecoming red, and for once she had no ready comeback.

Mollified, Gabe decided to soften the blow somewhat. His smile grew wider. "They're so ridiculously happy, I'm sure they'll be forever grateful for the little push you gave them."

Knowing she'd met her match, Sarah

turned away and pretended to give her attention to the rack of dime novels, while he finished arranging the cloth and sneaked another look out the window. Several children were wandering from the east end of town, which meant that school must have let out for the day. He watched Danny and Ben enter the restaurant.

He was placing canned peaches on the shelf when he saw Danny bound through the open portal, a wide smile on his face. "Hey, Gabe!" he said, running toward the counter.

Before Gabe could reply, Sarah shrilled, "Master Daniel Stone! That is no way to behave in a place of business!"

Danny skidded to a stop and stared at her with wide, frightened eyes.

Gabe set the crate of canned peaches on the counter. He knew what it was like to be full of life and excitement and to have that joy squelched with a few well-chosen words. "Danny."

Danny turned to look at him. "Sir?"

"It's all right. Come get one of the molasses cookies Abby made."

"Mr. Gentry!" Sarah barked as Danny moved to stand next to Gabe. "You do the boy no favors by encouraging him to act like a . . . a hooligan and then rewarding

151

him for his behavior!"

"Have no fear, Mrs. VanSickle. I hardly think Danny committed any grave social faux pas by running in the store, and I doubt seriously if my . . . influence will turn him into a hooligan."

Expecting another retort, Gabe was surprised to see a thoughtful expression creep into Sarah's eyes as she stared at him and Danny. He was sure it wouldn't be long before she regrouped and came at him in another verbal assault. She must be a miserable human being.

Gabe gave Danny a cookie and opened a bottle of sarsaparilla for him. If he was going to reward the boy for his bad behavior, he might as well do it up right. "Here you go," he said, lifting Danny onto the counter.

Danny's broad smile was all the thanks Gabe needed. "Wow! Thanks, Gabe."

Gabe gave a sideways glance at Sarah, who looked as if she wanted to say something about Danny's lack of respect by calling Gabe by his given name. Instead, she clenched her jaw and smiled a smile that could only be described as cunning.

While Gabe worked at placing the rest of the peaches on the shelf, he asked Danny if he wanted to go fishing one evening after the store closed. The invitation sparked a smile of such brilliance it was staggering.

"That would be great, thanks. How about Friday?"

"Sounds fine."

Smiling, Danny took another swig from the bottle of sarsaparilla. "Oh! I almost forgot. Mama wanted me to pick up that box of medicine and stuff she ordered."

"Sure thing. It's in the back," Gabe told him. "You finish up here, and I'll get it."

He gathered Rachel's items into a crate and was on his way back to the front of the store when he heard Danny call a greeting to his mother.

Rachel. Gabe paused and took a deep breath before pushing through the curtain that separated the store from the supply room. He hadn't spoken to her face-to-face in more than a week.

"Why, hello there, Rachel, my dear," he heard Sarah say in a sickeningly sweet tone that sent a chill of apprehension down Gabe's spine.

"Good afternoon, Mrs. VanSickle," Rachel said politely.

"I suppose you're aware that Mr. Gentry is spoiling your boy, but I guess that's to be expected . . . under the circumstances."

"And what circumstances would that be?"

Gabe decided it was time to get in there

and explain to Rachel about the cookie and carbonated drink. He didn't want Danny getting into trouble. He shouldered the curtain aside and met Sarah's spiteful gaze.

She looked from him to Rachel. "There's Mr. Gentry with your order now," she said with artificial pleasantry.

Rachel turned to Gabe, who smiled from the pleasure of just seeing her.

"Hello there. I just went to fetch your supplies."

"Thank you," she said, almost looking nervous. "I started thinking the box might be too heavy for Danny to carry to the wagon."

"It could be," Gabe said, setting the small wooden box on the counter. He gestured toward Danny, who was finishing his drink. "I hope you don't mind that I gave him a little something. I used to be starving when I got out of school."

Rachel shook her head. "That's fine." Her gaze clung to his.

"Danny is such a handsome young man," Sarah commented, her loud voice shattering the sweetness of the moment. "That dark, dark hair, those beautiful blue eyes and that cute little dimple in his chin."

"Thank you," Rachel said, turning to the older woman with a genuine smile. "I think

154

so, too."

Sarah tapped her lips with her finger and let her gaze move from Danny to Gabe and back again. "You know," she said with a little trill of laughter, "it's quite amazing, really."

"What's that?"

"How much Danny and Gabe resemble each other," Sarah said. Speaking over Rachel's gasp of surprise, she added, "Why, they look enough alike to be father and son."

From where Gabe stood, several things seemed to happen at once, and at first none of it made any sense. Danny's horrified gaze flew to Gabe's. Rachel's face drained of color and her panic-stricken look found his for just a moment. Then, with a strangled sound of torment, she snatched Danny from the countertop and set him on the floor. Grabbing his arm, she rushed for the door. Danny cast Gabe a worried look over his shoulder, and the truth exploded inside his mind.

Danny was his.

Rachel's expression and subsequent actions gave the claim all the validity Gabe needed. He suspected that Danny had known and had been afraid of his reaction. If he needed any further proof — which he didn't — it was there on the gossipy woman's triumphant face. She gave him a smug smile, and looking like the cat who'd just come upon a saucer of spilled cream, she turned and began to look through the fabric again.

Gabe turned away from her, his mind racing through a dozen facts and questions. First, the husband he had been so concerned about, the man he thought she'd loved, did not exist and never had. No wonder no one knew anything about him. The notion pleased him more than he could say.

Why hadn't Rachel told him she was expecting his child? Why had she told Danny and not him? And why hadn't *he* suspected the truth long before now? He felt worse than dim-witted. He possessed above-average intelligence and could add and subtract. In his defense, he had no way of knowing exactly how old Danny was. He was certainly no expert on children, but he did know they could be the result of what he and Rachel had done. His supreme arrogance and unending quest for pleasure had blinded him to the possibility that it could happen to him.

His stomach churned with a sick feeling that rose from his very soul. What a fool he'd been! So many things made perfect sense now — Rachel's anger and bitterness toward him, her unwillingness to forgive. He didn't blame her.

More questions surfaced. Where would the three of them go from here? Would God give him a chance to set things right, or would he be punished for his past? Gabe knew that Abby would tell him that he had been cleansed of his past sins, yet as much as he wanted to believe that and told himself he did, it was a hard concept to comprehend. Nevertheless, he hoped with all his heart that she was right.

First things first. He had to talk to Rachel and make sure she and Danny were okay. He shook his head in disbelief. That was ridiculous. Of course they weren't okay. Still, he had to go and see what, if anything, he could do to make things easier.

Rachel nearly ran to her buggy that was hitched to the rail in front of the restaurant where just moments ago she'd been enjoying the company of her best friends. Clutching Danny's hand, she pulled him along behind her, unaware that he had to run to keep up.

She fought the urge to bawl. No doubt about it, in a few hours her life would be in shambles . . . again. By dinnertime Sarah

157

would have told half the town Rachel's revealing reaction to the casual comment about Gabe and Danny. She wanted to scream at the unfairness of it, and she wanted to throttle Sarah.

She was afraid to look at Danny to gauge his reaction, and even more afraid of Gabe's, whatever it might be . . . whenever it might come. But come it would, and there was no longer any hope of escaping or delaying a reckoning.

"Get into the buggy, Danny," she snapped, untying the reins.

"It'll be okay, Mama," Danny said with supreme confidence as he clambered up into the seat. "Gabe likes me. I know he does. He asked me to go fishing with him on Friday."

Rachel looked into the too-serious eyes of her son, realizing for the first time that she and Gabe were not the only ones who would suffer from Sarah's spiteful tongue. Childlike, Danny saw only what his own limited perception perceived. How could she tell him that Gabe's liking had nothing to do with the reality of the situation?

She climbed up next to him, clucked to the horse and took off toward the house at a fast trot.

They were almost home when Danny

asked, "How did Mrs. VanSickle know about me, Mama? I thought just you, me and Pops knew."

An image of Sarah's gloating smile edged into Rachel's thoughts. She ground her teeth together. "Mrs. VanSickle is a very clever woman, Danny," she said, trying her best to hold her fury in check. "I suppose she saw how much alike the two of you look and figured it out."

"Do you think Gabe knew she was right? When I looked back at him, he just sort of stood there with his mouth hanging open."

"Oh, he knew," Rachel said with firm conviction. "Your father is very clever, too." It was the first time she had ever called Gabe Danny's father . . . at least to his face.

"Well, at least now you won't have to wait for the right time to tell him."

Danny actually looked pleased. She offered him a cynical half smile. "No," she replied with a hint of sarcasm. "I suppose there is that."

Anxious to close the store for an hour so that he could talk to Rachel, Gabe was debating whether or not to lambast Sarah for the misery she'd caused, or at the very least to ask her to leave, when she gave up the pretense of shopping and sashayed to the door, where she turned and gave him another sly smile.

"Well, I must say, Gabriel, this has been a most illuminating afternoon. I've learned so much."

"Yes, it has, Mrs. VanSickle. I've learned a lot, too, like just because a person goes to church every time the doors are open doesn't mean their hearts are right."

Looking as if she might have a fit of apoplexy, Sarah gave a mighty "humph!" and swept out. Gabe sighed, knowing he shouldn't have given in to his anger but feeling a certain satisfaction nonetheless.

With Sarah gone, he grabbed Rachel's box of supplies, turned the sign in the door to Closed, locked up and headed toward her house. Her buggy wasn't in sight, but Danny and Edward were sitting on the porch, which was edged with purple irises. Two pairs of eyes regarded him with thoughtful guardedness.

Gabe got down from the buggy and carried the box up the steps. "Danny. Edward."

"Hey," Danny said. Seeing the caution in his eyes, Gabe smiled. None of this was Danny's fault, and there was no reason for him to feel fearful or guilty. The tension in the boy's face relaxed.

"Good evening, Gabe. Have a seat,"

Edward Stone said, indicating the rocker next to his.

"I brought Rachel's supplies. Is she here?"

"No. She said she was going to talk to the preacher." He turned to his grandson. "Why don't you take that box into the office, Danny?"

He complied without a word.

"She told me what happened," Rachel's father said once the child was out of earshot.

"Did you know before?"

Edward nodded. "All these years, she refused to breathe a word about what happened or with whom, but when Simon brought you in and I saw how she reacted to you, it didn't take a genius to figure out why. My daughter isn't one to be so . . . hard and unforgiving."

It was Gabe's turn to nod. "Danny knew, too?"

"Yes, but only recently. I told Rachel she should tell him before something like today happened without him being prepared."

That explained a lot about the way he often caught Danny staring at him and the way he hung around wherever Gabe was. What must Danny — his son — be thinking?

His son.

The full impact of that hit him for the first

161

time. Until now, his mind had been filled with his own shock and the embarrassment Danny and Rachel must be feeling.

He had a son. An unexpected and fierce love for the boy flowed through him at the same time the burden of responsibility his new role demanded settled like a stone in his heart. Danny would soon grow into a man, and Gabe's own experience had taught him that the influence he exerted in the boy's life would help determine the kind of man he grew into.

If Rachel let him have any influence in Danny's life.

He plopped down in the rocker next to Edward with the heaviness of an old person. "They must both hate me."

Edward offered a wry smile. "Mind you, Rachel thinks she hates you, but she really doesn't. She's too much of a healer to hate, but I'd be lying if I told you your coming back hasn't taken a toll on her."

In a gesture just like his brother's, Gabe scraped both hands through his hair. "I can only imagine."

"She went through a tough time when she came home after medical school, and it's taken years for her to feel as if she's done enough to make up for her wrong-doings."

Gabe was surprised by Edward's lack of

anger. He couldn't begin to imagine what it must have been like to come back to Wolf Creek with a child born out of wedlock. No wonder she'd been so upset when he'd opened his eyes and seen her standing at his bedside. What had seemed like the culmination of a dream to him had been a nightmare to her.

"I'm sorry. I know it isn't enough and never will be, and I have no excuse, except that I wasn't a very good person back then. I think I've changed the past few months. I pray I have."

Edward smiled. "Oh, there's no doubt about that, and Rachel knows it. The forgiveness will come, I promise."

Gabe leaned forward, resting his forearms on his thighs, his hands clasped between his knees. "What about Danny? How did he take the news?"

"A funny thing, that," Edward mused. "Danny has been drawn to you from the first, almost as if he felt a connection between you, or maybe because he could picture you as the father he never had. I don't know. He's been asking questions about you ever since you arrived."

"Like what?" Gabe asked, both pleased and surprised.

"Like what you were like as a boy, what

163

you enjoyed doing, that sort of thing."

Gabe's mouth twisted into a disparaging smile. "And what did you say that made me sound . . . decent?"

"I told him you were plenty ornery, always getting into things you shouldn't and going places you had no business going . . . all pretty innocent."

"Thank you." They were silent for a moment before Gabe raked up the courage to say, "And what about you, sir?"

"Me?" Edward looked surprised.

Gabe's eyes met Edward's. "You must hate me for what I did to your daughter."

"Hate? No. I was disappointed. Heartsick. Selfishly, I thought about what people would say about *me* and her mother and how we'd brought her up." A crooked smile claimed Edward's lips. "Human nature, I suppose. If you're looking for someone to cast the first stone, you'll have to look elsewhere. The truth is that no one is perfect. We all make mistakes, some more than others. You and Rachel have made things right with God. If He's forgiven you, how can I do less?"

"Thank you." Gabe heard a noise at the screen door and saw Danny standing there. "Do you mind if I have a minute with Danny?" he asked.

"Certainly." Edward stood with his canes and went to the doorway. "Danny," he called, "your father wants to talk to you."

Wearing an expression that straddled the fence between apprehension and anticipation, Danny came out, held the door open for his grandfather and went to sit on the step. Gabe rose and sat down next to him. Where to start?

Before he could decide on how best to approach the subject, Danny said, "Mrs. Van-Sickle isn't very nice, is she?"

Gabe shot him a sharp sideways look, a bit surprised by the boy's grasp of the woman's character. Though he would like to say just what he thought about Sarah, he realized this was his first chance to exert a positive influence. "I think Mrs. VanSickle is a very unhappy woman, but you're right — many of the things she says and does are hurtful."

"You're not mad at her?"

"No." Gabe was a bit surprised to realize his heart was filled with so much regret that there was no room for anger.

"What about Mama? Are you mad at her?"

"Why would I be mad at her?" Gabe asked, taken aback by the question.

Danny looked away. "For not telling you about me."

Reaching out, Gabe turned Danny's head back toward him. "I left before she had a chance to tell me, and she didn't know how to find me. The truth is that I shouldn't have left her the way I did. I can't be mad at her for something that wasn't her fault."

"Why did you go? Where did you go when you left her?"

"I went to —" Gabe searched his memory "— to New Orleans, I believe. Why did I go? That's easy. I'd been in St. Louis for a few months, and back then, that was a long time for me to stay in one spot. I was ready to move on to new places and new people. I was always looking for something different back then, Danny. The next fun place, the next good time. I suppose I was looking for happiness."

"Was New Orleans fun?"

"I suppose it was, though I don't recall what I did there or if I was happy."

Danny's forehead furrowed in a frown. "How can you not remember?"

"After a while, what I thought were good times just sort of blended together in a blur of wasted years."

"Wasted?"

Gabe nodded. "The fun I was looking for was often the wrong kind. I hurt your mother, and I did things that God didn't like. I'm not proud of that."

Danny pondered that a moment before asking, "Why did you come back?"

"Because I've been very unhappy the past year or so, and I saw that what I once thought was fun wasn't anymore. I thought maybe if I came back and started over, I could find out what real contentment was like.

"When I was hurt, and I woke up and saw your mother standing beside the bed, I knew that the only time I was really happy was the time I spent with her." Gabe smiled sadly. "She gave me a lot of love, Danny, and I didn't realize how special that was. All I gave her was heartache."

Danny nodded. "She's got a lot of love inside her," he said with a nod, "and she's been crying a lot since you came."

A knife-sharp pain shot through Gabe's heart. He'd caused her enough suffering. If she'd let him, he'd spend the rest of his life making it up to her.

"She didn't want to tell you about me until we knew you were going to stay here. You are, aren't you?"

"I'm staying."

"And is it all right with you that I'm your son?" Danny's blue eyes were filled with uncertainty.

167

Slipping his arm around Danny's shoulders, Gabe pulled him close, humbled by his ready acceptance. He marveled at how such a simple thing like Danny relaxing against him in perfect trust could ease so much of the emptiness he'd felt for so many years.

"It's very much all right," he said. "More to the point, I hope you're all right having me for a father. I didn't get off to a good start, but I'll do my best to do better if your mother will let me."

Danny looked up at him and said solemnly, "I think you're doing all right, so far."

For the first time in nine years, Rachel felt the need to unburden herself to someone, only to find that the preacher was visiting a woman who'd just lost her husband. She needed to talk to someone she could trust and who would not be judgmental, someone who might understand the turmoil her emotions had undergone those many years ago. The only person who came to mind was Abby. Rachel headed the phaeton west, out of town.

Abby answered her knock, drying her hands on her apron. "What's wrong?" she blurted, seeing the expression on Rachel's face. "Danny? Edward?"

"They're fine," Rachel said. "At least I think Danny's okay." Her eyes filled with tears. "Do you have a minute to talk?"

Abby took Rachel's arm and pulled her through the door. "I have all the time you need. Come into the kitchen."

Rachel followed her friend through the house to the kitchen, truly the heart of this home. Eli slept in the cradle, and both Laura and Betsy were playing in the square penlike contraption Abby's first husband had constructed. Bread was rising at the back of the stove, and the mouthwatering aroma of chicken boiling escaped the lid of a cast-iron Dutch oven.

Rachel took a seat at the table, and Abby poured two glasses of lemonade before joining her. "Okay, what's happened?"

Rachel's voice was little more than a whisper. "I need to tell you something and ask your advice, but I'm so afraid it will change your opinion of me."

Abby reached out and touched Rachel's hand. "Nothing you've done or could ever do would make me think any less of you. Surely you know that."

She gave a reluctant nod. "I'll just give you the abridged version."

"However much you feel comfortable telling," Abby said.

Rachel drew in a deep breath. "When I was studying medicine in St. Louis, Gabe looked me up."

"Gabe?" Abby's surprise could not be hidden.

Rachel nodded. "He flattered me and wooed me for a few weeks and then he left with nothing but a note to say goodbye."

Abby raised her eyebrows. "Well, from what I've heard, that doesn't surprise me. A lot of unsuspecting girls have lost their hearts to bounders like Gabe Gentry."

Rachel dropped her gaze to the tabletop. "My heart wasn't the only thing I lost."

The statement fell into the room like the proverbial rock.

"I see." Abby tugged one of Rachel's hands free of the glass and clutched it in both of hers. "Look at me, Rachel."

She complied reluctantly.

"You're trying to tell me Danny is Gabe's son."

"Yes."

Uttering the simple word of confession seemed to open a floodgate of emotions. Anger and blame and even shame vanished before a gut-wrenching sorrow. A moan clawed its way up from her battered heart and long-denied tears broke free. It was not a pretty sight and made her crying the night she'd confessed to her father seem like nothing. Abby handed Rachel a clean diaper to mop away the moisture. After long moments, the crying dwindled to a trickle and an occasional shuddering sob.

"Did Gabe know?" Abby asked when Rachel had more or less regained her composure.

She shook her head. "He left before I even knew."

"Have you told him since he's been back?"

"No. But my dad figured things out and told me I should tell Danny before someone else put two and two together. When I found out Gabe was buying the mercantile and staying in town, I had no choice but to tell Danny."

"And what did he say?"

"Actually," Rachel said with a wan smile, "he was thrilled and wanted to know what happened. I told him that I was wrong to put my feelings for Gabe before God and that Gabe wasn't ready to be a father. He wanted to tell Gabe, but I said we should wait until the time was just right. I prayed that he would just leave town, but that didn't happen."

"Nothing's ever that simple, is it?"

"It seems not," Rachel said, swiping the

cloth across her still-damp cheeks.

"Obviously, something has happened."

"Sarah —"

Abby leaped to her feet, flinging up her hands in disgust. "I should have guessed that Sarah had something to do with your being in such a state! Tell me what happened."

Rachel sniffed. "Danny went to the mercantile to see if my medical supplies had come in. Evidently Sarah had been there long enough to see some interaction between Gabe and Danny, and when I walked in, she made the oh-so-innocent comment that they looked enough alike to be father and son."

"No!" Abby's eyes were wide with disbelief. "How could she?"

"Quite happily, it seemed."

"What happened then?"

"Gabe and Danny both looked stunned, Sarah looked inordinately pleased with herself, and I corroborated the statement by grabbing Danny and running out." She swiped her fingers across a fresh rush of tears that slipped down her cheeks. "What a mess!"

"I'm sure it seems that way, but all that matters in the end is how the three of you work things out. What did Danny say?"

"He was glad Gabe finally knew the truth. He said that now I wouldn't have to tell him and that it would be okay because Gabe really likes him."

"It will all be okay. I promise."

"How can it be? We'll be the talk of the town."

"Probably. At least until the next bit of gossip comes along. But at least you won't have to carry that burden alone anymore."

"Do you really think that Gabriel Gentry knowing the truth will lighten my load? More than likely he'll deny everything."

"I don't think so," Abby said with a shake of her head. "I've heard the stories about him, so I understand why you'd feel the way you do, especially since his actions with you seemed to confirm the gossip, but I truly believe he's doing his best to change, and both Caleb and I feel that he is taking his new commitments very seriously."

Rachel thought about that. Abby was right. How could she deny Gabe's sincerity when she could not see into his heart and everything she'd heard and seen the past few weeks pointed to a changed man?

"I've put all the blame on him all these years," she confessed. "It was easy. I told myself that he was worldly and knew all the tricks about how to seduce a girl, and I was innocent and shy and he swept me off my feet, but that isn't at all the way I remember it. He was the one who had to remind me that it was a mutual choice."

Abby smiled her gentle smile. "Sometimes it's hard for us to recognize our own part of the blame, but the fact that you have says a lot about how you'll handle things with Gabe from here on out."

"Handle things?"

"You have to talk to him, Rachel."

"I know I will sooner or later."

"The sooner the better," Abby insisted. "The two of you and your father need to stand united — if not for your own sake, for Danny's, because you're correct — there'll be talk aplenty for a while."

Rachel knew Abby was right, but the very idea of discussing the past with Gabe would be like ripping the scab off a partially healed wound. Since coming back to Wolf Creek, she had concentrated on building her reputation both as a physician and a solid, God-fearing citizen. Dredging up the past, both the good and the bad, meant examining every aspect of those three weeks with Gabe. Worse, it would leave her wide open for more heartbreak.

It was dusky dark when Rachel approached

the house. She had spent the better part of two hours with Abby and then more time with the preacher. He was not judgmental and told her that her repentance when she'd returned had put her back on the right track. When she asked why Gabe had chosen to come back to stay, the minister told her that no one understood how God worked in our lives, but we had to trust that He had a plan and that every day was within His control. She knew he was right, but she still dreaded her next meeting with Gabe.

Though she knew there were rocky times ahead, the relief she'd felt after telling her father about Gabe was nothing compared to the release she felt knowing that both Danny and Gabe knew the truth. Secrecy was a heavy burden. Now that Gabe knew and she'd accepted her own share of responsibility for their situation, her heart felt lighter than it had been in a very long time . . . perhaps since the time she'd spent with Gabe in St. Louis.

To her dismay, the first thing she saw when she crossed the railroad tracks in front of the house was Gabe sitting on the porch steps next to Danny. The tension holding her in its grip the past few hours eased when she saw there was no noticeable strain in either of them, and her heart gave a little lurch of something that wavered suspiciously between joy and hope.

Both of them were resting their elbows on the step behind them. Danny was clearly trying to mimic his father's posture and attitude. His face lit up when he saw her approach, his eyes sparkling with joy. Gabe's expression was unreadable. She wondered if her face reflected her uncertainty and was surprised that the antagonism that usually assaulted her when she saw him was absent. Perhaps her prayers were working. At least it would make dealing with him easier, which was good for Danny's sake. Abby was right. No matter how they felt or what they suffered the next few days and weeks, their main priority must be protecting Danny as much as possible.

As she pulled to a stop at the hitching post, Gabe leaned down and said something to Danny, who got up and went inside. Striding to the buggy with a loose, long-legged gait, Gabe lifted her down without giving her the opportunity to acquiesce or refuse.

His hands were warm at her waist.

Hers gripped his shoulders for balance and also in an effort to resist the almost overwhelming impulse to slide them up to cradle his lean cheeks between her palms.

Was it her imagination, or did his hands tighten? Searching for answers, signs, anything to give her a clue as to what he was feeling, she examined his face. He was still unbearably handsome, even with the new bump on his nose and the jagged scar scoring his cheek.

The intensity in his eyes was familiar. When Gabe gave his attention to something, it was complete and undivided. Just now that interest was focused on her. He searched her face, as if he, too, were looking for some way to gauge her frame of mind. Afraid that he would see the vulnerability she was feeling, she broke free and went to sit in one of the rockers.

He followed, crossing his arms over his wide chest and leaning against the porch post. "Why didn't you tell me?"

She'd expected him to broach the subject — though perhaps not quite so soon or in such a direct way. She had not expected the aching tenderness that accompanied the question.

"I didn't know until after you left," she confessed, staring down at the hands clasped in her lap. "And once I did, how was I supposed to find you in New Orleans?"

He had no ready answer.

"Would you have come back to me if you had known?" she asked, glancing upward.

"Yes."

His lack of hesitation surprised her.

"Yes? Are you actually saying you'd have stopped your wandering to be a husband and father?"

"Of course I would have." His expression said that he couldn't believe she'd asked such a thing. "You forget that I know what it's like to be abandoned by a parent. I would never intentionally put a child of mine through that."

Knowing his past and how deep were the scars left by his mother's departure, there was no doubting him. Random thoughts, startling in clarity, raced through her mind, disjointed images of how her life would have been if he'd stayed and they'd brought up Danny together.

Gabe hadn't loved her, had never claimed to. Could her love have held him when restlessness began to creep in? Would what he felt have been enough to keep him at her side when the inevitable trials of life began to edge into their utopia? Could a marriage between them have lasted? Would she have finished medical school or been forced to help support them?

She made a low sound of denial. Now was

not the time to indulge in what-might-have-been. "How's Danny?" she asked, curious about both her son's state of mind and how he was handling Sarah's stunning statement.

"He's fine. Perfect."

The enthusiasm in his voice buoyed her spirits. "I wouldn't say he's perfect," she contradicted, "but he's pretty close." The last was said with a proud smile that Gabe returned. The shared moment of parental pride seemed to bind them together somehow.

"From what I've observed, you've done a wonderful job with him," he told her. "I can't begin to imagine what it must have been like to come back here with a child, unmarried, and have the likes of Sarah Van-Sickle around to lord it over you."

"Actually, Sarah broke the news to the town before I ever came home."

"How on earth did she find out?"

"She made a trip to St. Louis to visit her sister and looked me up. I was almost at the end of the pregnancy when she showed up on my doorstep." Her mouth curved into a derisive smile.

"I can only imagine her glee," Gabe growled.

"She did seem to delight in my embarrassment, and of course, she knew I wasn't married. She couldn't wait to get home and tell everyone."

"I'll be the first to admit that I have more than my share of faults," Gabe said, "but for the life of me I can't imagine how anyone takes so much pleasure from deliberately dealing grief to others."

"I've given up trying to figure it out where she's concerned. At any rate, I hadn't breathed a word to my father about you and never intended to. My plan was to stay away from Wolf Creek until the baby was born, put it up for adoption, finish my schooling and then come home."

"You planned to give up the baby?"

She gave a deep sigh. "Believe me, it wasn't an easy choice. I did a lot of soul-searching and in the end I was convinced that giving him up would be best for everyone.

"What's that they say about the best laid plans of mice and men? When Pops showed up soon after Sarah went home and spilled the beans, he wouldn't hear of my giving up Danny. He said that I might have made a mistake, but that I wasn't going to compound it by giving away my child."

"Thank goodness."

The fervency in his voice sent Rachel's

gaze winging to his. His sincerity was as heartfelt as her relief. "Yes. Thank goodness he knows me so well. He knew I'd never forgive myself. So we stayed there until I got my diploma, and I've been trying to make it up to everyone ever since."

"What happened wasn't your fault," Gabe told her. "I took advantage of you."

Rachel looked at him thoughtfully. She'd spent years convincing herself that what he said was true, but now she knew that it had been a mutual longing. Perhaps in the beginning his masculine beauty and charm had played a part, and yes, she was lonely and he had made her feel beautiful and special. But she knew right from wrong and had not been without the tools to withstand his advances if she'd wanted to. She hadn't wanted to, because she'd loved him and believed he loved her.

"No, you were right," she argued. "I was every bit as much to blame as you. I have no excuse except that I loved you and because of that I turned my back on God and everything I'd been taught." Her voice broke, and tears began to slip down her pale cheeks.

Gabe pushed away from the porch railing and took a step toward her, but she held him back with an upraised hand and a shake of her head. Despite her attempts to keep him away, he knelt next to the rocker. Despite her attempts not to, she couldn't help looking at him. The agony and remorse she'd carried so long darkened her eyes to almost black.

"I've been so angry with you," she whispered. "I loved you so much, and you hurt me so badly."

He reached out and covered the hands twisting in her lap with one of his. "I cared for you, too, Rachel, but —"

"Don't!" she said and then made a deliberate attempt to soften her tone. She was unaware that her fingers had curled around his, that she was holding him at arm's length and yet still keeping him close. "Whatever we shared is all in the past, so just . . . don't try to woo me with lies and pretty words again," she begged. "Please."

Gabe reached out and lifted her chin with his free hand. "No more lies, Rachel. And no more pretty words unless I truly feel them and think you want to hear them."

The truth of his promise was reflected in his eyes. His fingertips moved gently over her cheek, and his thumb traced the curve of her lower lip as it had the day in the mercantile. "For now, just let me tell you the truth as I've come to know it."

She nodded and waited for him to find the right words.

"Even though I was stupid and self-centered and thoughtless back then, I had enough sense to know you were a very special person. I'm not claiming it was love — I've never had much experience with that emotion, but whatever it was I couldn't deal with it, and so I treated it, and you, with the same casual disregard I did everything."

"Gabe, you don't —"

"Sh," he said, placing a finger against her lips. "I need to say this. I've needed to say it for a very long time."

She pressed her lips together and he continued.

"When I finally came to my senses and realized my life was a shambles and I was no happier than when I left here, I started thinking about you. I dredged up memories of every moment we'd spent together, everything we'd said, done, felt. I knew then that I'd had something special within grasp — maybe my only chance to find real happiness — and I'd tossed it aside.

"I started thinking about my relationship with Caleb, too. We were never close, and as I looked back I began to see that he was the one who got the short end of the stick because I was such a slacker. About a year ago I started playing with the notion of coming back to try to make things right with you and him and anyone else I might have hurt.

"When I woke up and saw you standing at my bedside, I knew beyond a doubt that the time we spent together in St. Louis was the best of my life, and that *you* were the best thing that ever happened to me. I'm truly sorry. For everything. But at the same time, I'm not sorry that I had those few weeks with you, wrong though they were."

Rachel wanted to believe him. She knew he believed what he was saying, that he meant it. But how long before the siren of wanderlust began singing her tempting song in his ear?

She wasn't aware that she'd spoken the words aloud until he smiled and said, "I've heard all her songs and they don't pull at me anymore."

"What if she whispers that Dallas is where you really need to be," Rachel murmured, "or that California has sights you haven't seen?"

"I've been to both of those places and have no desire to go again. At least not alone."

Was he implying he would like to go with her? "How long before some other woman catches your attention, and you begin to wonder what her arms would feel like around you?"

"The only woman whose arms I can even remember is you. Your arms."

How she wanted to believe him, but there was so much at stake. It was time she stopped running on emotion where Gabe was concerned, time she started using her common sense and intellect. She didn't think she could survive if she gave him her heart and he waltzed out of her life a second time. Risking Danny's heart was out of the question. What she could do was grant Gabe forgiveness and move on with her life.

"If it's forgiveness you want, Gabe, you have it." She choked out a breathless sob of laughter. Pressing her hand to her heart, she gave him a tremulous smile. "You don't know what a burden has been lifted just saying those words. I feel so . . . so free."

"I'm glad."

She sobered suddenly. "This isn't just about you and me and what we felt or may feel now. It's about Danny. It's been about him ever since they laid him in my arms."

"I'm beginning to understand that. Maybe you'll think I'm crazy, but I love him, Rachel. I never had any idea how much you could love a child until he put his arms around me and told me I was doing fine as a father."

Seeing her skepticism, he asked, "Why should women be the only ones who feel that special bond? I want to be part of his life. Please say you'll let me."

She chewed on her bottom lip, her mind racing. How could she deny him this, when his eyes held such earnestness? Yet how could she say yes when she was so afraid?

As if he could read her mind, he said, "There's nothing I can do to undo my wrongs, and I know you have plenty of reason to doubt me, but you can believe me when I tell you that I'm not going any-where."

She stared at him, wanting to believe, uncertain if the statement was reassuring or distressing.

CHAPTER SEVEN

For the next few days gossip around town was worse than a feeding frenzy, and it seemed to Gabe that almost everyone who came into the mercantile sneaked furtive glances at him. Some turned away when he tried to make eye contact. A few regular customers stopped coming by, but he wasn't too worried since he was the only store in town. They'd have to come back sooner or later, unless they wanted to travel to Murfreesboro or Gurdon for supplies.

He figured there was plenty of speculation about him and Rachel at the town's dinner tables, which he supposed was to be expected, but for the most part, his customers treated him as they always had. As he'd overheard one of the old men tell one of his checkers cohorts, it was a rite of passage for young men to sow a few wild oats.

The offhand comment only made Gabe feel worse, especially when the old codger added that he was just a bit surprised that Doc's girl had been involved. That was Gabe's true shame. He deserved everything being said about him, but he was heartsick at the knowledge that Rachel was being talked about.

Besides her and her family, the ones whose opinions meant the most were Caleb and Abby. After Gabe and Rachel talked, he'd rented a buggy and driven to the farm, hoping to break the news to them in his own way. He was flabbergasted to find that Rachel had already confided to Abby, who had told Caleb. Though Gabe expected censure and worse from his brother, he was surprised by his willingness to listen without interruption or reproach.

Gabe told them about his earlier talk with Rachel and ended by confessing, "I don't know what to do to make things right."

"You've already taken the first step," Abby assured him. "You've put your trust and your future in God. You have to turn this over to Him and let Him work this out however it's meant to be."

"She's right. It will all turn out the way He wants it to," Caleb said. "That's one thing Abby taught me. I came up with all sorts of reasons about why I wasn't good enough to make a life with her. I didn't have a relationship with God, I wasn't good husband and father material, I wasn't like William, and I couldn't relate to Ben. The list went on and on, so I did my best to drive her away."

"What!"

Caleb smiled. "That's a story for another day. Let it suffice for now that, thankfully, God and Abby had other plans. There's something to be said about a woman who has a mind of her own and isn't afraid to speak it. If things between you and Rachel don't turn out the way you want, you'll have to trust that it's the Lord's will, accept it and move on. That will be the hardest part."

Abby smiled. "Caleb's right, but I'm an incurable romantic, and I find it hard to believe that He has brought the two of you to this place after so much time and pain and in such a dramatic way just to tear you apart. Even if you decide you don't suit, I can't believe He doesn't want you to be a part of Danny's life. You do want that, don't you?"

"More than anything," Gabe told her. "Except for Rachel and me to have a life together."

"You love her, then?" Abby asked, smiling her gentle smile.

"I do. But she's made it very clear that

189

she doesn't want to hear anything like that from me and has assured me that I won't play her the fool a second time."

"But if you love her, you wouldn't be."

"I know that, but she doesn't. All she knows is that I walked away from her once." He blew out a deep breath. "The thing is that as good-for-nothing that I was, I'd never have walked out on her if I'd known there was a baby. I'd never do to a child of mine what our mother did to us. I know how badly that hurts and how deep those scars go."

Caleb shot a look to Abby, who nodded.

"What?" Gabe asked, sensing something afoot.

"Frank told me a story about that, and maybe when you hear it, you'll be a bit more sympathetic to our mother."

Gabe gave a disbelieving snort, a bit surprised by Caleb calling Libby "mother." Neither of them had called her anything but her name for years, and their father had always been Lucas.

"I doubt that," he said, "but feel free to enlighten me."

"The way I remember it is that Lucas led us to believe that Mom fell for this guy, wanted to go away with him and just walked away from us," Caleb said.

"That's the way I remember it."

"Frank says that isn't the truth. She wanted to take us to Boston for a visit, but Lucas wouldn't let her. So some visitors came to visit from back East. Lucas claimed she fell for the guy and caught them together in a compromising situation. Frank had a hard time believing that, since he said she'd never been anything but the devoted wife and mother."

"Okay . . ." Gabe looked at his brother. "So what did happen?"

"By all accounts, Lucas beat the guy up, which Frank says Edward Stone can verify, and told Mom he wanted her gone. She packed up everything, including you, and the wagons were loaded to go to the train station. They were going to pick me up at school when they got to town.

"When they were ready to pull out, Lucas ordered Frank to unload our trunks and bring you to him. He said there was no way Libby was going to take his sons away from him."

Gabe's frowning gaze focused on his brother. "He forced her to leave without us?"

Caleb nodded. "Frank said Mom went a little crazy, trying to grab you back, pleading, crying and yelling that he couldn't do that to her. He told Frank and Micah that if they didn't do what he said, he'd see to it that they never worked around here again. He told her there was no way she could fight him, so for her just to go back East and make herself a new life. He'd see about the divorce. Do you remember any of that?"

Gabe shook his head, though a wisp of memory — a beautiful dark-haired woman cradling his face while tears streamed down hers — drifted through his mind like smoke on a capricious breeze. Was it real or only an image that flashed into his mind as his brother described the day that defined his entire life?

"She said that if she couldn't take us, she wouldn't leave, and Lucas told her that if she didn't go quietly, he'd see to it that she and her family paid."

Gabe regarded Caleb in disbelief. "So she didn't leave us behind because she didn't want us."

Caleb shook his head. "She left because she knew Lucas was right, that there was no way she could win against his money and power. After she was gone, he gathered up everything she'd left behind and burned it. What wouldn't burn he buried out back."

"That place we always thought was an animal grave?" Gabe queried.

"Yep." One corner of Caleb's mouth lifted into a derisive smile. "Sort of puts things into a whole different perspective, doesn't it, little brother?"

"Yes." Gabe frowned. "Do you think that's why Lucas treated us the way he did?"

"Who knows?"

"I wonder if that's why he paid me to leave?"

Caleb and Abby exchanged confused looks. "What do you mean, paid you to leave? You went to him and asked for your inheritance."

"Where did you get that idea?" Gabe asked. "I was so fed up one day that I spouted off to him. Nothing unusual about that, right? I told him I couldn't stand the sight of him, and I couldn't wait for him to die so that I could get my inheritance and put him and Wolf Creek far behind me." He shrugged. "I think I hoped it might hurt him, to pay him back for the way he was always hurting us.

"Whatever I hoped for didn't work. He didn't look like it fazed him one little bit. He stared at me while he chewed on the end of his cheroot. Then he said he was sick to death of the sight of me, too, because every time he looked at me he saw Mama's face. Then he just walked away.

"I figured everything would go back the way it was in a day or two, but the next afternoon he handed me a wad of cash and told me what arrangements he'd made at the bank for me to get the rest of it. Then he told me to pack my bags and get out, the sooner the better, and he specifically told me to never come back as long as he was alive, so I didn't."

Caleb and Abby looked as if they'd just been knocked for a loop. Caleb shook his head. "I had no idea. I knew the two of you were mad at each other, but that was pretty common. I've always thought you asked him for your part."

"Not exactly," Gabe said. "When I looked back later, it was almost as if he was glad to see me go, like it would be a relief to be rid of me. I tried writing a few times, but I figured out pretty quick he had no intention of answering, so I stopped. I'm not going to lie about it. I had a great time for several years. But it gets old."

"What? Traveling?"

"The traveling was great. Seeing all those places was fantastic, though I'm not sure I really appreciated them at the time. What gets old is trying to satisfy every one of your heart's desires. It loses its luster after a while." He smiled at his brother and sister-in-law. "Like I said before, you were the lucky one. You have everything that's worth anything right here in this house."

Caleb reached out and took Abby's hand. "You're right," he said. "I do."

Rachel entered the parlor, her spirits low, her feet dragging.

"Not much need my asking how your day went," Edward said, taking in his daughter's countenance with one quick glance. "Bad, I gather."

"Worse than bad. A couple of ladies actually turned their backs on me when I spoke to them on the street, and Mrs. Taylor canceled the appointment for Sophie's follow-up on her sore throat."

"They'll put aside all that holier-than-thou snobbishness the first time someone gets bad sick and they need a doctor."

"I suppose you're right." Rachel tugged off her bonnet and dropped it onto a chair. "Then, to pile on the agony, I was leaving Ellie's and who should walk in but Sarah herself. To see her face plastered with that smirk of hers while she looked me over with that superior expression, people would never know she'd done her best to ruin three people's lives. She was so sickeningly sweet to me I thought I might upchuck.

Dreadful woman!"

Edward laughed. "Pour yourself a cup of coffee, my dear, and settle down. This, too, will pass."

"Do you really think so?"

"I do."

Rachel poured her coffee, added her requisite two spoons of sugar and a dollop of cream and plopped down across the table from her father. "Where's Danny?"

"He wanted to go see Gabe."

"And you let him?" Rachel almost screeched.

"I thought the two of you had agreed that Gabe could be in Danny's life, at least in a limited way."

"We did, but . . ."

"But someone will see him there and there will be more talk," Edward said, an expression of mock horror on his face. "They probably will, but the die is cast, Rachel. Any harm that's going to happen has already been done, and if Gabe is to be part of Danny's life, it follows that they'll be seen together. Besides, I have a feeling that he and Gabe can handle anyone who gets out of line."

"Do you think so?"

"I know so. When I look at Gabe Gentry now, I see a man who is finally coming into who God meant him to be, and I believe with all my heart that he loves Danny, and that he will protect him as best he can." He smiled. "Besides, I think Danny is pretty good at taking up for himself when he needs to."

"I suppose," she said, but she didn't sound convinced.

The objects of Rachel's concerns, all three of them, were at that moment in the mercantile. Danny was learning the intricacies of chess from old Mr. Jessup. Gabe was putting out a new order of abalone buttons in the dry-goods section, longing for the last hour to pass so he could close the store and take Danny fishing. Sarah was looking through the rack of new spring dresses that had arrived the day before.

Even knowing that she was the creator of the tension that fairly crackled through the air, nothing would alter Sarah's regular excursions to the store, since she couldn't bear the notion that something new might come in and she wouldn't be the first in town to have it. Gabe didn't mind. She was a good customer, and as he'd told Caleb, he could be nice to anyone — well, almost anyone — for an hour or so. No sense cutting off his nose to spite his face, and it gave him a chance to practice forgiveness.

It was hard, but the preacher had told him and Rachel that it was important to perform the outward acts of forgiveness while praying and waiting for God to make them feel it in their hearts. He'd explained that in his experience, only a rare few could be cut to the quick by another and immediately cede pardon to the person responsible for inflicting that pain.

As a reminder to himself and his customers that everything said and done affected others in either a good or bad way, Gabe had bought a big framed slate and wrote a daily scripture on it. He also listed people in town who were in need of prayer for one reason or another.

The day's scripture from Proverbs read: "Pleasant words are a honeycomb sweet to the soul and healing to the bones." As a reminder to do the right thing, he glanced at it often as his gaze followed Sarah's meanderings through the store.

"Hey, Gabe!" Danny called. "Mr. Jessup says I'm gonna make a whale of a chess player one of these days. He says I'm catchin' on faster than anyone he's ever tried to teach."

Before Gabe could respond, Sarah exclaimed, "Master Daniel Stone! I'm sure you know better than to call an adult by his first name. That is 'Mr. Gentry' to you." She flashed a sly smile toward Gabe. "Or perhaps you should call Mr. Gentry *Father*."

Uncertain how to answer, Danny's wide-eyed gaze sought Gabe's. Literally grinding his teeth, he winked at the child and cast a quick look at the scripture on the wall. *Please, dear Lord, give me the right words.*

"You know, Mrs. VanSickle, I do believe you're right," he acknowledged in as near-to-pleasant a tone as he could manage. He would love nothing better than for Danny to call him Dad, but before giving him permission to do so, he would have to get Rachel's consent. "By the way, have you seen the new blouse patterns that came in?"

Nonplussed that for once she had failed to draw blood, Sarah swished over to the rack holding the dress patterns. When she brought her purchases to the counter a bit later, Gabe cocked his head to the side and asked, "Did you notice my new sign?"

"I did." She said no more, and Gabe didn't press the matter. He rang up her purchases, took her money and bade her good day, reminding her that he would have a new shipment of Saratoga chips on the next train. The Emersons had told him of Sarah's penchant for the crunchy chip made

199

from deep-frying thinly sliced potatoes, and he tried to keep them in stock for her. Secretly he thought her insatiable consumption of the chips was at least part of the reason for her tendency to portliness.

Mollified somewhat by his remembering her preferences, Sarah left. Gabe heaved a sigh. Finally. He pulled his watch from his pocket and saw that it was almost time to shut down for the day. As he carried the empty crates to the back, he thought about her snide remarks. Something she'd said brought up another issue, albeit unintentionally. She'd called Danny by Stone, when in reality he was a Gentry. Would Rachel consent to Danny calling him Dad and taking the Gentry name?

"You can't be serious!"

She regarded Gabe with patent disbelief.

He stood leaning against the parlor doorframe, dangerously attractive in a faded chambray shirt, denim Levis and a pair of boots that looked as if they had more than a brief acquaintance with work. His arms were folded across the impressive expanse of his chest.

"I can't be serious about what? Letting Danny call me Dad, wanting him to have the Gentry name, or you going fishing with us?"

"All of them!" Rachel snapped, whirling toward the kitchen doorway to escape the teasing glint in his eyes. It had far too powerful an effect on her for her comfort.

She never heard him cross the large braided rug covering the floor, but the weight of his hands on her shoulders stopped her midstride. She took a deep breath and wished she hadn't when the scent of his spicy cologne began its subtle assault on her senses. Her eyes drifted shut.

"Did anyone ever tell you that those little curls at the nape of your neck make it look extremely kissable?"

She sucked in a shallow breath and stood very still, her hands fisted at her sides, fighting the impulse to tip her head forward the slightest bit. . . . Common sense returned in a flash. She'd taken that path once and look what had happened.

"You've told me," she said with feigned patience. "Often. And you promised me you wouldn't say things like that."

"I promised not to say it if I didn't mean it, and I do." He blew out a frustrated breath. "Okay. Back to the problem at hand. What would it hurt for Danny to call me Dad? We'd both like it."

His voice held a gentle persuasion, and it sounded closer. She imagined she felt the soft whisper of his breath stirring loose tendrils of her hair. *Had* he leaned nearer?

"Everyone would . . ." Determined to regain her composure, she turned to face him and made the mistake of looking into his eyes. She immediately forgot what it was she meant to say. Like Danny, he had the most outrageously long eyelashes.

"Know?" Gabe said, picking up her thought. "Guess what, pretty girl, they already do. Let's not try to hide anything else. By taking control and doing what we think is right for us and for Danny, we keep the busybodies from manipulating the situation. Let everyone think what they want. They will anyway."

It was true. "It's just that we'd be confirming things."

"I can't see how we can do anything else, can you?"

The news was already out, so . . . "No. Not really."

One battle won, Gabe thought. "About the Gentry name. I don't —"

"Stop it, Gabe," she commanded, glaring at him. "Don't push your luck. I am not changing Danny's name. He will be Danny Stone until such time as I marry, if I do.

Then he can take that man's name, if that's what they both want."

He nodded, very serious. "I see," he said with a nod. "Angling for a proposal, now, are you?"

"What!" she cried, marveling at the sheer audacity of the man. Then, seeing the familiar teasing twinkle in his eyes, she narrowed her own to angry slits. "Wretched, wretched man!" She brushed past him.

"But you still think I'm handsome."

She heard the laughter in his voice, and a dozen memories rushed through her mind, only to be squelched by reality. "I think you're incredibly conceited and full of yourself," she said over her shoulder and suppressed a shiver when she felt his fingers against her neck as he toyed with one of the errant curls.

"Does that mean you won't go fishing with us?"

She stopped in her tracks. Heaven help her. There seemed no escape from his determination, and that, she admitted with a sigh, was what worried her. Gabe Gentry with a goal was hard to deny. Worse, the more time she spent with him, she was becoming less and less certain that she wanted to resist.

I wonder what he'd have said if you'd told

him that you were pressing for a proposal? How fast and how far do you think he'd have run? She shoved the thought aside and said over her shoulder, "It's my night to cook. I have to fix dinner for Pops."

"I'll have Ellie send over something from the café, and while I'm at it, she can make us up a picnic supper. And will you please turn around to talk to me. I'd much rather talk to your pretty face than your back. Besides, your neck is too much of a temptation to resist much longer."

That sent her whirling around. His smile was broad, mischievous and as endearing as Danny's. He *was* very, very handsome. And charming. And he knew it.

Which was extremely maddening.

She gnawed at her bottom lip in indecision. It had been a terrible few days, and fishing was not her favorite pastime. She had agreed to let Danny spend time with Gabe, and even though she was convinced he loved Danny, she was still concerned about letting him spend too much time with him. So didn't it make a strange sort of sense to go fishing with them and see to it that Wolf Creek's prodigal didn't corrupt her son?

Pushing aside the little voice that whispered she was lying to herself and that she was really going so she could spend time with Gabe herself, she said, "All right. I'll go."

"Well, you don't have to sound so thrilled about it," Gabe said matter-of-factly. "You might turn my head."

Wolf Creek was running high from all the spring rains. From the whoops of laughter and excited shouts, Danny and Gabe were having a marvelous time. Never a fan of threading worms on hooks just to watch them drown, Rachel lay on her stomach on a quilt she'd brought, reading the latest installment of a serial she'd been following in *Frank Leslie's Popular Monthly.*

Finished with the story, she closed the magazine and set it aside, resting her chin on her palms and watching the two males connecting over the "manly" pursuit as sons and fathers had been doing since the beginning of time.

As she watched, Danny jerked another fish, his third, onto the bank. Gabe helped put it on the forked stick they were using as a stringer, and Danny raked through the bucket with grimy hands, looking for another of the huge worms they'd found hiding in the fertile soil beneath the damp leaves.

"Hey, Mom!" he cried. "You're gonna cook these for me tomorrow, aren't you?" They were small perch, and there wouldn't be much left when they were cleaned, but he was so precious with his hair standing on end and his eyes alight with excitement over catching them, there was no way she could refuse. He was every bit as hard to resist as his father.

"If you clean them, I'll cook them," she promised. Tossing Gabe an innocent look, she said, "Unless I'm mistaken, cleaning fish falls into the father department."

As soon as she spoke the words, she longed to call them back. Why had she deliberately made reference to the situation in a way that only reinforced it?

"Yes, ma'am, it is," he said with a pleased smile.

Irritated with herself for being so suscep-tible to his magnetism, irritated with Danny for being so happy when she was so miser-able, irritated with Gabe for . . . well, for being Gabe, she stifled a groan and rolled to her back, flinging her forearm across her eyes to block the late-afternoon sunlight that sifted through the canopy of new green leaves.

Why was he still able to make her heart pound and her pulse race with nothing but that teasing smile of his? She'd hated him for so long, blamed him for everything, but once she'd seen him hurt and bleeding, her resentment had begun to dissipate. As if that weren't bad enough, she found that the tender feelings she'd buried so painstakingly beneath layers of loathing and disgust were reemerging slowly, like the brave crocuses that pushed their tender heads up toward the sun despite the discouragement of being buried beneath layers of leaves and snow.

Just because he'd explained why he'd walked away from her and she accepted and believed him didn't mean that she was ready to give him a second chance. He had proved lethal to both her emotional and spiritual well-being. He'd hurt her so badly she hadn't been certain she would ever recover. She'd known she would probably never find the courage to trust her heart to another man and doubted she would ever find one whose touch stirred her as Gabe's did.

But she'd had Danny, and through him she had a part of Gabe, maybe the best part. She was thankful for that. Even though he seemed a changed man, she could not let Gabe Gentry wear down her defenses again. To do so would be insanity. So why was the notion so very tempting?

CHAPTER EIGHT

Gabe was taking cash from the register to pay Claudia Fremont for a basket filled with dozens of large brown eggs he would resell when Artie Baker, one of his chess and checkers "regulars," burst through the doors.

"Slow down there, Artie," Gabe said with a smile. "What are you in such an all-fired hurry about?"

"I was just checkin' to see if you'd heard the news. Figured if you hadn't you ought to."

Willing to humor the old man, Gabe said, "I heard that Paul Gillespie's milk cow died."

"Naw," Artie said, with a shake of his grizzled head. "That's old news."

"Guess I haven't heard it, then."

"Joe Carpenter over at the telegraph station said yer mama's comin' in on the nine-o'clock train in the morning."

Gabe felt as if someone had landed a hard right to his gut. "My mother?" He wondered if the question was actually as stupid as it sounded.

"If Libby Gentry is yer mama, then that's who I'm talkin' about," Artie said as if Gabe was more than a bit dim. "Hattie's all atwitter about it. Says she got a letter just yesterday from Libby saying she was coming and would need rooms for two other people she was bringing with her. Hattie figures they're Libby's kids."

Kids. His mother had other children. He wasn't sure why that came as a shock. If she and Lucas had divorced, there was no reason she would not have married again and started another family. Still, that notion was as alien as the fact that the mother he'd resented most of his life was actually coming back after all these years and that he would have to face her.

Another fact slammed into him. If the young couple were his mother's children, they would be his and Caleb's brothers or sisters. How would he and his new siblings react to each other? Half-formed visions of what might transpire the next few days began to race through his mind. What would he say to the woman who had birthed him? Even knowing that he'd been wrong about so much of their past, he wondered what she could possibly have to say to him and Caleb.

Gabe's stomach churned. He and Rachel were already the talk of the town, and Libby's coming would only be more grist for the gossip mill. Between them, he and Caleb had contributed more than their fair share of natter for the rumormongers the past year or so. There was no doubt that his brother and Abby would be affected by the news. Danny, too. Coming on the heels of Sarah's bombshell, it was too much.

He was vaguely aware that Artie and Claudia were looking at him expectantly, waiting for him to make some sort of response. He wasn't aware that he'd mumbled something under his breath until Artie cupped a hand around his ear and asked, "What's that?"

Knowing he was expected to treat this mind-boggling news with his usual easygoing composure, Gabe forced a smile. "It looks like the Gentry family will be providing some more chin-wag for the gossipmongers."

He wondered if Caleb had heard the news yet. As soon as he could close up, he'd ride out and tell him.

Seeing that they weren't likely to get much

more response from Gabe, both Artie and Claudia took their leave, no doubt to spread the word that Wolf Creek's most notorious resident was coming back for a visit.

Gabe was sitting on a stool behind the counter, nursing a cup of rancid coffee and trying to figure out who he could get to watch the store so he could ride out to Caleb's, when his brother walked through the door. His intense gaze zeroed in on Gabe.

"You've heard." They spoke the words almost in tandem.

Gabe nodded and watched Caleb take a blue spatterware mug and pour himself a cup of the sludge from the coffeepot. Gabe raised his eyebrows and grimaced. "I can't recommend that."

Caleb's mouth quirked into something that, with a lot of stretching, might pass as a smile. "Since marrying Abby, I've discovered I like living dangerously. Besides, misery loves company, right?"

"You bet." Gabe joined his brother at the table where the old-timers played their games. He chose to postpone the serious talk for a bit and frowned at Caleb instead. "How can you imply that marriage to an angel like Abby is dangerous?"

"You ever try shoeing a horse after spending most of the night walking the floor with a colicky baby? Or getting all dressed up for church and having an infant spew all over your clean shirt?"

Gabe bit back a smile. "Can't say I have."

No matter how much he grumbled, Gabe knew Caleb loved his life. They stared at their coffee in silence for a few moments before Caleb took a sip. He shuddered, got up and added three spoonfuls of sugar to his before taking another tentative sip. Frowning, he asked, "You got any of that condensed milk?"

"I do." The thick, sweetened milk was a favorite of his brother's.

"How about we break out a can? Add it to my bill."

Gabe got the milk and punched a couple of holes in the top with his pocketknife. They doctored their coffees and settled into the ladder-back chairs, their long legs stretched out in front of them.

"How did you find out?" Gabe asked.

"I was about to order lunch at the café when Pete Chalmers came in and asked if we'd heard the news. I canceled lunch and came straight over here." His stomach growled.

Without a word, Gabe got up, cut two small wedges of red rind cheese, ripped a length of brown paper off of a large roll and scooped a handful of crackers from the barrel. Then he snagged a jar of Mrs. Pritchard's homemade sweet pickles from the shelf. They ate in silence for a while, chewing on more than their impromptu lunch. They were both aware that this was the first time in years — maybe ever — that they had shared a common problem.

"Why do you suppose she's coming back?" Gabe asked at last, taking a bite of cracker and cheese and washing it down with a swig of coffee.

"Maybe because Abby wrote to her," Caleb offered, concentrating on spearing a pickle.

"She what!" Gabe yelled, jerking upright and sloshing coffee all over the checkerboard he'd neglected to move. "That interfering little brat!" he muttered, wiping at the spill with a pristine white hankie he fished from his pocket.

Caleb cast him a mocking sideways look. "A minute ago, she was an angel."

"I've changed my mind," Gabe grumbled. "She's a menace. Worse than a dog with a bone when she gets one of her notions."

"Tell me something I don't know," Caleb said, putting another chunk of cheese on a cracker.

"You're serious about this? She actually

did write to Libby?"   •

Caleb stared at the cracker and cheese as if it held the secrets of the universe. "I'm not sure, but I suspect as much. She kept after me to do it, and I kept saying no. Knowing my wife, I expect she did it for me."

"Why would she do that?"

Caleb shrugged. "Come to dinner this evening. We'll ask her."

"I did it because it's high time the two of you got rid of all those hard feelings you've been carrying around all your lives," Abby confessed that evening as they sat down to eat. "I just wrote introducing myself and telling her about Emily and Betsy and my marriage to Caleb." Seeing the irritation in Caleb's eyes, she added tartly, "Well, if my daughter-in-law had died and I had a grand-child, I'd want to know about it."

"So when did you write this letter?" Caleb asked.

"Last spring sometime," Abby told them. "I thought there was a chance she'd answer, but she never did. Then when Eli came along, I sent another telling her about him, but I certainly never expected her to come, since she didn't bother to write back after the first letter." She sighed. "Are you really so furious with me?"

Caleb's scowl eased. "Not furious," he said. "Maybe mildly irritated. I was hoping to get more of a rise out of you, though."

Abby's shoulders slumped in relief. She looked from him to Gabe. "For some strange reason, he —" she cut her eyes toward Caleb "— gets a kick out of making me angry." With her forefinger extended, she made circles near her ear, as if to indicate her husband was a bit crazy.

Gabe laughed. That was one of the strangest things he'd ever heard.

"Seriously," Abby said, "you both need to see her, look her in the eye and ask her about her side of things."

Gabe thought of Rachel confessing how easy it had been to put all the blame on him until he'd come back and she was forced to face him. As she'd said, it was easier to stoke the fires of bitterness and hard feelings from a distance.

"Frank told us the truth, so we know that she didn't leave us out of selfish reasons, like we'd always thought. Gabe and I can live with that," Caleb said.

"With all due respect to Frank, he only knows what he saw the day she left and what was being bandied all over town." Again she looked from one brother to the other. "You owe it to yourselves to hear what she has to say. And you owe it to your children to give them a chance to know their grandmother."

Grandmother. Danny. Gabe didn't relish the idea of telling Rachel and Danny about Libby's return. Of course, by now, they'd no doubt heard the news. What would Rachel think about telling Danny he had a brand-new grandmother when he'd just learned he had a father? What would Danny think?

He sighed. He suspected Abby was right, but it didn't make the idea of meeting Libby any less disturbing. What did you say to a mother you hadn't set eyes on in nearly a quarter of a century?

Danny was all agog with excitement when Rachel walked into the house from making her rounds out in the country.

"I have a grandma!" he cried, his smile so wide it threatened to split his freckled face.

Weary, unsuspecting, Rachel set her bag onto the seat of the hall tree and wandered toward the kitchen, where she knew she'd find her father working on supper. "Really?" she said, riffling Danny's hair as he skipped along beside her. "Just where did this grandma come from?"

"Boston, I think, but she's not here yet.

She's coming on the train in the morning."

Rachel shot a confused look at her father, who was peeling potatoes at the table. His smile was overly bright.

"Danny, do you mind playing outside for a few minutes? I need to talk to Pops."

Danny opened his mouth as if to argue, but she gave him the look, and he mumbled, "Yes, ma'am," and then he headed for the door.

Feeling the beginnings of a headache coming on, Rachel sat down across from her father. "What was that all about?"

"This, dear readers," Edward intoned melodramatically, "is the next installment of our serial, 'The Trials and Tribulations of Dr. Rachel Stone.' "

"What now?" she asked, resting her elbows on the table and massaging her temples.

"It appears that Libby Gentry Granville and two companions will be arriving in our fair city on the morning train from Boston."

"Libby Gentry Gran . . ." Rachel's eyes widened with recognition.

"Exactly," Edward said. "Caleb and Gabe's long-lost mother. The one who allegedly left them for another man."

"Allegedly?" Rachel parroted with raised eyebrows.

"Innocent until proven guilty, my dear,"

Edward reminded her. "I never took Libby for a woman who would betray her wedding vows. Of course, it might have been because I was half in love with her myself at the time."

Rachel's face turned scarlet. "Daddy! What about Mama?"

"Your mother and I weren't an item when Libby first came to town, and I think all the young bucks were smitten with her to some degree. As soon as it became apparent that she had eyes only for Lucas — or rather, that he intended to land her — I zeroed in on your mother."

Rachel smiled. "Thank goodness."

"Yes," Edward agreed with a smile, "thank goodness."

"Why do you think she's coming back?"

"To try to make things right with her sons, I would imagine."

"It seems there's a lot of that going around these days."

"As well there should be. Life is too short for grudges and hard feelings. I believe God wants us to make amends whenever we can."

"You're right," she agreed with a nod. "Who are these 'companions' she's bringing with her?"

Edward shrugged. "Speculation around

town ranges from her other children to a couple of high-toned Boston attorneys come to *wrest* the Gentry farm from Caleb." Edward's theatrical tone had returned. He sobered suddenly. "My guess would be her children."

Frowning, Rachel chewed on her lower lip. "Do you think she'll want to meet Danny?"

"Of course she will, once she learns about him."

Rachel swallowed a lump in her throat. "One more person to hear about my ill-fated relationship with Gabe."

One more person to judge her. Gabe's mother, no less! How would she ever be able to face Libby Gentry Granville? Even her name sounded intimidating.

She must have spoken her fears aloud, because Edward replied, "Intimidating? Libby?" He laughed. "Believe me, she was never an ogre, my dear. I actually remember her being very nice. Put yourself in her shoes. It can't be easy for *her* to come back to a town that has thought of her as an adulterer for two decades and face the children she abandoned."

Rachel sat up straighter. "I never thought of it that way. I'm sure you're right. How do you think Gabe and Caleb are taking the news?"

"I'm sure they're both as upset about it as you are, and no matter how it turns out, I give Libby high marks for having the courage to do it."

Rachel caught her lower lip between her teeth and considered that. Here she was, worried about more gossip, a rather insignificant problem compared to what Gabe and Caleb were facing. How were they feeling knowing that the mother who'd walked out of their lives was about to return? Did she realize that her arrival would dredge up all the old anguish?

"What do you mean, 'no matter how it turns out'?"

Edward shrugged. "Caleb and Gabe might refuse to see her or forgive her."

Concerned only with her own feelings, she hadn't thought of that, either. Would Gabe listen to what his mother had to say? She hoped he would at least hear her out. She knew firsthand how much better she'd felt after they had cleared the air and put their feelings aside to do what was right for Danny.

She glanced at the watch hanging from the chain around her neck. Almost closing time for the mercantile. She looked at her father. "Do you think I should go over and talk to him?"

"It can't hurt," Edward said. "And while you're at it, why not invite him to supper? There's plenty."

Rachel paused. The suggestion seemed almost as if Edward were giving his stamp of approval to her forming a more intimate relationship with Gabe.

"You wouldn't be trying to play matchmaker, would you?"

"There's no need. Even when you're fighting him tooth and nail, a blind man could see that the two of you still have feelings for each other . . . that whatever it was that you felt isn't over." Seeing that she was about to object, he continued. "Whether you like it or not."

"I don't like it." There was no reason to deny what he'd said. Edward was too smart, and he knew her far too well. She sighed. "I suppose you think I'm completely barmy to feel anything for him after the way he used and abandoned me," she said, her voice a shamed whisper.

"I've never been a big believer in coincidence," he said, a thoughtful expression on his still-attractive face. "So what I think is that God is working in both your lives and that He has given you a second chance."

Her dark eyes held query and a tiny smidgen of hope. "And Gabe? You . . . you really think he feels something for me?"

Edward winked at her. "If I were a gambling man, I'd make book on it."

Edward's words followed Rachel as she made her way across the railroad tracks, past the hotel to Antioch Street. Was her father right? Did Gabe really care for her? Oh, she knew he was attracted to her and held a certain fondness for her, but was he only being nice so that she would grant him greater access to their son? She didn't think so. He seemed to enjoy the time they spent together with Danny — more and more time the past couple of weeks, and though he sometimes flirted, never once had he done or said anything inappropriate.

Recalling his peppermint-scented breath against her nape that day in the store and the huskiness of his voice when he'd told her it looked kissable, she felt a little shiver scamper down her spine. She was an educated woman, certainly smart enough to know *that* was not love, but was it possible that her father was right and Gabe did still care? Was that caring love? The possibility was both thrilling and alarming.

She was just approaching the store when

the object of her thoughts stepped through the aperture, key in hand. He smiled, the automatic action bringing the pleasing crinkles at the corners of his eyes into play. "Hello there!" he said. "I was just on my way to your place. Do you need something? I can let you in."

Rachel took a steadying breath and rammed her hands into the pockets of her dark blue skirt. "No. I just wanted to talk to you."

He raised his eyebrows. "It must be serious if you're looking for me."

"Serious enough," she said. "What did you need to see me about?"

Did she imagine the shadow that flickered across his face? "Something's come up. Would you like to go to Ellie's and get a cup of coffee or a glass of lemonade?"

Where everyone would see them together. That would just add more fuel to the fire! "No, thank you," she said. "Actually, Pops wanted to know if you'd like to join us for supper."

Gabe couldn't hide his surprise, or miss the reluctance in her voice. "Supper doesn't include a hefty dose of arsenic, does it? Or maybe hemlock?"

"I don't find that in the least bit funny."

"I can see that," he said somberly. "I'll

make a note in my book of Rachel Stone observations." He turned his palm up and pretended to write with his finger. "Don't try to tease the great Dr. Stone, since clearly she has no funny bone." He glanced up, his eyebrows raised in sham surprise. "My, my, I do believe I have the start of a poem."

"Are you ever serious?"

"Do you ever have fun?" he countered. "The Bible says there are times to laugh, Rachel — remember?"

"I remember. Are you coming or not?"

"Of course I'm coming. How can I turn down such a gracious invitation?" he mocked. "What time?"

"Come now. We need to talk."

"So you said. About?"

"Something's come up," she said cryptically, tossing his own answer back at him. She turned to walk away, and after making sure the door was locked, Gabe followed. His loose, long-legged stride soon brought him to her side, and they walked down the street together, both with their hands stuffed into their pockets.

At the corner, they passed Mrs. Carmody and her brood of six. The frazzled housewife looked from Rachel to Gabe and actually pulled her skirt aside as if she would somehow be contaminated if she allowed the fabric to brush against Rachel. She did speak, though her mouth was pinched with disapproval, and only after Gabe made it a point to greet her and her children with his customary good manners.

They were in front of the hotel when Meg Thomerson came out, balancing a basket filled with soiled linens on her hip.

"Let me get that, Meg," Gabe said, taking the basket from the woman whose husband treated her as a sparring partner.

"Thank you, Mr. Gentry," she said, pushing a stray strand of hair from her astonishing green eyes. "And thank you again for letting me have some more time on my bill at the store."

"That's not a problem," he said gruffly.

What a wonderful thing to do, Rachel thought, trying to meet his eyes. Everyone in town knew that Elton Thomerson was a deadbeat, and there were few people willing to extend him credit. It was up to Meg to take up the slack.

Three years and two children ago, she was considered more than pretty, but the time with Elton had taken its toll. There were premature lines at the corners of her eyes, and barely three months past her latest delivery, she looked far too thin. Even so, her smile seemed never far from the surface.

She beamed at Rachel with her usual friendliness while Gabe deposited the basket into the bed of the buggy alongside three others. Rachel knew she would deliver the sheets and towels the following afternoon all clean and ironed wrinkle free. She didn't know how the petite woman managed to stay so positive, except that she never failed to make a church service unless she or one of the children was ailing.

"I should have part of my bill when I finish up Millie's laundry," she told Gabe before looking at Rachel. "And I should be able to pay off Seth's sore-throat bill next week."

"Don't worry about it, Meg. I'm not hurting for it."

The woman's eyes filled with tears. "Thank you, Dr. Rachel. I don't know what this town would do without you." She looked from Rachel to Gabe. "And I think it's so wonderful that the two of you have found each other again after all these years."

Rachel cast a sideways glance at Gabe, who was rearranging the baskets and giving a good impression of being deaf. She offered Meg a weak smile. Wondering how to reply, she settled for a simple "Thank you."

Gabe helped Meg into her buggy and they watched her make a left turn at the corner and disappear. Wisely, he chose not to comment and fell into step beside Rachel.

"Giving Meg time to pay her bill is very nice of you."

"Yep," he quipped, making light of it. "No doubt they're casting a bronze statue of me even as we speak."

"Well, it isn't that big a thing," she teased.

"She needs help," he said, suddenly serious. "I feel sorry for her. And we all need a hand at some time in our lives."

Knowing that was all he'd say, they walked in silence for a moment. "What's come up?" Rachel asked finally, tilting her head to look at him. The heat of the late-afternoon sun coaxed out the red tones hiding in her dark hair.

"Ladies first."

Looking askance at him, she drew a fortifying breath and plunged. "I hear your mother is coming to town tomorrow."

"I hear the same thing." A wry half smile lifted one side of his mouth.

"And?"

"And it's a bit disconcerting to say the least."

"You didn't know she was coming?"

"No. Neither did Caleb."

"Hmm." Rachel shot him a frowning glance. "I wonder why she decided to come after so many years."

"Probably because Abby wrote to her to tell her about Emily, Betsy and her own marriage to Caleb."

Rachel lifted a hand to shield her eyes. "Abby knew she was coming, then?"

"Actually, she didn't," he said, switching sides with her so he could block her from the sun's rays. "She never heard a word back, but she wrote Libby again when Eli was born, and it seems that for some reason, Libby has now decided to pay a visit."

"You call your mother Libby?"

"Caleb and I stopped calling her Mother after she left us."

There was no need to ask why. "How do you feel about her coming?"

"I have mixed emotions," he confessed. "Both Caleb and I grew up believing she left us with no backward glance, but we recently found out that Lucas wouldn't let her take us. That puts a different slant on things, at least for me." He sighed. "As for how I feel about it, I keep coming back to the notion that maybe I'm feeling a little like Danny must have felt when he found out about me."

Rachel considered that and thought he could be right. She recalled Danny's excitement as well as his trepidation and curiosity. As he had, Gabe was no doubt wondering what Libby Gentry Granville would think of the person he'd become. He would be wondering if she loved him, and if they could ever forge a meaningful relationship. Yes, it was easy to see that Gabe and Danny would share parallel feelings.

"And Caleb?"

"You know Caleb. He doesn't give away much about what he's feeling."

"Will you tell her about . . . Danny?"

Gabe turned toward her, completely blocking out the sun. He studied her face before answering. "Yes, Rachel, I'll tell her about Danny. And you. And how I managed to mess up the best thing that ever happened to me."

Rachel ducked her head and started walking again, before he noticed the tears that sprang into her eyes. The frankness of the statement tugged at her heart in a way that threatened to set her bawling her eyes out. Of all the things he'd said to her about their past . . . explanations, apologies or whatever else, there was no doubt that those simply spoken words and the emotions driving them were genuine.

They'd reached the whitewashed arbor that sat at the end of the path leading to the front of her house. Covered with clusters of pale yellow roses, it stood near the road, its delicate curve inviting people in. As she started to step through, he grasped her arm in a gentle grip.

Releasing his hold on her, he framed her face with his hands, the pads of his thumbs riding the crests of her cheekbones, his spread fingers cradling her head. She didn't try to pull free, wasn't sure she could have if she wanted to. Tipping back her head, he met her troubled gaze.

"You're worried about Danny meeting her."

She nodded.

"Danny is her grandson. They have the right to meet each other. What happens beyond that is up to them, just as what happens between me and Danny is up to us. That's fair, don't you think?"

"Yes," she said with reluctant acquiescence.

Leaning forward a bit, he rested his forehead against hers. Their noses bumped. The scent of the ever-present peppermint he seemed so attached to mingled with the masculine aroma of his aftershave, something that reminded her of far-off lands.

Her eyes drifted shut.

He took a deep breath and straightened. His hands slid to her shoulders. "What else?" he asked, showing an astonishing insight into her thoughts and emotions, an insight she'd noticed during their time in St. Louis.

"Ah," he said after a moment. "You're worried about what she'll think of you, right?"

"Yes," she admitted, allowing him access to even more of her feelings.

Holding herself very still, she breathed in the scent of him and fought the onslaught of memories that swept through her. It would be so easy to let her arms slide around his hard middle and lean into him. So tempting to rest her head against that broad chest and let him support her for a while.

"The whole town has believed for twenty-plus years that she was unfaithful to my father. I have no idea what really happened, but whether she's a vamp or a victim, I can't picture her as the kind of person to judge others."

Rachel stepped back. There was no teasing about him now, nothing but the intensity she remembered. Never mind that he had been irresponsible, thoughtless and selfish nine years ago. At that moment, all that mattered was that he understood exactly how she felt and was doing his best to ease her mind.

It worked until he lowered his head and kissed her.

Chapter Nine

The kiss was the softest whisper of his lips against hers, as delicate as the brush of a butterfly wing, as insubstantial as the beat of a hummingbird heart. There was no persuasive technique involved. No insistence or demand. Instead there was hesitation and promise. It was nothing at all how she remembered his kisses.

If there was any last lingering resentment, it faded to nothingness, and the last remnant of her resolve melted away. She knew there would be no more manipulating her feelings, no pretending or trying to deny them by pushing them aside. She gave in and gave up to the love she felt, and it felt so very good. And scary.

Just when she feared she might somehow give herself away, he stepped back with a last almost-as-if-he-couldn't-help-himself stroke of his thumb against her lower lip, a

tender gesture that was fast becoming familiar.

"Why did you do that?" she asked, hearing the breathlessness in her voice.

That he was dead serious at that moment
was undeniable. He was not teasing or test-
ing her. She did see a hint of remorse, as if
he were torn between wanting to kiss her
and being sorry he had.

He lifted his shoulders in a half hearted
shrug. "I couldn't seem to help myself. I'm
sorry if I offended you."

"You didn't." Was it her imagination, or
did her denial surprise him? He might have
said something else, but Danny burst
through the front door, raced down the
steps and launched himself at Gabe, who
knelt and caught the child up in a tight
embrace. Rachel felt her heart constrict in
sudden painful perception. Danny adored
Gabe. Gabe adored Danny.

"Is it true?" Danny asked, resting his
hands on his father's shoulders and leaning
back to look at him. "Do I really have a
grandma?"

"It seems you do," Gabe said, smiling.

"Tell me all about her."

"I don't know much about her," Gabe
confessed. "She . . . left when I was just a
little boy, younger than you."

Danny stared at Gabe for long moments, giving the statement serious thought. Then Gabe stood, and Danny moved between his parents. He turned to face them, grabbed one of Gabe's hands and one of Rachel's in his and tugged them along the path to the house, confident that even though he could not see where he was going, they would not let him fall.

"It'll be okay, Dad," he said with a tone of grave certainty. "I 'spect she left because she just wasn't ready for the responsibility of a family, the way you weren't ready back then."

Rachel's face flamed at hearing the words she'd spoken to Danny repeated to Gabe. She glanced at him and saw him looking at her with a thoughtful expression that soon turned to one of gratitude. At that moment she knew that he realized what she'd done and appreciated the fact that she had not painted him the villain of their particular story.

"She's been gone a long time and growed up a bunch I'll bet," Danny said, offering a child's simplistic reasoning to the situation. "I 'spect that once she gets to know and love you, she'll be ready to settle down and be a mom. I just hope she likes me, too."

"How could she not?" Gabe said with a

laugh, delighted with his son's logic. The joyous sound and Danny's answering smile filled Rachel's heart with joy. An image of them together around the table — a family — slipped like a will-o'-the-wisp into her mind.

Pipe dreams.

Though she admitted to loving him, she was no longer the shy innocent of her youth, and she was certainly no worldly sophisticate, nothing like the kind of woman Gabe was accustomed to. She was not charming, playful or clever. On the contrary, she was often considered too plainspoken and stuffy, and she had the added disadvantage of possessing above-average intelligence, something most men did not appreciate in a woman.

She was just Dr. Rachel, pretty enough she supposed, but still a small-town girl whose biggest goal was to heal those she could, and to be the best person she could be. No matter how much Gabe might have changed, she was just too afraid of disappointing him, too afraid of being hurt a second time to trust him with her heart. If that happened, she knew that she would never recover.

After a supper of ham, boiled potatoes with

butter, buttermilk biscuits and fresh green beans, everyone pitched in to clean the kitchen.

Afterward, Edward challenged Danny to a game of dominoes while Rachel and Gabe retired to the front porch. They sat side by side in matching rockers that overlooked the front yard and the buildings across the railroad tracks. The corner of the hotel was in plain view, and beyond that, they could hear the occasional rattle of a wagon on Antioch Street.

Neither spoke, content to sit and listen to the serenade of tree frogs and insect songs that were punctuated by the strident, plagiarized melodies of a mockingbird ensconced on the rose trellis.

"I hear the box lunch is coming up next weekend," Gabe said at last. "Are you taking part?"

"I always do. It's more or less expected that everyone do something. It's mandatory if you're an unattached woman." She offered an ironic smile. "It's supposed to be an unobtrusive way to bring unmarried folk together. Not that it works very often."

"I imagine the bids on your boxes are high," he commented with a questioning lift of his eyebrows.

"I do all right."

"You're bound to be the prettiest single lady in town."

She laughed. "Actually, Ellie and I are considered the town's spinsters, even though everyone says we're pretty enough for *mature* ladies."

"Mature, hmm?"

"Yes." She actually laughed, a sound that sounded awfully close to a giggle. "I believe that's a creative way of saying we're over the hill."

Gabe threw back his head and laughed, too, amused at the thought that two of the prettiest women in town were considered past their prime.

"Believe me, it's no laughing matter. The men who bid on my boxes are usually the more *mature* gentlemen." This was said with a definite hint of amusement in her brown eyes. "Most of them are widowers looking for someone to take care of them in their old age. Who better than the town doctor?"

Gabe chuckled again. "Well, I'll be sure to give them a run for their money this year."

It sounded like a promise. Her mind moved ahead to that day and the possibilities it might bring. Quiet between them returned. She recalled that even in St. Louis, when he was taking her around to show her the many sights, they'd had the ability to share time together with no need to fill the silence with meaningless conversation. It had surprised her then, and still did.

"I'd like to thank you for what you told Danny."

Even though they were attuned at the moment, she was so lost in thought that she didn't immediately grasp what he was referring to.

"What he said about my mother not being ready to take on a family," he explained. "I know you must have said the exact thing to him about me."

She answered with her customary directness. "I told him what I felt was the truth."

That took him by surprise. "Well, I appreciate it, especially since it's clear that you held a lot of resentment toward me. You could have said a lot of things to prejudice him against me."

"I would never do that, no matter how I felt. As you reminded me, I'm hardly without fault in the matter, and as you also said, whatever develops between two people should be just that — between them. It's not my way to force my opinion on someone else."

"Has it changed?" he asked, his voice as soft as the gathering shadows.

"What?"

"Your opinion of me."

Instead of answering, she stared at him for long seconds. "I'm still observing," she said at last.

"Fair enough." He looked at the buildings across the way, their edges softened by the gathering shadows. "I'd best get back before it gets too dark to put one foot in front of the other."

She stood, and he followed suit. "Thank you for the supper. It was delicious."

"You're welcome." She wondered if he would try to kiss her again and wondered what she would do if he did. Instead, he reached out and trailed a finger down her cheek, smiled a bit ruefully and went down the steps.

She watched him go through the rose arbor. "Gabe!" she called.

He turned.

"Will you let me know how things go . . . with Libby, so I'll know what to expect for Danny?"

He gave her a wave of acknowledgment she could barely make out and strode toward buildings across the way.

Libby Gentry Granville had arrived.

According to the gossip — and there were plenty of folks eager to keep Gabe in the loop — The Southwest Arkansas and Indian Territory train chugged into town from Gurdon at precisely nine o'clock, belching black smoke and spitting sparks as the wheels ground to a stop.

Moments later, a magnificently dressed older woman had descended the train, followed by a younger woman who looked to be in her early twenties and a man whose age was somewhere in between. At exactly 9:05, two people burst through the door of the mercantile, almost knocking each other over in their haste to deliver the news.

Gabe thanked them and sent them on their way. He was certain that his seeming disinterest would be added to the mix of reports as word spread around town.

He wondered who the man could be. Rumor had it he looked about Caleb's age, so he couldn't be another brother, though the young woman must be his sister. Funny. He was just getting used to having a relationship with his estranged brother and now there would be another sibling to get to know . . . if he were so inclined.

A grim smile hiked one corner of his mouth. It was highly unlikely that Libby would come all this way and not insist on spending some time together. The reality was that his mother's unannounced visit could not have come at a worse time. He was still adjusting to meeting Rachel after so many years and reeling from the knowledge that he had a child. All that while learning how to establish a new business and trying to carve out a place in a town that considered him a dissolute wastrel.

Caleb, bowing to the wishes of his headstrong and tenderhearted wife, had come by earlier to see if Gabe would like to go to the station to meet the train with him and his family.

"I don't think so," Gabe told him, still uncertain how he felt about the whole thing and what he could possibly say to the visitors, knowing there would be dozens of pairs of eyes watching the whole shebang. "I don't think I can find anyone to run the store on such short notice."

"I understand," Caleb said. "I've been fighting Abby on this since yesterday, but she finally wore me down."

Abby wins again, Gabe thought with a smile. She was doing a bang-up job of transforming her husband into a more social human being.

"You're not getting cold feet, are you?"

Drat it! Caleb was far too astute to fool for long. "I suppose you could call it that," Gabe hedged. "It's just that I've had more than my share of notoriety, and I have no desire for more. I don't want our first meeting to be discussed over the dinner table. Whatever happens between us at our first meeting should be relatively private."

"Then at least come out to the farm for dinner," Caleb pressed. "Abby is planning a huge family feast."

Seeing the familiar tightening of his brother's jaw, Gabe figured he'd better accept.

"Sure," he said. "That would be great. You know I never turn down Abby's cooking."

"Wonderful!" Caleb's rare smile made a brief appearance. "Make sure you rent a nicely sprung buggy so they'll be comfortable for the drive out."

"Whoa! What do you mean 'they'?" Gabe asked, though the question was completely unnecessary.

Caleb gave a nonchalant lift of his shoulders. "Since you're coming, it seems logical for you to collect everyone and drive them to the farm, since they have no idea how to get there." He portrayed an excellent impression of innocence.

Duped and manipulated and no way out of the situation! "Fine," he told Caleb ungraciously. "I'll do that." Gabe pointed a finger at Caleb. "But you owe me, big brother, and don't you forget it."

Caleb had only laughed and left.

Now, as he worked about the store, he wondered how the reunion was going. Caleb claimed he no longer harbored any hard feelings toward their mother, but as mellow as he'd become, good Christian that he was trying to be, and as much as he claimed to have forgiven her, Gabe couldn't see his brother welcoming Libby with open arms.

At least he had guts enough to go meet her, while you're here hiding behind a pitiful excuse.

True.

He supposed that Libby would want to meet before he picked them up to go to the country, but he never dreamed she would walk through the doors of the mercantile.

His back was to the door and he was arranging a new shipment of chambray shirts by size when he heard a woman speak his name.

As soon as the weather permitted, he'd started opening both doors to let in the springtime breeze, which meant there was no jangle of bells to announce a customer. He'd compensated by adding a bell on the counter, like the one Hattie had at the hotel, so that he would know someone needed help if he was working in the storeroom.

Hearing his name, he froze, his hands smoothing a collar. Though it seemed inconceivable, he immediately recognized the soft, melodious voice. He remembered hearing her laugh — though rarely, it seemed now. A hazy recollection of her crooning a lullaby to him and Caleb as she sat on the edge of their bed at night swirled through his mind like a wisp of smoke. He recalled that clear sweet voice explaining that his father wasn't angry at him; he was just angry . . . or worried, or whatever feeble reason she could think of to distract him from his tears and Caleb from his gradual retreat into stoic solitude.

Wondering if the rest of her was as he remembered, Gabe turned. She stood just inside the door, flanked on either side by her companions. The young woman wore a celery-green dress with a tiered lace overlay and three-quarter-length sleeves ending with a double lace frill.

The man was clad in the latest fashion — charcoal flannel trousers topped with a burgundy waistcoat beneath a casual jacket of muted black, gray and burgundy plaid. The girl was looking at Gabe with wide, uncertain eyes while the man regarded him with a careful scrutiny, almost as if Gabe were a prime example of horseflesh he was thinking to purchase.

From what Gabe could tell from the distance separating them, his mother was little changed. She was still the tall, slender, elegantly beautiful woman of his faded memories and still bore herself with a straight, upright carriage. Out of the blue he remembered her admonishing him and Caleb not to slump.

Instead of the everyday cotton dresses he recalled her wearing, she was gowned in a day dress of some royal-blue fabric with a knife-pleated skirt, a small bustle, a fitted bodice with set-in sleeves and a high stand collar. A waterfall of delicate lace cascaded down the front. The trio exemplified big-city wealth.

While he was recovering from his shock and trying to sort out how he was feeling, Libby murmured, "Oh, Gabe!" and crossed the room, weaving between the aisles and displays, her steps impatient, an eager smile on her face.

Something akin to panic gripped him. It felt as if his heart seized up and he found it hard to breathe. She must have sensed something was amiss, because she stopped a few feet from him, her smile dying a slow death. Her eyes, as blue as his own, roamed over his face, as if she were trying to assess the changes the years had made while also trying to judge his mood. Even from where she stood, he detected the faintest, well-remembered smell of her favorite scent, lilac.

All the love he'd felt as a child came rushing back, and he suddenly wanted to hug her, to feel the comfort and peace he'd always felt when enfolded in the warmth of her embrace. Fast following that was the memory of him crying himself to sleep after he and Caleb were told she'd left them. He could almost hear the sound of his sobbing in the silence of their darkened bedroom, could almost see Caleb lying stiffly next to him, his face turned to the wall, as if to block out the world.

The tenuous tenderness passed. The quiet grew near unbearable as they stood there staring at each other. He should say something, but what? At a total loss for perhaps the first time in his life, he extended his hand to shake hers. The stilted action was the height of formality. "Hello, Mother. I trust your trip was comfortable."

The anguish in her eyes was palpable, and he felt like a cad for causing it. He might have hurt people in the past, but never with it as a goal.

Hearing the tonal inflection in his voice

seemed to settle something in her mind. She fixed a bright smile on her face and, still clinging to his hand, pulled him toward the couple standing near the door, both of whom were regarding him with less-than-friendly expressions.

"Gabe, this is your sister, Blythe, and my stepson, Winston Granville. Blythe, Win, this is my younger son, Gabe."

Blythe extended a small, lace-gloved hand. "How do you do, Mr. Gentry," she said, her voice tinted with the same formality as his own.

Dismay filled him. He knew she was miffed that he was treating her mother with obvious coolness. He didn't blame her. He didn't want there to be conflict between him and his half sister, or conflict between him and his mother, for that matter. He'd had enough discord and anger to last a lifetime.

Hoping to ease the awkwardness, he said to his sister, "I'm doing quite well, thank you, but I'd do a lot better if you called me Gabe."

A blush spread up her throat to her face. It seemed his little sister was a shy one.

Then he turned to the man, who regarded him with the supreme composure that seemed to accompany being born with money. Gabe was somewhat surprised that

Win seemed very protective of his step-mother. Gabe liked that. He extended a hand, which was met with a firm grip. "Win. It was good of you to accompany Mother." As he spoke, he realized he meant the words.

"I'm always glad to help Mother however I can. And this is one trip I wouldn't have missed," Granville said, a hint of steel both in his tone and his tawny eyes.

Strangely it wasn't the veiled antagonism that rankled. It was Win Granville calling Libby "Mother." Of course, truth to tell, she had spent far more time being a mother to this man than she had her own sons. Gabe was the real outsider, not Win Gran-ville.

Striving for a bit of normalcy in an unconventional situation, Gabe said, "I understand I'm to drive us all out to Caleb's for supper."

"Yes," Libby said, adding, "if it isn't too much of an imposition."

He managed a smile. "None at all. Actually, you're in for a treat. Abby is not only a wonderful wife and mother, she's an excellent cook."

"My first impression was that she is very sweet and genuine," Libby said. "It's good to have my opinion reinforced." Her almost wistful gaze met his. "Caleb seems happy."

Even though they'd been apart most of his life, spending time with Rachel and Danny had taught him just how much a mother was invested in the happiness of her children. "I believe he's very happy, thanks to Abby."

"And you've never married?" Libby asked.

"No."

But I have a son. He'd have to tell her soon, he supposed, otherwise someone else would beat him to the punch, just as they would with the sordid details of his life while he was away.

"Hard to please?" she asked with a smile.

"Too self-indulgent for too many years," he corrected and plunged in. "I may as well tell you, since if you haven't heard, you will. I've been away the past nine years and my behavior during that time was —" he expelled a harsh breath "— less than sterling, I'm afraid."

He watched as they tried to absorb what he'd said. His mother looked troubled by his confession. Win seemed speculative. Blythe was clearly scandalized. He could almost see her innocent mind trying to visualize what that behavior might have included. It was easy to see there would be no hero worship of her big brother. At least not this one.

Lew Jessup strolled through the doors, bypassing the checkers tables and heading toward the new shirts, casting a curious glance at the foursome. Gabe wasn't the least surprised at his timing. When Artie Baker followed in a matter of seconds, Gabe stifled a groan. The two must have been sent as spies for the rest of the town.

Unlike Sarah, though, there would be no maliciousness connected to their reporting on the actions of the newcomers. Still, Gabe would rather have any meaningful conversations with his mother and siblings conducted in private.

He offered his extended family a dry smile and gave a slight jerk of his chin toward the two men. "Now doesn't seem the best time to discuss this since it seems business is picking up."

Win understood perfectly.

"Hattie at the hotel serves a light lunch, and Ellie at the café across the street is open from daylight until dusk. I can personally recommend either place. I'll pick you up for Caleb's after I close — say about six?"

Gabe was aware that he was rambling, but he really just wanted them to leave before some other disaster occurred.

The thought had no more than crossed his mind when a denim-clad tornado burst

251

through the doors. All eyes turned toward the sound of bare feet slapping against the wooden floor. Gabe's heart stopped. Danny. His dark hair stood on end, and a smudge of dirt smeared his right cheek and the bib of his overalls. His hands and feet were as filthy as the tin can he clutched. His gaze zipped past the visitors and zeroed in on Gabe. A wide smile echoed the excitement sparkling in his eyes.

"You oughta see the big ol' worms I found, Dad. I thought maybe Grandma would like to go fishin' with us while she's here."

Three pairs of eyes turned toward Gabe. He wasn't sure whether he should laugh or cry. No doubt about it, God had a fantastic sense of timing, as well as an incredible sense of humor. Gabe motioned Danny closer. As he passed the trio, he looked up, his eyes growing wide with comprehension. He stopped in front of Gabe, who rested his hands on Danny's shoulders. He swiveled his head back and up and whispered loudly. "Is that her?"

Gabe nodded and let his own gaze move from his mother to his sister and stepbrother. "Mother, Blythe, Win . . . this is Danny. My son."

With his uncanny aptitude to size up a

situation in nothing flat, Danny instinctively realized he needed to make a good impression. He set the can on the floor, scrubbed his hands down his thighs and finger-combed his hair to smooth it, succeeding only in adding a smudge of dirt to his forehead.

Win's expression was unreadable. Blythe's eyes were as large as silver dollars, and the shock on his mother's face transitioned to a smile as she watched Danny's impromptu toilette.

"Pleased to meet you," Danny said, extending a grubby hand. Seeing how dirty it was, he quickly withdrew it and offered his grandmother a blinding smile instead.

To Gabe's surprise, the well-dressed Mrs. Granville sat back on her heels in front of Danny, putting them at eye level. He couldn't tell if the sheen in her eyes was pleasure or tears. She held out her own hand, and Danny cast an inquiring look at Gabe. When he gave a single slight nod, the boy thrust out his hand once more.

Libby cradled the dirty hand in both of hers. "I'm very pleased to meet you as well, Danny," she said, clearly captivated with the child. "And I would love to go fishing with you. Perhaps tomorrow afternoon after I have time to rest up from my trip?"

"That'd be great," Danny said, "but it will have to be after church and the box lunch."

"Box lunch?" Win queried.

"It's an annual event," Libby explained. "They auction off box lunches the ladies have made, and the money is used to help people around town. After everyone eats, there will be games and just a general good time."

"Some of us are gonna sneak off and go fishing," Danny offered. "It's a lot of fun." He looked up at Blythe and Win. "I don't know who you are, but if you're with my grandma, I guess you can come, too, if you want." He gave Win a considering look. "You might want to bid on my mom's box. She's making fried chicken, and next to Ellie's, it's the best in town."

"Maybe I'll do that," Win said, his expression giving away nothing of what was going on inside his head. "And as for who we are, since I am a brother of sorts to your father, it appears that I am your uncle Win."

Danny looked at Gabe. "Caleb is your brother. Is he my uncle, too?"

The subject of how everyone was related hadn't yet come up in all the hubbub of the gossip. "Yes."

"So Abby is my aunt."

"Right."

Danny scrunched up his short freckled nose and squinted, trying to work out the familial ties. "So me and Ben are *cousins.*"

" 'Ben and I are cousins,' " Gabe corrected automatically.

"No, Dad," Danny said, all seriousness. "You can't be Ben's cousin. If Caleb is my uncle, then you're Ben's uncle."

The trio of new relatives laughed, clearly delighted with the child. As well they should be, Gabe thought with a surge of fatherly pride.

Win smiled at Danny. "I'd be happy to go with you and your grandma fishing. It promises to be an entertaining time. Blythe?"

Her gaze traveled from one person to the next. "Well, uh, certainly," she said, almost managing to suppress a delicate shudder. "I'd be happy to go along. I'm your aunt Blythe, by the way."

That settled to his satisfaction, Danny narrowed his eyes in perfect mimicry of his mother. "I'll bet you need someone to put your worms on the hook, don't you, Aunt Blythe?"

"I . . . I'm afraid so," she confessed, turning a pretty hue of pink.

Danny shrugged and shook his head in typical male disgust. "Girls."

It was Win who, seeing the curious onlookers, ended the fiasco. He held out his hand to help Libby to her feet. "I think we should go back to the hotel and rest a bit before lunch. It's been quite an eventful morning. We'll have plenty of time to . . . discuss things."

"True," Libby said, rising. "It isn't every day a woman acquires five wonderful grandchildren." She ran her hand lovingly over Danny's sweaty head, but she was looking at Gabe as she spoke, her way of saying that whatever the situation, it would be all right.

"I'll expect the whole story later, Gabriel." She placed a finger beneath Danny's chin, tilting his face upward. Her voice trembled as she looked at Gabe and said, "He's so much like you it's amazing."

Then, regarding Danny thoughtfully, she asked, "Do you have any other grandparents?"

"Just Pops, my mom's dad. My mom's the doctor."

Libby regarded Gabe with a lift of her eyebrows. Clearly Danny had piqued her interest with the announcement about his mother. "I thought Edward Stone was the doctor."

"He used to be," Danny offered. "But now my mom is."

Libby looked thoughtful, working out more family ties. Then, as if the conversation had not taken a brief turn, she said, "So you call Edward Pops. I like that. Instead of Grandma, do you think you could call me Pip?"

Gabe couldn't imagine a less likely name for a woman of such elegance and refinement. A memory surfaced. He could almost see Grandpa Harcourt looking at his daughter, his eyes alight with love and pride as he said, *"Isn't she a real pip?"*

"Sure," Danny said, "but it's a really funny name."

"Maybe so," Libby said, "but my father called me that, and it's been such a long time since anyone else has used it, I think I would like it very much if you and the other children did."

"Pip and Pops. I like it," Danny said, offering another of those wide smiles.

That settled, Libby gave the grubby child a hug, not a bit concerned that he would ruin her beautiful walking dress. The trio started toward the door, Gabe promising again to pick them up at six. They had almost made the opening when Sarah swept through. It seemed God wasn't finished with him yet.

"Why, hello, Libby," she gushed. "I heard

you were in town."

"I imagine you did," Gabe's mother said. "Sarah, I'd like you to meet my daughter, Blythe, and my stepson, Win. Children, Sarah VanSickle."

The Granvilles made the polite, appropriate responses, but Sarah hardly noticed. She was too busy looking around the room to see who was present.

"I see you met your grandson," she said with a triumphant smile. If she was hoping to hear something negative about Gabe's conduct or Danny, she was disappointed.

"I did," Libby said, her features schooled to serenity. "Isn't he the cutest thing?" She brushed past Sarah as if she were something distasteful. "If you'll excuse me, we really must run."

"How long will you be in town?" Sarah called after her.

"As long as it takes."

"To do what?" Sarah pressed. "I was hoping we could get together."

Just outside the doorway, Libby turned. Gabe could almost see his mother biting her tongue. It was an expression he'd seen often enough on his brother's face.

"Oh, we will, Sarah," she said in a pleasant voice. "But when we do, I want us to have a nice private conversation." With that, she turned and started down the sidewalk as if she hadn't a care in the world, Blythe and Win trailing behind.

Gabe's gaze shifted to Sarah, who looked as if she were about to suffer a fit of apoplexy. What beef could his mother possibly have with Sarah VanSickle that she was intent on discussing? Whatever it might be, it was clear that Libby was wise to the viperous woman's tricks and had no intention of allowing Sarah to make the past, and whatever dicey tidbits it entailed, a public spectacle.

CHAPTER TEN

Gabe made it through the rest of the day and the gauntlet of questions thrown at him by almost everyone who came to make a purchase. Somehow he managed to deflect or ignore most of them with generic answers or the pretext of needing to help another customer.

Danny had returned to the mercantile after going home to tell Edward that he'd met his grandmother and informed Gabe that Rachel was out in the country checking on a patient. He drew a sigh of relief. He'd been granted a brief reprieve before facing Rachel to tell her that Danny had spilled the beans about who his mother was.

He was about to close when he saw Rachel coming down the sidewalk. She looked tired, frazzled and troubled. He wanted to pull her into his arms and tell her that everything would be all right, that his mother was not the least bit intimidating and that whatever happened he would be right beside her so she would not have to bear this newest crisis alone. But even though there had been a definite softening in her attitude lately, she'd made it clear that Danny was her primary concern. The rare times he'd felt they were connecting on a more personal level, he had been so afraid of her returning to her former scornful attitude that he'd backed down, afraid to push too hard.

He waited until she got inside before locking the doors and turning the sign to Closed.

"Danny told me he met his grandmother," she said without preamble.

"Quite by accident, but yes, he did."

"He also told me she really liked him and said something about an aunt and uncle and everyone going fishing tomorrow."

"All true."

Rachel's expression seesawed between relief and disbelief. "Do you mind giving me your version? Our son is a master at glossing over anything he feels might upset me or that might put him in a bad light. Somehow, I can't believe it —" she waved her hands through the air in a vague gesture "— was the happy occasion he portrayed."

"Actually, it was," Gabe said. "More or

261

less." He gave her a condensed version of everything that had transpired, including Sarah's contribution to the drama. He finished with, "Libby asked him to call her Pip, which was her father's pet name for her."

"And she seemed to accept Danny, no questions asked?"

Gabe smiled. "Oh, there will be plenty of questions. Count on it. But there was no hiding the fact that she was quite taken with him, even though he was absolutely filthy."

Rachel's dismay was unmistakable. "I wanted him to be nice and clean and on his best behavior when they met for the first time," she wailed. Then she asked, "How dirty was he?"

"Extremely," Gabe said, a smile surfacing at the memory of Danny's grimy condition.

Seeing how the corners of his mouth hiked up in amusement, she said, "This is not funny, Gabriel Gentry, though I can see how someone like you might see the humor in it."

He refused to take offense at a statement he realized was rooted in some sort of motherly embarrassment.

"Danny had been digging worms," he explained, "and he'd brought them with him. However, he *was* on his best behavior.

Quite the young gentleman, in fact."

"Really?" She still looked somewhat distressed, but her whole posture was more relaxed.

"You should have seen him, Rachel," he said with a soft laugh. "It was very funny. He smoothed his hair." Gabe mimicked the action. "And smeared more dirt on his face in the process, and when he started to shake her hand and saw how dirty it was, he stuck it behind his back instead."

"Oh, no!"

He reached and took her hands in his, drawing her closer. For once she didn't resist. "She adored him, Rachel," he told her, his eyes smiling into hers. "Who wouldn't?"

He brought her hands to his lips and pressed kisses to her palms. "Trust me when I say that everything will be fine." He released his hold on her and drew his watch out of his pocket. "Unfortunately, I have to run you off right now because I'm supposed to take everyone to Caleb's for dinner."

"What about you and Libby?"

He shrugged and gave her hands a squeeze. "We didn't really have a chance to talk. There were too many curiosity seekers milling about. I'll have a better grasp of things after tonight, and you and I will talk tomorrow, while we share your box lunch."

"You seem very confident that you'll be the highest bidder," she said, almost playfully.

"Confident enough."

Libby was enchanted by Caleb and Abby's brood. She spent time talking to Ben about his trapping, telling him how much Caleb had liked it as a boy, and cuddling Laura — both were Abby's children from her marriage to William Carter.

After Abby put the children to bed, the adults retired to the parlor to enjoy coffee and a slice of Abby's buttermilk pie so that Libby could tell her side of the story, which was, she insisted, one of the reasons she'd come back to Wolf Creek. As it turned out, Frank *had* been correct in setting the story straight as far as he knew the truth. Libby filled in the blanks.

"I fell for Lucas Gentry the first time I saw him," she said, a reminiscent smile on her face. "With my very different . . . upbringing, he was the antithesis of everything familiar, which I found quite exciting. He wasn't a handsome man in the traditional sense, but he was ruggedly goodlooking, and there was an attractive brashness and self-confidence about him that drew me, at least in the beginning."

A pensive smile softened her features. "I loved it here, too. I'd been brought up a city girl, but there was something about the rolling hills and the fresh air and the close-knit community I found appealing."

"A blessing and a curse," Abby volunteered.

Libby's smile held a touch of irony. "You're right, of course. I had no idea in the beginning that that closeness could also be a detriment, since it was next to impossible to keep a secret for long."

She looked at Caleb. "When I came to town, Sarah Davis — Sarah VanSickle now — and Lucas were expected to marry, though there had been no formal announcement."

Gabe and Caleb shared a look of disbelief.

"When it became apparent that he was interested in me, she was furious," Libby said. "He ended things with her, and for the remainder of my visit, he pursued me rather intensely."

"I don't doubt that," Caleb said with barely concealed hostility. "Once he got hold of an idea, he didn't let it go."

"No," Libby said, "he didn't. The night before we were to go back to Boston, he proposed, and I said yes. My parents were unhappy that things had moved so fast, and my father was . . . oh, I don't know . . . There was something about Lucas he just didn't trust. But I was marrying age, so they agreed. They delayed their return for two weeks until we could put together a small wedding that was fancy enough to satisfy my mother."

She drew in a deep breath. "Lucas was like a chameleon, able to adapt to a situation with very little effort. He became whatever he needed to be to get what he wanted, and then he changed into something . . . someone else. Once he had me, it was off to the next item on his list. At first he was generous with everything but his time, but it didn't take long for me to realize how he used his generosity for control."

She looked from one of her boys to the other. "I know what you're wondering, but he was never abusive, at least not in the beginning."

Caleb's face looked like a thundercloud. "Are you saying he hit you?"

She reached out and patted his hand. "No, nothing like that. But abuse can take many forms. You came along ten months after the wedding and Gabe four years after that. You boys gave me a reason to get up every morning. You helped fill the lonely hours that being alone so much created.

"Lucas was too busy making a name to have time for us. He was either working or off trying to buy more cattle or land — anything to make more money or gain an edge. He thrived on the power it afforded him. When I look back now, I see that his being away so much was really a blessing of sorts."

"He did like having people in his debt and kowtowing to him," Caleb said. "I remember that."

"Yes," Libby said. "He took us to Boston for a visit once, but he refused to go again, saying that he could have bought another parcel of land for what the visit cost. He wouldn't let me go alone with you boys, claiming it would be too hard on me.

"He became quite miserly, too. The three of us dressed like peasants except when he wanted to show us off, and he went around on a prize stallion decked out in the latest and finest so that he would look more impressive for his wheeling and dealing."

"Did Grandmother and Grandfather Harcourt know how things were?" Blythe asked her mother, clearly stunned by her mother's confession.

"I never told them, but I think they suspected. They came as often as they could, but it wasn't enough. I have to say the church was a big support, but I'd been taught not to air my dirty laundry, and besides, it was too embarrassing. I didn't want anyone suspecting what my life was really like, and I don't think Lucas would have taken kindly to my exposing his true colors to the world."

"He sounds like a terrible person," Abby said, scooting closer to Caleb and taking his hand.

"It sounds as if *terrible* doesn't begin to cover it," Win added.

"All I can say is that money and power became his gods." She sniffed and continued. "One autumn when you boys were three and seven my parents came to visit and brought along my older brother, Tad, his wife, Ada, and her brother, who just happened to be Sam Granville."

A collective gasp filled the room, and Libby offered a wan smile. "Sam's wife had died a couple of years earlier, and he was left with his two boys, Win and Philip. Sam was handsome and funny, and he made me laugh. . . ."

Gabe and Caleb exchanged troubled looks but did not interrupt. Blythe's face wore a reminiscent smile, no doubt remembering her father.

"Lucas was jealous, though I'm not sure why, since by this time, our marriage was over in every way that mattered. The old dog-in-a-manger adage, I suppose. We lived in the same house. I cooked, took care of everyone, and he made more money and gathered more . . . of everything.

"One night Tad, Ada, Sam and I went for a walk down by the creek while my parents kept an eye on you boys. Lucas had gone somewhere and hadn't bothered returning for supper. We were walking back, and it was getting chilly. Tad and Ada hurried home, but Sam and I dragged behind, talking about plays and art and music . . ."

Her voice trailed away and she looked at her sons again. "As much as I loved you, it was nice to have a bit of time free of responsibility and to be able to carry on a conversation about things outside this house, this town. When I mentioned being chilly, he took off his jacket and put it around me, and there was one of those moments that seem —" she shrugged "— suspended in time."

A muscle in Gabe's cheek worked. He wanted to ask if Sam Granville had kissed her, but before he could say anything, Libby's control broke and tears began to slide down her cheeks.

"At precisely that moment, your father came thundering out of the woods on that demon horse of his. The timing was so perfect I always wondered if he'd been watching and waiting for just a moment like that.

"I want you to know that Sam didn't kiss me. I took my marriage vows too seriously. I would never have let him even if Lucas hadn't arrived when he did." She swiped at her eyes and blinked fast. "Of course, Lucas was furious. He got off the horse and . . . said a lot of terrible things to me and to Sam . . . accusing us of things I would never do. And then he hit him and hit him and —"

"Enough!" Gabe commanded. His stomach churned at the images filling his mind. He didn't need to hear any more. Frank had told Caleb that Lucas had almost killed the man he'd suspected his wife of cheating with. There was no need for a blow-by-blow description.

She nodded. "It was months before he healed," Libby said, "and even then, he never walked quite the same. Some injury to his spine, I suspect. His last few years were spent in a wheelchair."

Despite the pain of what he'd thought was her rejection, despite the troubled years,

Gabe believed her, and if the expression on Caleb's face was anything to go by, so did his brother. But whether or not he believed her, Gabe's behavior left him in no position to cast stones.

His mother had wanted to make things up to him and Caleb, just as he'd wanted to make things right with Caleb and Rachel. She'd taken that all-important first step, and it was up to him to meet her halfway.

Standing, he reached out and drew her to her feet and into his arms in an awkward gesture of comfort. He heard her sob and felt her arms close around his middle, felt her press her cheek against his shirtfront and her tears wet the fabric.

Fighting the emotion thickening his own throat, he whispered senseless, meaningless words of comfort and crooned soft soothing sounds. It was a language universal in origin, one that God Himself had designed for the hearts and minds and lips of mothers. They were tender words and gentle murmurs passed down from generation to generation, a distinctive means of communication that some few men — those who did not consider themselves too manly for such nonsense — might awkwardly adopt for just such an occasion.

Blindly, Libby reached out an arm to Caleb, who rose and allowed her to draw him close. Gabe, who had never seen his brother shed a tear during their growing-up years, thought Caleb's eyes looked overbright.

After a few moments, she pulled back, gathering herself and her emotions. He remembered that about her, too. Libby Gentry seldom got emotional, but when she did, she masked it as soon as possible. At one time or another they'd all learned that showing Lucas any weakness only made it easier for him to inflict more pain.

Taking the handkerchief Gabe offered, Libby wiped her eyes and waved them back to their chairs. "Sit please," she urged. "There's more."

Rachel dressed for church, her stomach filling with butterflies at the thought of meeting Gabe's mother for the first time. Facing a woman who had conversed with the child whose existence was proof of your disreputable past was not only nerve-racking, it filled Rachel with renewed shame.

She regarded herself in the mirror, her gaze fixed on the woman who stared back from its silvery depths. She wore a pale lavender dress with a white piqué V-shaped insert trimmed with purple piping. White cuffs and collar similarly trimmed finished the simple tailored dress that she felt befitted her station in town. She looked every bit the country doctor and nothing at all like the woman Libby Granville no doubt thought she was.

How her life had changed since she'd gone to Simon's wagon and discovered her past lying bleeding inside! Until then, her days had been uncomplicated and fulfilling, though perhaps a bit uneventful. She'd seldom shared time with a man and often wondered if anyone would ever come along to town to capture her interest. When the sheriff arrived, she'd gotten her hopes up, but it hadn't taken long for them to realize that there was not one spark of excitement when they were together.

Unlike the way the air fairly crackled when she was with Gabe.

He had only to enter a room and her lonely heart refused to listen to the sensible warnings of her head. She could not fault his behavior. He was everything a woman dreamed of in a man. Attentive. Caring. Helpful. Danny loved him with every fiber of his being, which should have been a consolation but in actuality frightened her for her son.

Gabe said he wasn't going anywhere, but what if his business venture failed and he had to go somewhere else to make a living? What if he found no one in town to love and went to another city to find a bride? What if that wife didn't care for Danny, or was jealous of their relationship? What if this unknown woman refused to live in the same town as the scarlet woman who would be a constant reminder of his past? Gabe might have to move, and Danny . . .

She shook her head in despair. It was an impossible situation, and she had no idea what to do about it. She'd asked God for His guidance, but He had given her no visible sign of what to do.

Sufficient unto the day is the evil thereof.

The words from the sixth chapter of Matthew echoed in her head, derailing the troubling turn of her thoughts. She paused in the act of stabbing the filigreed hatpin through her hat and into her upswept hair, thinking about the real meaning of the familiar passage. It was one she often quoted — sometimes almost flippantly — when day-to-day concerns seemed to be piling up to insurmountable heights.

There *was* no reason to worry about the future, since no one had a guarantee of what the next moment might bring, as Caleb had found out when what should have been the joyous occasion of his daughter's birth was mitigated by his wife's death.

Rachel told herself that she believed the Lord was with her no matter what, but she wondered if her life reflected that belief. Strong-willed and fond of being in control, she found it hard to surrender her will to Him, often trying to solve problems herself without waiting to see what He had in mind.

It all came down to whether or not she believed that God was working His plan in her life, taking her down the road He wanted despite the times she wandered off track or willfully chose to walk away from Him, determined to do it her way. Did she believe He was all-powerful, able to make adjustments to counteract her wrong moves?

If she didn't, she should.

She closed her eyes, a prayer of sorrow and supplication for a greater understanding and a stronger faith filling her mind. When she was finished, she had accepted that no amount of worry would change His plan. The best way to deal with the evils of life was one day at a time.

As soon as Rachel stepped through the doorway of the church, Gabe took her by the elbow. "I need to talk to you."

The weariness she saw in his eyes spoke of a sleepless night and suggested he'd learned something about his mother's leaving he hadn't known before, something he was having trouble coming to terms with even twelve hours later.

"Danny, will you please help Pops get settled?" she asked, not wanting little ears to hear whatever it was Gabe needed to tell her. When they'd gone, she looked around at the stream of arrivals.

"It's getting pretty crowded in here," she whispered, looking around at the knots of people mingling around them. "And since you're so sure you'll be the top bidder for my box lunch, we can talk while we eat."

Seeing his surprise, she realized that his thoughts were centered on something completely different. "Don't tell me you forgot one of the biggest events of the year?"

"It's been a peculiar couple of days," he murmured, "and last night was . . . very enlightening to say the least, but it did fill in a lot of blanks for both me and Caleb."

"What is it?" she asked sotto voce, intrigued in spite of herself.

Gabe lowered his voice. "Libby didn't have the affair — Lucas did."

With her mind still reeling from Gabe's pronouncement, Rachel passed down the aisle and took her seat in the pew next to

276

her father. She'd been there no more than a moment when a soft hum rippled through the gathering, and heads began to turn toward the back of the room.

Despite her reluctance to meet her, Rachel felt a surge of sympathy for Libby Granville. Perhaps more than anyone else, Rachel understood what Libby must be suffering. She recalled her own experience — the thudding heart, trembling hands and nausea that had churned inside her, the same nausea that was no doubt roiling inside Gabe's mother as she made her way toward the pew where her family was seated.

The service passed by in a haze and was over before Rachel knew it. There was a mass exodus as everyone hurried to fetch their boxes or baskets before heading to Jacksons' Grove. Rachel saw to it that Danny and Edward and his chair were settled in the preacher's wagon before driving to the house and collecting her own basket.

There was plenty of time for catching up with friends and neighbors and lots of lemonade and fruit punch to drink during the time it took for everyone to arrive. The air was filled with the shouts and laughter of happy children and the hum of dozens of conversations. At day's end, everyone would go home filled with good food and new memories.

The auction might be a way to pair up the single people, but the boxes made up by the married women fetched good prices, too, since good-natured bidding often broke out between a husband and his brothers or brothers-in-law.

The older women kept the children entertained and provided food for them and those too old to be interested in the bidding, while the adults drifted away to share their meals. The afternoon would be whiled away with games of horseshoes, baseball and tag, while others meandered to the creek or found a quiet spot beneath the shade of a tree and indulged in a nap.

Rachel and Danny were wandering through the crowd, speaking to people she knew while he chatted with his friends. She saw him give a handful of wildflowers to eleven-year-old Bethany Carpenter, Ellie's daughter. He always went out of his way to show her some kindness. She saw a smiling Sheriff Garrett talking to Ellie, and a strained-looking Meg Thomerson, the baby in her arms and little Seth clinging to her skirts. Elton stood next to her, looking surly and already three sheets to the wind. Rachel said a quick prayer that he would not lose control again.

She glanced over to her father's vantage point beneath a large oak from which he had chosen to observe the festivities. It was close enough to the action of the bidding to observe what was happening but far enough away to be out of the throng.

He was smiling with pleasure; problems did not seem to be the insurmountable obstacles for him they did for Rachel.

She was about to turn back to check on Danny when she saw Libby Granville approach Edward's wheelchair. As Rachel watched, Libby smiled at Edward and extended both hands in greeting. Their mutual pleasure was evident, and the faint sounds of their laughter drifted across the meadow, along with the buzz of friendly chatter, squealing children and birdsong.

Rachel watched as Gabe and two strangers joined the pair. The siblings made an attractive trio. Blythe was dressed in a pretty summer frock of rose-hued organdy. With his dark blond hair and golden eyes, Win was as handsome as Gabe, but in an entirely different way. Elegant and self-possessed, he was the epitome of Boston fashion in a pale gray pinstripe suit.

Gabe said something and Rachel saw her father give a shrug and a vague wave. Gabe turned to scan the throng and spied her in the midst of the crowd. His serious expression transformed into the amazing smile that never failed to cause her heart to flutter. Despite the scar that grew fainter every day, he was a gorgeous man and would still be handsome when he was her father's age.

Day by day she was learning that there was more to him than a pretty face and inborn charm. She'd noticed many of them all those years ago, but when he left her, she'd thought he only pretended to have those qualities she'd fallen in love with.

He was kind and generous and blessed with patience and a dry sense of humor that popped up when she least expected it. He truly liked interacting with people, especially women. He paid close attention to their opinions, which she believed was the reason the new line of ladies' clothing he'd added to his inventory was so successful. He'd been blessed beyond most. It just wasn't fair.

"What isn't fair?"

The sound of his voice pulled her from her daydreams. She must have been deep in thought if she hadn't seen him coming. As he stood there smiling down at her as if neither had a care in the world, she suddenly felt nothing like a successful physician who dealt in life and death, and more like a gauche miss just out of the school-room. But then, she'd always felt that way around Gabe.

"It's nothing."

"You didn't look as if it were nothing. You looked . . . dismayed."

"Can you blame me with everything that's going on?" she asked, hoping to switch the conversation from one unacceptable topic to another.

"Hey!" He chucked her beneath the chin. "It's not that bad. We all had a very reveal-ing talk last night, and Caleb and I know exactly what happened. My mother said she didn't have an affair."

"And you believe her?"

"I do. So does Caleb. I'll tell you all about it later. Right now, why don't you come and meet her. I took all the blame for what hap-pened between us, and she was more than happy to let me."

"You talked to her about us?" Rachel cried in a scandalized whisper.

"I told you I would, and you know it had to be said. There was no way around it."

She turned her face away. "I imagine she thinks I am some sort of hussy who —"

"She most certainly does not. Now stop

281

trying to see the bad in this and look at the good."

"What good?" she asked, turning to face him again.

Before he could answer, Danny raced up and grabbed Gabe around the waist. "Dad, can Ben and Caleb go fishing with us when we go?"

"Certainly," Gabe said, "but it will be later, after we all have our picnic."

"Okay," he said, already off and running toward his friends.

Gabe's face wore a smile of complete satisfaction. "There went the good."

He meant it. He didn't see Danny as a burden or something to be ashamed of. He was truly thrilled about being a father, thrilled to be Danny's father. That much *was* good. In fact, it was wonderful.

He held out his elbow for her to take. "Ready?"

"I suppose we might as well get this over with," she said crossly, tucking her hand into the crook of his arm.

He laughed at her distinct lack of enthusiasm and gave her hand a pat. "That's the spirit!"

The laughter drew attention to them, though it seemed that they'd attracted a gaggle of gawkers just by standing there.

282

"Excuse me for not being too keen on the idea, but it's more than a bit humiliating."

"Don't I know it? Don't forget that it's an experience I was subjected to when I had to face your father. Thankfully he didn't shoot me, and I promise that my mother won't attack you, either."

Rachel glowered at him.

"She isn't going away any time soon, sweetheart," he said, smiling that easy smile. "Come on. We'll face the music together."

She was hardly aware of their progress across the green field with its patches of yellow and purple wildflowers. She was too rattled by his casual use of the endearment. *Sweetheart.*

If only I were his sweetheart.

Where had that come from? she thought irritably. It was one thing to vow to be kinder and more forgiving. She could even love him, as long as he didn't suspect how she felt. That would be disastrous, something she had to remind herself of several times a day.

Everyone in the group surrounding her father was laughing, but they turned as one as Rachel and Gabe drew nearer. Expressions ranged from pleasant inquiry to guardedness to thoughtful. Emotions that fit the circumstance, depending on one's perspective, Rachel thought. To her surprise, it was her father who spoke up instead of Gabe.

"Rachel, this is Libby Granville, Gabe's mother — which I'm sure you know," he added with a cheerful grin. "Libby, this is my daughter, Rachel, Danny's mother."

Rachel offered her hand and Libby took it in a light grasp. "I'm so pleased to meet you, Rachel. Gabe has told me a lot about you, and you've certainly done a fine job with Danny."

Rachel wondered if her face blanched at the woman's directness. Clearly Libby Granville was not one to beat around the bush. Having that frankness focused on her, she found, was a bit disconcerting.

"Thank you, Mrs. Granville. He's a wonderful little boy, but he can be a handful sometimes."

"He wouldn't be his father's son if he wasn't a handful," Libby said with a rueful smile. "And please call me Libby. Mrs. Granville was my mother-in-law." She gestured toward the couple standing nearby. "This is my stepson, Win, and my daughter, Blythe."

Blythe shook her hand somewhat awkwardly. Win's grasp was warm and firm, and she wondered if it was her imagination that

he held her hand a tad longer than necessary. His tawny eyes brimmed with good
humor. "My pleasure, Dr. Stone."

"Thank you. And everyone please call me
Rachel. We don't stand on ceremony in Wolf
Creek."

"Rachel, then," he said.

Rachel's glance encompassed them all.
"So how are you finding our town so far?
I'm sure it's quite a change from Boston."

"It is very different," Win agreed, "but it
does have its points of interest. Mother has
been excited about coming ever since Abby
wrote to her more than a year ago."

"I wanted to come so badly then, but Sam
was very ill, and there was no way I could
leave him," Libby explained. Her eyes
darkened with sorrow. "He passed away just
after Christmas, and when Abby wrote telling me about Eli, I told Win and Blythe I
simply had to come back. They both wanted
to meet Gabe and Caleb, so here we are."

The conversation fizzled for a moment,
and Rachel scoured her mind for something
else to say. Unfortunately, her brain appeared to have turned to mush.

Gabe came to the rescue. "Everyone is going fishing with Danny after the auction and
picnic," he said, coming to her rescue.
"Would you and Edward like to join us?"

She was about to open her mouth to say that she had things to do when Edward spoke up.

"We'd love to."

"Are you sure you'll be up to it?" Rachel hedged, appalled at the thought of spending any significant time with the Granvilles. "It will make a long day."

"But a good one," Edward assured her. "Libby and I have a lot of catching up to do. I'll be fine, I promise."

He did spend too much time inside, she thought. Mostly because she wasn't always there to see to it that he got out and about as he should. And he was also tied down with watching Danny and being responsible for starting the evening meal. She shouldn't begrudge him this short time with a friend, even if she knew she would be miserable.

She mustered a smile. "If you're sure we won't be intruding, we'd be glad to join you."

As everyone was expressing their pleasure, someone rang a dinner bell and announced that the auction was about to begin. Mayor Talbot had been designated as the auctioneer, and bidding on the first basket started with a description of what was in it and who'd contributed it. Offers flew briskly, and cheers went up when Abe Caldwell had to pay three dollars for his wife's box.

Abby's was up next, and to everyone's surprise, Win got into the spirit of the day and joined in the battle, raising Caleb's every bid so that he was forced to pay seven dollars to share lunch with his wife. Gabe and Win were laughing so hard they could hardly catch their breath.

Caleb's face looked like a thundercloud as he paid the money, but Abby turned toward Win and gave him a wide smile and a wave. She was still laughing as she and Caleb sauntered off to find a spot down by the creek.

"It isn't like he can't afford it," Gabe offered, pulling out a monogrammed handkerchief and wiping his eyes.

Three more boxes sold, and then Rachel's came up.

"This basket was donated by Dr. Rachel Stone." Homer Talbot lifted the blue-patterned feed-sack dish towel and peeked inside. "Looks like fried chicken, homemade biscuits, pickled beets, a jar of slaw, some of Edward's famous lime pickles and pound cake with — What's this, Rachel?" he asked, holding up a pint jar.

"It's called 'lemon curd.' Something I haven't tried before."

"Looks dee-licious!" the mayor said.

"Some gentleman out there is going to have a real treat." He looked directly at Gabe. "Who'll start the bidding at fifty cents?"

Gabe raised his hand, and someone across the way raised him a dime. Then, from behind Rachel, a voice said calmly but firmly, "Five."

The crowd gasped, and Rachel and Gabe both turned to see Win standing leaning against a tree, his eyes alight with mischief.

"What do you think you're doing?" Gabe snapped.

"Bidding on the lady's basket," he said. "It all sounds delicious, and I haven't had any lemon curd since I was in London a few months ago."

"Let's keep things moving," Homer said. "Do I hear five-fifty?"

Glaring at his stepbrother, Gabe held up his hand. "Eight," he said over the murmur of the crowd.

Win's gaze locked with Gabe's. "Ten."

Gabe's face was as red as the jar of beets in the basket. "This isn't funny. What kind of game do you think you're playing, *brother*?"

"You thought it was funny when Caleb had to pay, *brother*," Win reminded him. "And it's no game. It's just that when I see something I want, I go after it."

CHAPTER ELEVEN

Gabe bid twelve dollars and Win relented with a shrug. The crowd was abuzz over the spirited bidding rivalry and curious about what it might mean to Dr. Stone and Gabe's relationship.

It was a ridiculously high price to pay, but there was no way Gabe was going to let the aristocratic Bostonian share a lunch with Rachel. Who did that blue-blooded upstart think he was, anyway? Just because the Granvilles were somebody back in Boston didn't mean Win could come into Gabe's neck of the woods and try to snatch the woman he loved out from under his nose. If Win was entertaining some half-cocked notion to "go after" Rachel, he'd soon find out that he'd have another battle on his hands!

Gabe pulled the cash from his wallet and went to pay the fee to Ruby Talbot. Collecting the basket of food amid a chorus of good-natured ribbing, he stalked toward the group gathered beneath the trees.

A sudden thought struck him. Was it possible Win was thinking of spending more time in Wolf Creek than he let on?

The previous evening, his stepbrother's conversation seemed centered around the town. He appeared to have looked things over since arriving and had asked a lot of questions about businesses or storefronts for sale, about what the town needed and what possible avenues for growth there might be not only in Wolf Creek, but in the surrounding area.

At the time, Gabe had assumed Win was just making conversation and had listened but offered little to the discussion. Caleb had lived here his whole life and had his fingers on the pulse of what was happening. He'd answered Win's questions without reserve, discussing several possibilities for new businesses.

Now that Win had all but come out and announced his interest in Rachel, Gabe wondered if he'd misjudged the older man. Was he attracted to her enough to be a true rival? Enough to relocate his business?

Stalking along toward the group beneath the trees, Gabe's stomach twisted beneath the reality of the situation. Maybe she would rather have someone like the upstanding Granville heir than a ne'er-do-well who'd done everything in his power to mess up his life. And hers.

He approached the gathering, automatically looking for the outsider. Win was still lounging against the tree, regarding him with an amused expression. Though he'd seemed okay at first, Gabe wasn't sure he liked his stepbrother overmuch. He was sure of one thing, though. His plan had been to take things slow and not pressure Rachel, but with Win in the picture, maybe it was time to move things along. He was going to ask her to marry him. Soon. The worst that could happen was that she would say no.

Rachel picked up a quilt she'd brought and her wary gaze moved from one man to the other. "Will you make sure Danny gets something to eat, Dad?" she asked Edward.

"Of course I will."

"Don't worry about a thing. Your father and I have it well in hand," Libby said. "I'll even fix Edward a plate." She gave a shooing wave of her hands. "You two go on now and enjoy your meal."

"Thank you," Rachel said and hurried to catch up with Gabe, who evidently had no qualms about leaving her behind.

"What was that all about?" she asked, as she fell into step with the irritating man.

His face held wide-eyed innocence. "What was what all about?"

"Don't pretend you don't know what I mean, Gabriel Gentry. What was that between you and Win?"

Gabe shot her an irritated look. "You heard him. When he sees something he wants, he goes after it. Meaning you, of course."

The notion that Win Granville might be interested in her was stunning. He was too self-confident, too sophisticated, too everything she would not be interested in. She laughed. "He was just stirring up a bit of controversy for the fun of it — he does seem to have a wicked sense of humor — or he was just helping out the town by bidding up the price of the baskets."

Gabe stopped and turned to her. "That's a very generous observation, and one anyone who knows you would expect you to make, but don't be naive," he said. "You must know that you're a very beautiful woman, even though you make me want to bang my head against the wall most of the time."

She stared at him, uncertain whether to laugh at his frustration, thank him for thinking she was beautiful or smack him for saying that she drove him crazy. Then she saw the uncertainty in his eyes.

She pressed a palm to her heart that gave a ridiculous little flip of joy. Oh, my! It would be easier to believe that the world would stop turning before believing she would ever see what her eyes were telling her now.

He was jealous.

More than that, for perhaps the first time in his life, he was unsure of himself. Her heart thudded beneath her hand. He'd kissed her and told her he cared and she'd believed him as far as it went, but was it possible that he really truly cared for her? The thought was almost overwhelming.

"You're imagining things," she said, willing her voice to steadiness. "And I may be naive, but I'm not silly enough to fall for the likes of Win Granville. The man is as handsome as sin, but he definitely has heartbreak written all over him."

Pressing his lips together as if he were afraid he might say something to add to the volatility of the conversation, Gabe turned and started walking. Rachel followed, searching for a topic that might restore some harmony for the next hour or so. After a moment or two, he stopped beneath the spreading branches of a huge oak tree. The nearby creek gurgled and bubbled and rushed headlong over the rocky bottom.

"How's this?" he asked, frowning at her.

"Perfect." She unfurled the red, white and blue quilt she'd brought along. "You were right. Your mother isn't at all judgmental. I like her."

Gabe put down the basket and lowered himself Indian style. Rachel sank down on her knees, her skirt billowing out around her. Their gazes locked as she waited for him to respond.

"I like her, too," he admitted. "And I didn't expect to."

There was no need for him to explain, and she was thankful to see that his grumpiness had disappeared. "You said earlier that Libby didn't have an affair — Lucas did."

"Right." While she set out the lunch, he told her everything that had transpired the evening before.

"You'll never in a million years guess who he was seeing."

"I can't imagine . . ."

"Sarah VanSickle."

They'd reached the dessert portion of the meal, and dropping that bit of news into the conversation almost caused the piece of pound cake Rachel had just sliced to slip from her fingers.

"Sarah VanSickle?" she echoed, putting the cake onto a delicate saucer trimmed with clusters of forget-me-nots. She thrust the plate at him.

"It surprised me, too, although knowing her as I do, I'm not sure why," Gabe admitted. He held out the cake while Rachel added a dollop of the lemon curd.

She fumed as she fixed her own dessert. How could anyone deliberately come between a husband and wife? How could anyone destroy a family through sheer malice? No one should have to suffer what Libby and her boys had gone through, all because of one man's ego and one woman's vindictiveness.

That any of them had come out of it with as few scars as they had was nothing short of a miracle. She saw God's hand in sending Frank, the only person to offer two young boys what comfort and love they'd received during their youth. Frank had done what he could to counteract Lucas's callousness, somehow managing to instill good old-fashioned decency in them.

She saw God's plan in the way He'd brought Caleb and Abby together, and how through Abby, He'd worked to reunite a mother to her sons and grandchildren. It was so easy to see and trust Him working in the lives of others, but did she dare trust that He was working in hers and Gabe's? Had it been God's plan for Gabe to be attacked on his journey home last December? Had Simon been sent just so he could bring Gabe to her doorstep? Was it His intent for them to work through their troubled past and become a family?

"What are you thinking?" Gabe asked, bringing her convoluted thoughts back to the present.

She lifted her gaze to his. "I'm thinking that life is very complicated. It's unfair and often downright ugly, and only by the grace of God do we manage to come through it relatively unscathed."

He frowned. "Those are pretty weighty observations."

"Well," she said with a self-deprecating smile, "as you well know, I am not a featherbrain by reputation."

She took her first bite of cake. Gabe had finished his while she was woolgathering. "Do you think Libby will confront Sarah now that there's no one around to stop her?" she asked.

"Oh, you can count on it."

She finished her cake and busied herself with gathering and wrapping the soiled plates and flatware in a plain dish towel to transport them back home.

"Do you know what really infuriates me?" he asked, pitching the dregs of his lemonade into the grass and handing her the glass.

From her perspective it was all infuriating. "What?"

"That Sarah can go around and deliberately pick people's lives to pieces when she's guilty of far worse than most of them."

"Maybe she's asked for forgiveness for what she did to your family," Rachel said, striving for fairness.

He made a scoffing sound. "If so, I'm sure she got it, but what about the things she's done since?"

"We all sin, and most of us commit the same sins over and over," Rachel said. "At least I do. Seventy times seven, remember?"

"I understand that, but there's a difference. When we ask for forgiveness and mean it, we may inadvertently fall back into that old sin. The difference is when you ask for forgiveness all the while *intending* to go out and do the same thing at the next opportunity."

Rachel thought of how Sarah's wicked tongue had forced Caleb and Abby into marriage, and how her spitefulness had caused her to spread the news about Danny's paternity to the four corners of the county. How many other lives had she ruined through the years? Would she ever stop her campaign of malice?

That question triggered another, troubling idea about her life. She had almost let her anger and animosity devour her. If Gabe had not returned, would she have become like Sarah? The thought was sobering, frightening. Like Sarah, she attended services regularly, but by harboring hostility toward Gabe, wasn't she just as wrong?

"You're right," she told him, searching for the right words for Gabe. "What she does is wrong, but instead of lowering ourselves to her level and maligning her, we should —"

"— pray for her," he said in disgust. "I know."

"Yes," Rachel said, unable to hide a smile. "But you really should have a better attitude when you do."

Seeing the mirth in her eyes and knowing she was right, he offered her a halfhearted smile in return. "I know you're right, but I have a way to go with this Christianity thing."

Rachel sobered, knowing that she, too, had a long way to go. "Coming from someone with years of firsthand experience, I can promise you that we'll never get it right, and it isn't always easy. The thing that matters is that we keep giving it our best, which I haven't always done, even though I should know better."

"What are you talking about? You're one of the best people I know."

"I wasn't very Christ-like when you came to town, was I?"

Gabe's expression held no condemnation. "You had reason to . . . hate me."

"I didn't hate you, but every time I looked at you, it all came back to me. The shame and guilt and how alone I was when you left me with nothing but an offhand good-bye." She drew in a shaky breath. "And as much as I tried, as much as I *wanted* to, I didn't really hate you. I don't."

Gabe's eyes held an indefinable tenderness that she had opened up to him. He was sorry to have been the one to cause her so much pain. "What do you feel, Rachel?" he whispered, leaning toward her.

Their gazes met and held. "I don't know." She shook her head. "That isn't true. I think I do know, but I'm afraid."

The trembling words came straight from the heart.

He moved closer, and as he had the day outside her house, he rested his forehead against hers. Her eyes drifted shut.

"Don't be afraid, Rachel," he said. "I do know what I feel, and it's as real and true as the sunrise, because that's what you are. Real. True. Back in St. Louis I wasn't thinking about anyone but Gabe Gentry, but this time everything's different. What I feel isn't going away, and neither am I. We have all the time in the world."

"How can you be sure it won't go away?"

He dropped a quick kiss to the tip of her nose.

"Because my heart is involved this time. Because Danny's heart is involved. I pray yours is. And because this feels so right that it scares *me* to death sometimes. I ran from what you made me feel once. Not again."

He was scared? She drew back to get a better look at him. "Why would you be scared?"

"I'm scared that despite everything I do and no matter how hard I try, that when I finally do ask you to spend the rest of your life with me — and I will ask you — that you'll say no."

Rachel couldn't speak for the knot of emotion in her throat. It was what she'd dreamed of nine years ago. But time and circumstances had changed. They had both changed. When he asked, what would she say?

"Stop trying to figure out what you'll do," he said, almost as if he could read her mind. "I'm not asking you for anything today. And I promise you that whatever your answer is, I will do everything in my power to never cause you that kind of pain again."

"The woman is impossible!" Libby said, stalking across Caleb's parlor. Another week had passed and they were all congregated at the farm to share another meal. This time Rachel, Edward and Danny were in attendance, even though Rachel felt like an outsider.

With the meal over, the dishes washed and put away, and the little ones down for an afternoon nap, the grownups were gathered to hear the details of Libby's confrontation with Sarah the evening before.

"Be specific, Mother." Win sprawled in a wingback chair, his long legs crossed at the ankles, regarding the contrasting tips of his shining shoes. He glanced up. "Surely she listened to what you had to say."

"Oh, she listened," Libby said, whirling around to face her family. "I told her that I'd always known about her and Lucas. She had the gall to tell me that if I'd been the right kind of wife, he would never have strayed."

301

"That's interesting." Edward said. "Especially since it's common knowledge that he broke off with Sarah and took up with a woman from Murfreesboro not a month after you left."

Rachel and Gabe exchanged surprised looks. This was new information and said even more about what a rogue Lucas Gentry had been.

"Serves her right," Libby snapped, clearly in a huff. "Then when I confronted her with starting the gossip about Caleb and Abby even though her accusations were groundless, she informed me that we were supposed to 'abstain from all *appearance* of evil,' and she felt it was her Christian duty to bring awareness to the situation, so that it could be set straight."

Caleb's jaw clenched, and he opened his mouth to say something, but Abby stopped him with a hand on his arm. "And here we are," she said, meeting his heated gaze with a smiling one. "As happy as two fat cats in the sunshine."

"It could have turned out far differently," Caleb groused.

"Could have, but didn't."

Rachel saw that Libby looked at her new daughter-in-law with unabashed affection.

"All's well that ends well, then," Blythe

said. Though she seemed painfully shy, as her time in Wolf Creek had passed and she got to know her brothers and their families better, she seemed more comfortable contributing to the conversations.

"I don't mind telling you that I was furious," Libby continued. "She was totally unrepentant about anything she'd done. When I brought up Rachel and Gabe and told her she had no right to blather her suspicions about Danny to everyone in town, she just laughed. 'Your sins will find you out,' she said, to which I replied that she was twisting scripture and what she had done was motivated by pure meanness — not goodness. Then I reminded her that we are to 'keep our tongue from evil.' "

"And?" Gabe asked, fighting the urge to smile as he listened to his mother go on about her confrontation with her archenemy.

"She told me not to preach to her and stalked away. I realized then that I was casting pearls before swine and —"

Edward's sudden hoot of laughter silenced her in midsentence. Planting her hands on her slender hips, Libby glared at him, but then when she realized how ridiculous the idea of her and Sarah tossing scripture back and forth in the heat of an argument must sound, she joined him.

"You can't reason with unreasonable people, my dear," he told her. "I'm afraid that unless something drastic happens to make Sarah see the error of her ways, she'll never change. It's a reality you'll have to deal with if you do decide to move here."

Caleb, Abby and Gabe looked as shocked by the casual comment as Rachel felt. The animation on Blythe's pretty face vanished, and her hands tightened in her lap. As usual, Win's expression gave away little, but Rachel thought he seemed watchful beneath the nonchalance, as if he were inordinately interested in everyone's response.

Frowning, Caleb addressed Win. "I know we talked about this some, but I thought you were just making conversation, showing interest in town. Are you really considering a move from Boston?"

Win gestured toward Libby, who sat down in a chair next to Edward's.

"Well, I am. At least for part of the year. With Sam gone, there's no reason I can't go where I wish. So why not? Win is perfectly capable of overseeing the family businesses."

"Which are?" Gabe asked.

"Actually, Win worked with his father's newspaper and printing endeavor, and Sam handled the furniture-manufacturing facility," she said. "Since he died, Win has taken it on, too. Along with Philip's help, of course. He's an attorney."

Gabe was impressed in spite of himself.

"Win and Blythe have had me for more than twenty years, and I feel I have so much to make up for with you two boys and the grandchildren here. I would miss Win and Blythe terribly, of course, which is why I'm considering equal time at both places."

"Unless Blythe and I decide to come, too," Win added, casting a quick glance at Gabe, who felt a sudden urge to smash his fist into his stepbrother's aristocratic nose.

"I don't want to move," Blythe said, her lips forming a pout that made her look younger than her twenty-two years. "Wolf Creek is a nice little town, but after living in the city all my life, I can't imagine being happy with no theaters, museums or parks and no eating establishments but the hotel and Ellie's café."

"The choices are a bit limited," Win said, "but I think that's exactly why this might be a good place to branch out. It seems to me that the area could use a new business or two. What about an attorney? There are bound to be legal issues that crop up, even with so few people."

"Are you saying your brother might move,

too, if the rest of you come?"

"Not Philip!" Win said with an emphatic shake of his head.

"I agree," Libby added. "I can't see him ever leaving the city, but some young lawyer out there will settle here one day."

"So it's really all still up in the air," Caleb said. "What would you do with your days, Mother? As Blythe said, we don't have much to do in the way of activities, and there isn't much of a social scene. I don't see that changing any time soon."

"I'm not sure. I'll be somewhat limited being gone half the year, but I'll think of something. Maybe Ellie would let me help her part of the day."

"You'd work in a café?" Rachel asked, astounded at the thought that the stylish woman sitting across from her would lower herself to work in an eating establishment.

"Well, I'm a pretty fair cook, and I had a lot of practice before I went to Boston. I'm certainly not above it, just because my husband left me with a lot of money," she said with a shrug. "It doesn't matter what we do. It matters that we do something and that we're happy doing it. I happen to like being busy and I love to cook and bake."

"I don't know, Mother," Win kidded her. "I'm not sure your piecrust is up to Ellie's standards. Her food is pretty wonderful. Not to mention she's a real stunner. What I can't figure out is why someone hasn't snatched her up."

"Sheriff Garrett is working on it," Gabe said, giving Win a pointed look. "They've hit a bump or two lately, but it's nothing they can't resolve, I'm sure."

"What kind of bumps?"

Abby looked around the room. "Well, I don't want to gossip . . ."

"For pity's sake, Abby!" Caleb said. "Just tell the truth. Colt is a good man, but his children are wretched little brats."

"I can vouch for that," Gabe said. "I actually shudder when I see them come through the doors at the store."

"They are a handful," Rachel added. "But that isn't the biggest problem."

Everyone looked at her expectantly.

"Ellie's daughter, Beth, is a Mongoloid. Ellie's husband took one look at her and disappeared. She hasn't seen him since, so Ellie isn't divorced, and she isn't a widow. Until her husband is located or declared dead, she couldn't marry again if she wanted to."

Over the next few days, every moment Rachel was not treating someone's ailment, she was thinking about her conversation with Gabe and his mother's announcement that she might return to Wolf Creek. She wasn't sure how she felt about that, but she understood the older woman's need to reconnect with her sons and establish relationships with her grandchildren. She would think less of Libby had she not felt the way she did.

As for everyone else, they were fine with the idea. Neither Danny nor Ben was accustomed to having a grandmother around and were ecstatic about the notion. No doubt the younger children would be just as happy once they figured out exactly what having a grandmother meant.

Two days before the Granvilles were scheduled to return to Boston, Edward asked them to the house for dinner. Win and Blythe declined, stating that Ellie was having chicken and dumplings at the café, a dish they hadn't tried before coming to the South and one they declared was so good as to be "positively sinful." Though they might be right about how good it was, Rachel suspected there was something more behind their refusal. She also suspected that that something more was Libby wanting to spend some special time with Danny before she left.

But it wasn't only Danny Libby wanted to spend time with. When the supper dishes were done and put away, Edward challenged Danny to a game of checkers and Libby suggested that she and Rachel sit on the porch. Nervous, though she wasn't sure why, Rachel acquiesced.

"I wanted a chance to talk to you alone before I leave," Libby said.

"I understand."

Libby smiled. "I'm not sure you do. I imagine there are all sorts of things running through your mind, including wondering what I really think of you." She reached out and patted the hands Rachel clutched in her lap.

"I've talked to Gabe, and he told me about St. Louis. After hearing about his antics through the years, I was a bit surprised that he took the entire blame for what happened."

"You kept up with him and Caleb?" Rachel asked, surprised.

"Some," she said with a nod. "Enough to know that Caleb was turning into a sour recluse and Gabe was running amok. When he left here, I lost track of him except for what few things made the papers back East. I never heard a word about you and Danny, though."

"There's no way anyone could have known about me and Danny until Sarah spoke up." Rachel said. "I never even told my father who Danny's father was."

"So Edward said."

"Who kept you informed? Surely not Lucas."

"No, not Lucas," Libby said with a laugh. "It was Frank, actually, but I only heard from him a time or two a year, since reading and writing aren't his strong suits. And when there was some medical problem, your dad would drop me a line through Frank. It was all very hush-hush. I couldn't have Lucas finding out that I was keeping up with them."

Rachel liked Libby even more, knowing she'd done what she could to keep up with her sons' development.

"Do Caleb and Gabe know?"

"Yes."

"I appreciate your openness, Libby, and I especially appreciate your acceptance of Danny. It was very gentlemanly of Gabe to take sole responsibility for what happened. For years I told myself that he was the only one responsible, but the truth is that I was as much in the wrong as he was." She took a deep breath and met Libby's gaze. "Suffice it to say that he's very hard to withstand when he puts his mind to something — not that that is an excuse."

"He always was hard to resist," Libby agreed with a gentle smile. "When Caleb got into trouble, he got all serious and helpful and did any and everything to get back in my good graces. Gabe turned on the charm and wooed me back into a good mood by entertaining me with some sort of foolishness or another."

Rachel had no problem envisioning that, since Danny was pretty adept at the same thing.

"Since coming back and hearing about how truly appalling their time with Lucas was, I'm ashamed of not having tried harder to do something to get them back. Sam had money. I should have found a good attorney and . . . done something."

"Lucas Gentry was a powerful man," Rachel said, wanting to ease the pain reflected in the older woman's eyes. "Even more daunting than his fortune is the fact that he was very politically connected, from local attorneys to the governor. He wouldn't have hesitated to use that influence against you."

"Thank you for pointing that out. I know you're right. It's just that I hate what happened to them, and I worry about how it affected them as they grew up."

"Lucas's behavior had a profound effect on everyone's life, including yours," Rachel reminded her. "Thank God you've come through it, stronger. You've made a wonderful new life and have Win and Blythe. Caleb is like a new man since Abby came along, and I truly believe Gabe is on his way to happiness, so stop worrying. Dad always says that worry is like a rocking chair. You can rock all day and never get anywhere. One thing I've realized is that we can't undo the past. All we can do is take the lessons we learn from our mistakes and apply them to future situations."

"As you've done."

She shrugged. "As tough as Caleb and Gabe's life was, it has made them the men they are. Imperfect, certainly, but basically good men. That goodness had to come from you, from the memories of you they never let go."

Libby's eyes shimmered with tears. "He loves you, you know, and the longer I'm here, the more I understand why."

Rachel's breath caught. "He loves Danny."

"Don't sell yourself short, my dear."

Rachel felt her own eyes fill with tears. "How can you be so nice to me?" she whispered. "When you know . . ."

"I'm not here to cast stones," Libby said.

312

"We all fall short, and no matter how much we'd like there to be, there are no little sins and big sins. Just sins.

"She may never acknowledge it, but Sarah's gossiping tongue is just as bad as what happened between you and Gabe. The two of you have learned from your mistakes and have made things right with God. You're trying to live good lives. It's a heart thing, something Sarah just doesn't get."

"So you've forgiven her?" Rachel asked.

"I'm working on it," Libby said with another of those dry smiles. "So!" She swiped her fingertips beneath her eyes and her voice took on brisk purpose. "Now that we have that cleared up, do you have any objections to my moving here?"

"What I think has no bearing on your decision," Rachel said, surprised that Libby would seek her approval.

"Of course it does. I'll have a lot of contact not only with Caleb and Gabe, but with the children. How do you feel about my being part of Danny's life?"

Touched that she cared about her feelings, Rachel said, "I think it would be wonderful for him to have a grandmother. As long as you don't spoil him too much," she added.

Libby's eyes widened and she placed a

palm against her chest as if the comment had inflicted a mortal wound. "But spoiling is what grandmothers are for, and I have so much catching up to do."

Seeing the genuine dismay in Rachel's eyes, Libby laughed and leaned forward to give her a quick hug. "I'll try."

Knowing she was fighting a losing battle, Rachel gave in to the inevitable. She would now not only have to share Danny with Gabe but with his mother, and possibly Win and Blythe.

Not necessarily a bad thing.

Reluctantly, she agreed with the little voice whispering inside her.

CHAPTER TWELVE

Libby was long gone and everyone else in the house was sleeping soundly. A shaft of moonlight slanted across Rachel's bed, and a whisper of air drifted through the partially open window, causing the lace curtains to ripple gently. She lay there thinking of her conversation with Gabe's mother and conjuring up images of what it would be like with Libby Granville in town. In her life.

Libby claimed Gabe loved her, and with those words running through her mind, Rachel began to dream of re-creating some of the funny, tender moments she and Gabe had once shared and building a life with their son. Would it ever happen? She'd begun to nurture the tiny, tentative hope that it might.

She often thought of Gabe's statement on the day of the box-lunch picnic. He was going to ask her to marry him. When? What would she say if he did? According to his mother and her father, Gabe loved her. Could she trust it was true? Could she trust *him* again?

She heard the sudden patter of raindrops and sighed in pleasure. She loved hearing rain against the rooftop. Then, realizing that the window was half-open, she scrambled to a sitting position and swung her legs over the side of the bed. She'd almost reached the window when she heard another soft clatter and realized it wasn't rain at all. Someone was throwing gravel.

Grabbing the shawl that was draped over the back of a nearby chair, she flung it around her shoulders and poked her head out the window. Gabe stood near her mama's rosebush with his hands on his hips, his head tipped back watching to see if she would answer his summons.

"What are you doing here?" she screeched in a loud whisper. She was appalled by his presence yet unaccountably pleased to see him. What a scandal it would be if anyone else saw him! Thank goodness Danny, not her father, had the room next to hers. Unlike Edward, Danny slept like the dead.

"I haven't seen you all day, and I wanted to tell you that I . . ."

Her breath hung suspended and her heart seemed to stop midbeat.

". . . I miss you."

"Gabe," she all but groaned. Then, pushing aside a ridiculous rush of pleasure, she summoned her most professional tone. "Go home. I'll see you tomorrow."

"Did anyone ever tell you that you're a heartless woman, Rachel Stone? Where will I see you tomorrow? At the store or between the times before you hurry off to see a patient? Where's the romance in that?"

"Romance?" She croaked the single word in a low, stunned voice.

"Yes, romance. Obviously you've never been courted before."

The insidious, ridiculous pleasure blossomed inside her. "Really? What was St. Louis?"

"That doesn't count because I didn't know what I was doing or why," he said in a low undertone. "This —" he spread his arms wide "— is the real thing. I told you."

She chewed on her lower lip. Uncertainty lent stridency to her voice. "If someone sees you here, it won't be pleasant."

"What can they do? Talk about us?" he challenged.

She resisted the urge to giggle. "Go home, Gabe."

"So practical," he said with a low chuckle and a shake of his head. "We need to work on that." He took a step backward. "Tomorrow, then. I have to take a load of grain out to Mr. Connor after I close, but when I come back, I'm going to ask you to walk with me down by the creek and I'm going to ask you a very important question, so you'd better be ready. Preferably with the answer I want to hear." He pivoted to leave.

"Gabe!"

He turned.

"What if you don't get the answer you want?"

"Then I'll try harder." She saw the flash of his smile in the moonlight. "I'd like tomorrow better than next month or next year, but I'm learning that I can be a very patient man, and I have it on good authority that women can't resist me, so it's only a matter of time."

She smiled at the teasing tone of his voice, her heart light with promise.

"You're a very conceited man," she told him, but there was no real condemnation in the words.

"I prefer to think of it as confidence. And it's part of why you love me. You do, you know."

He sketched a jaunty salute, turned and left her dangling out the window, her mouth hanging open. She watched him disappear into the trees behind the house, knowing he was right, drat him. She was even starting to believe that her love was returned, but neither fact altered the nagging fear of whether or not she was ready to trust that love enough to take a second chance.

The sun was still plenty high in the western sky when Gabe drove his wagon back toward Wolf Creek the next day. He'd told Rachel he wouldn't rush her, but he wanted her to know how he felt. As anxious as he was to have the upcoming conversation with her, he'd needed the extra couple of hours to settle his nerves. He couldn't recall ever feeling so scared about what a woman would say.

She well knew that he was no innocent. She might be more inclined to say yes if he were blameless and they had no past to come between them, but no matter what she said, he didn't regret that time. It had taken him years to realize that if he hadn't looked her up in St. Louis, he might have gone on with his aimless life indefinitely.

She was like no woman he'd ever met. Serious and still somewhat shy, yet decisive and professional. She was dedicated to her goals. Intelligent and innately good. After all these years, he understood why he had turned his back on her. Once she had given him her heart, she had given him everything else she possessed with utmost trust. Even as self-serving as he'd been, he was smart enough to realize how special that was. What did a man like him do with love like that? How was he to return it? His only knowledge of love was the vague memories of his mother, who had left him. And so he'd panicked, written her a note and disappeared.

What a fool he'd been! But when he'd awakened with her name on his lips and his eyes wet with tears long after she should have been nothing but a hazy memory, he'd realized what an impact she'd had on him. That was when he'd gathered the courage to come home.

And here they were, almost six months later. If he thought it had taken courage for him to return, he couldn't imagine how brave she'd been to come home with an illegitimate child. Yet she had endured the whispers and speculation. She had restored her good name and was well respected in the community. Did he have the right to jeopardize that by asking her to share his life? Maybe not, but he intended to anyway.

The sound of shouting and neighing horses up ahead jolted him back to the present. He thought he heard a woman scream. What was going on? he wondered, slapping the reins against his horse's back, urging it to speed up.

The road curved, and as he rounded the slight bend, he saw that a surrey had been forced off the side of the road. Two horsemen with bandannas pulled up over their faces had dismounted and were yelling at a stout woman, but he was too far away to make out what they were saying.

He recognized the buggy at the same time one of the men reached out and tugged an earbob from one of the woman's ears. Sarah VanSickle! And it looked as if she was being robbed. Even as the thoughts came together, Gabe saw her knock her attacker's hand away from her other ear. When the man grabbed at her reticule, she stepped backward and received a couple of blows for her effort.

Recalling his own encounter with bandits on this very stretch of road — possibly these same two — he urged the gelding to a tooth-rattling pace that launched him up from the bench seat every time the wheels hit a bump. As he neared the scene and pulled his horse to a stop, Sarah recognized him.

"Gabe! Help! Please!" She was holding

her abdomen, and her lip was bleeding.

When he leaped to the ground, the thief who was watching Sarah's abuse at the hands of his cohort turned to face him. The familiar coal-black eyes above the bandanna's edge were filled with a chilling malevolence. "Well, well, well. Back for more, are you?"

The eyes and the gravelly voice breached the entrance to a memory Gabe had slammed the door on. These were definitely the same men. Even if the robber hadn't uttered the telling statement, he would never forget that voice.

"Yeah," he said. "And I'm not hungover this time."

Lunging forward, he hit the outlaw's midsection with his shoulder, wrapping his arms around him and using his forward momentum to bring him down. The men hit the ground with loud grunts. They wrestled, rolling over and over, one on top and then the other, exchanging blow for blow. During the struggle, the stranger's kerchief slipped down, but Gabe didn't recognize him. He looked Indian, though.

He paid for his lack of attention with a particularly hard punch to the kidney and another to the eye. With blood running down his face, he hauled back and landed a well-aimed strike to his opponent's face. The man's grip loosened, and with his lungs heaving, Gabe struggled to regain his footing. He swiped at the blood dripping off his chin and faced the man who held a handful of Sarah's ruffled bodice in one hand and a bowie knife in the other.

"Give him your reticule, Sarah," Gabe told her, angling closer. From the corner of his eyes, he saw the man he'd fought roll to his knees and draw his Colt. "Give them what they want."

Sarah looked at him as if he'd grown two heads. "Don't be ridiculous, Gabriel! I'll do nothing of the sort."

"It's only jewelry. It can be replaced."

"Jewelry Randolph worked long hours to pay for," she snapped.

The man jerked suddenly and she went careening forward. The action was accompanied by the sound of rending cloth. As she staggered to regain her footing, the big man's hand came away with a handful of fabric.

"My brooch!" With no thought of the knife in his hand, she leaped forward, her hands curled into claws. She meant to scratch out his eyes, Gabe thought. Unfortunately, she only managed to drag the handkerchief down. She gasped when she saw who it was. Another blow sent her sprawling onto the ground.

The man Gabe had fought let go a string of curses. "They've seen us, Elton."

"So they have, and that's no good at all."

From the look in his eyes, there was no telling what he'd do. Unaware that they were both near death, Sarah struggled to her feet and rushed her assailant once more, swinging her reticule like a lasso.

"Give me my earrings!"

Gabe cast a quick look at the other desperado and saw that he'd turned his weapon toward Sarah. Gabe sprang forward, hoping to knock her out of the line of fire.

Several things seemed to happen simultaneously. Two loud *boom*s shattered the evening air. Sarah screamed and then just . . . disappeared. Something seared his side. Almost simultaneously an intense pain blossomed in his head. He heard both men yelling and cursing. He knew he needed to help Sarah but was having a hard time battling back the shadows stealing over at him. As the all-consuming pain and blessed darkness carried him away, he thought he heard Sarah screaming and the clatter of hooves pounding down the gravel road.

"Gabriel!"

The sharp voice sounded familiar. He didn't like it. Something stung his face, and he forced his eyes open a crack. A grotesque face stared down at him. Pale. A bruised eye. Mouth swollen to twice its size. Scraggly hair. A fancy hat sitting at a cockeyed angle on her head. A ridiculous pheasant feather dangling down.

He must be in the middle of a nightmare. If he didn't know better he would say it was Sarah VanSickle leaning over him, calling his name in sharp, demanding tones and slapping his cheeks, insisting that he get up.

He heard her. Trouble was, he couldn't. He hurt too badly, and the shadows were pulling at him again.

It was just before candle lighting, and there was no sign of Gabe. Rachel was sitting in the parlor, pretending to read the newest copy of *Woman's Home Journal* while a tedious refrain chased through her mind: *He's changed his mind. He's changed his mind . . . changed his mind . . .*

The sounds of half a dozen yelling voices interrupted the litany, followed by the loud clatter of wagon wheels rumbling across the railroad tracks. More crying out ensued, shouts that were accompanied by the sound of a whip cracking through the air and hoof beats thundering toward the rear of the house.

Someone was making quite a ruckus, which meant that whatever it was must be serious. Leaping to her feet and calling for her father, she headed for the office. All thoughts of Gabe vanished as she mentally prepared herself to deal with this newest crisis. Patients arrived at all hours of the day and night, and she needed to be clear-headed to attend them.

No amount of preparation could have equipped her for what she saw when she flung open the door. The wagon Gabe used to make deliveries sat there, but it was Sarah VanSickle who held the reins. Her tear-streaked face was battered and bruised and smeared with blood. Her expensive hat was askew, and one feather dangled by her ear.

"Sarah!" Rachel said, rushing forward. "What on earth happened?"

"Robbed outside Antoine," she said, sobbing as her tenuous hold on her dwindling stamina slipped away.

"Robbed?" Edward said from the doorway. "Who . . . ?"

"Elton Thomerson!" she cried. "I didn't know the other one."

Elton Thomerson? Meg's husband? Stunned by the information, Rachel had no time to dwell on it. "Let me help you down," she said.

"I can't walk," Sarah said with a shake of her head. "I think I broke my ankle when I went over the side of the gully. It's Gabe you need to help. He's been shot."

Blood drained from Rachel's head and she swayed with sudden dizziness.

"Rachel!" The sharpness of her father's voice dissipated the gathering fog. "Go check on him. I'll get the stretcher."

Thank God for her father, she thought. He always seemed to be there when she needed him most. She spied Danny in the doorway next to his grandfather. His frightened eyes were wide and glittered with unshed tears. She knew what must be going through his mind. He had just found his father. Was he about to lose him? He needed a task that would divert his mind from the news that Gabe had been shot.

"Danny!" She heard the same brisk command in her voice that she'd heard in her father's. Like a true Stone, Danny's head snapped up and he gave her his full attention.

"Run get Roland. I need someone to help me get your father inside. Then go tell your grandmother and the others. They need to know what's happened. Run like the wind."

Danny took off, passing Roland, who was just rounding the corner of the house. If there had been time, Rachel would have hugged him in relief.

"I heard all the commotion and headed this direction. Figured you might need some help," he said, already moving toward the rear of the wagon. "There's a passel of folks headed this way to see what's going on."

Grabbing her skirt in one hand, she hurried to join him. When Roland saw who it was, he raised his troubled gaze to hers. She knew he was remembering the other time a beaten, bloody Gabe had been brought for her to patch up.

Edward returned, dragging the stretcher behind him. Rachel slid it into the wagon bed and Roland climbed in, lifting Gabe's upper torso while Rachel took his feet. Every molecule of her body was telling her to hurry, yet common sense urged her to take care.

A quick visual once-over told her that he'd been in another fight — were there more broken ribs? — and confirmed that he had indeed been shot. Twice. One bullet had struck him low in the side. The other had grazed his skull just above his left eyebrow. It had bled profusely, which was normal for a scalp wound. The bleeding had slowed to a sluggish ooze. She didn't want to think that if it had been an inch over he would be dead. She didn't want to think of possible brain trauma.

Together, she and Roland got Gabe into the surgery and onto the table. She gave Roland a quick smile of thanks. "Go get Mrs. VanSickle and take her into the bedroom. She thinks she's broken her ankle. Dad will have to handle that while I take care of Gabe. Then stay close in case we need you."

Knowing Roland would do her bidding, she gave Gabe a whiff of ether to keep him from waking while she treated him, then scrubbed her hands. She cut away his shirt and vest and pushed the fabric aside to examine the wound on his side. Luckily the bullet had entered the soft tissue near his waist. She rounded the table and heaved him to his side. Spotting the exit wound, she knew the bullet had traveled straight through. She was cleaning the injury when her father came into the room.

"How about some help?"

"That would be great, but what about Sarah's ankle?"

Edward was already scrubbing his hands. "It isn't broken, just a really nasty sprain. I gave her a little laudanum to ease the pain, so she'll be fine until we get to her. From the looks of things, Gabe needs us worse than she does."

"He does," Rachel said, probing with sterile tweezers for any bits of fabric that might have been drawn into the cavity by the expansion and contraction of the surrounding flesh.

While she worked on the soft-tissue wound, Edward irrigated the head injury and probed the area with his finger. "I'm pretty sure there's no fracture or bone splinters," he said. "And the bullet missed all the big vessels. He'll have a massive headache when he wakes up, but barring infection, he should be fine with a few stitches."

Still as white as a sheet, Rachel looked up from her own work and flashed him an uneasy smile. *Barring infection* . . . The unknown element that doctors always worried about. But Gabe was strong and healthy, and she'd done a thorough job of cleaning his wound, as she knew Edward had. *Please, God* . . .

When she finished bandaging Gabe's side, she determined that besides a few bruises on his face, he had no other injuries. Then she poured some fresh water, fetched a clean cloth and began to wash away the blood.

Her touch was as gentle as if he were a newborn, as she cleansed the reminder of the ordeal and revealed the face she loved so much. She smoothed the cloth over a cheekbone, trailing it over his eyebrows and the grooves in his cheeks.

"Rachel."

She looked up to see her father's smiling face.

"Maybe you ought to marry the boy so you can keep an eye on him. We can't have this happening every six months."

"What makes you think he wants to marry me?" she asked, amazed by the breathlessness she heard in her voice and surprised that her father had brought up what she'd supposed would be a touchy subject.

"Because he's already asked me if I'd mind."

Rachel had no time to think about what her father had said. After they checked Sarah over and treated her cuts and scrapes, Rachel immobilized the swollen ankle. Sarah would spend a miserable few days, but her injuries were not serious, and Rachel released the groggy female into the care of her husband and son, telling them that if they needed her in the night, not to hesitate coming for her.

Secure in the knowledge that she and her father had done all they could for their patients, she cleaned and straightened the bedroom and treatment room. Rock steady and able to rely on her skill and knowledge in a crisis, she was less professional if the patient was someone she cared about, often assaulted by a ridiculous panic and shakiness once the emergency had passed. Mundane tasks helped steady her.

After peeping in on Gabe once more, she and her father went into the parlor, where the Granvilles and the preacher sat waiting for news of his condition. Someone had made coffee and served the leftover peach cobbler she'd made for supper.

Libby, who was cuddling Danny on her lap, looked up as soon as she spied them in the doorway. Worry added years to her pretty face. Danny, too, looked anxious. Thank goodness his grandmother had been here to comfort him.

"How is he?" Libby demanded. "Danny said he'd been shot."

"Yes."

"Who would do such a thing?"

"Sarah said it was Elton Thomerson and another man."

"A local, I assume?" Win asked.

"Yes. Sarah told Dad she was being robbed and Gabe came to help, but that's all we know at the moment. There was no time to ask too many questions since he needed immediate attention. We'll have to wait until one of them is lucid enough to tell us more."

Weary from standing so long, Edward, who had traded his canes for his wheelchair, rolled himself over to Libby and gave her hand a reassuring squeeze. "Barring infection or trauma to the brain, he should be fine."

"Trauma to the brain?" Win echoed. For the first time since meeting him, Rachel saw a breach in his supreme self-possession.

"He sustained a gunshot wound to his side." Rachel put her hand on her own side to indicate the approximate location. "The bullet went all the way through. I cleaned it as best I could and removed a few cloth fragments. But infection is always a concern.

"It appears the second bullet grazed his scalp." Again, she pointed out the spot. "Dad didn't detect any bone fragments, and we don't expect any other damage at this point, but we can't be completely sure. Unfortunately, we have no way of looking beneath the skull to assess any other injury."

"Is he gonna be all right?"

The question was asked by Danny, who looked at her with the fearful expression of someone who realized that his world had been turned upside down and he had no way to set it aright.

Rachel crossed over to him and squatted down. Danny catapulted from his grandmother's lap into his mother's embrace, flinging his arms around her neck.

"I hope so, Danny," she said, holding him close and inhaling the little-boy scent of him. Dirt and sweat. A smell she could breathe in all day. One Libby had been robbed of by Lucas Gentry. She blinked back the sudden sting of tears. "You know Pops and I will do everything we can to make him better, but it's in God's hands."

He pulled back to look at her. "Then we should pray, shouldn't we?"

"We have been," Blythe offered. "But we can certainly pray now if you like." She looked at the minister. "Brother McAdams, would you lead us, please?"

"I'd be glad to."

The preacher led the request to God, praying for returned health for both Gabe and Sarah, for the capture of the men who'd caused the injuries and for strength for the families and protection for the community from further incidents. When he'd finished, Danny seemed comforted and asked if he could see Gabe.

"Of course you can," Rachel said, standing and taking Danny's hand. "I'll go with you."

"If it's okay with you, I think Pip should go," he said and gave a shrug. "I mean, Dad is her little boy, and I know she's worried about him."

"You're right, of course," Rachel told him, meeting Libby's gaze. Like Danny, Libby had just found Gabe. If her heart was aching half as much as Rachel's, she was in a lot of pain.

Rachel followed Libby and Danny to the room where Roland had put Gabe after Sarah was taken home. She stopped in the aperture and leaned against the doorframe. Libby went straight to the bed and reached out to brush back an errant lock of Gabe's hair. Danny stood in the doorway watching, almost as if he were gathering the courage to face Gabe's injuries.

Finally he took a tentative step and then another. Libby held out her hand to him and pulled him to her side. Rachel watched as he looked from the bandage wrapped around Gabe's head, over his bruised face to the one circling his middle. He swallowed hard.

"He looks really sick, doesn't he, Pip?" he asked in a low, trembling voice.

"He does," she agreed, pulling up the sheet to hide the disturbing picture from Danny.

Rachel approved of the answer and gesture. There was no sense denying the obvious.

"Do you think he'll be all right?" he asked in a quavering voice.

"I do." The statement held firm conviction. "His father was as tough as nails, and I come from sturdy New England stock, and your mother and grandpa are very good doctors. Besides he's already come through one round with those robbers, so I can't imagine him letting this get him down, can you? He has too much to look forward to."

Danny angled his head and looked up at her. "Like what?"

"Like being a father to you, for one thing. I know it's in God's hands, but I just can't believe that He would bring your father back to his family and not allow you to have a life together."

"Like God sent him back here on purpose?"

"I really think so," she said, brushing Danny's hair away from his forehead as she'd done for Gabe. "God works in our lives, Danny, even when we don't do what He wants. He says, 'You didn't do what I wanted, and now look what a mess you've made of things! But don't worry, I can fix it if you'll only trust me and let me have control of your life.' "

She smoothed his hair again. "People usually understand things better and change as they grow older. Often they try to fix their mistakes by doing the right thing. I believe that when they do, it's God working in their lives."

He nodded. "Is that what He's doing with Mom and Dad? Mom said they made a mistake a long time ago. Do you think God is trying to help them fix it?"

Rachel blinked and swallowed the lump that suddenly clogged her throat. From across the room, Libby's eyes met hers.

"I do," she said with the same conviction she'd used earlier. "I really do."

CHAPTER THIRTEEN

It was almost midnight when Rachel finally convinced the Granvilles that Gabe was stable and they all should go back to the hotel for some sleep since they would be leaving for Boston the following day. When he arrived, Caleb joined her in trying to convince his mother. Libby finally agreed to get some rest but vowed that nothing could persuade her to leave town until she knew for certain that Gabe was on the road to recovery. Understanding the maternal mindset, Rachel offered no further argument.

Once she had donned her gown and robe, she went into Gabe's room and made another thorough check of him. His pulse was steady, and both injuries had all but stopped bleeding. He stirred as she listened to his chest.

"Lie still," she said, gently pressing a hand to his shoulder.

At the sound of her voice, he opened his

eyes, glassy with pain and dulled by the anesthesia she'd given him. "Rachel."

His voice sounded as if he'd swallowed gravel.

"Don't talk."

"Not going anywhere."

"Not for a while," she said, removing the earpieces and looping the stethoscope around her neck. She started to turn away, and his hand moved with surprising speed to grasp her wrist.

"Don't go."

"I'll be right here," she said.

"Promise."

"I promise." The vow seemed to satisfy him, and he closed his eyes. She slipped from his loose grasp, and convinced that he was holding his own, she lay down on the cot.

Drawing a deep breath, she forced the hands fisted at her sides to unclench and folded them over her middle. Using a technique her father had taught her, she started at her toes and willed every part of her body to relax, releasing her not only from the tension, but also the "doctor mode." Once she was filled with calmness instead of cool objectivity, she could try to process the past few hours and all they meant. One thing stood out above all else.

Gabe might have been killed.

She wasn't aware that the tears she'd imprisoned behind a facade of professionalism had escaped and were running down her temples. She had waffled over her feelings for weeks now, knowing she loved him but telling herself she wasn't sure she could trust him or that love, feeling he had to prove that he had changed and that he intended to stay no matter what, so that she and Danny would not get hurt.

What a cockamamy notion! She either loved him or she didn't. Real love didn't set rules. It didn't depend on stipulations: *Promise you will never do anything to make me angry or hurt me. Prove that you won't repeat the same transgressions so that I can trust that you mean what you say. Do all these things and I'll love you.*

Ridiculous and naive.

Love just *was.*

Loving someone and sharing a life was fraught with pitfalls that guaranteed pain. Whether it was sudden and passionate, tender and gentle, or based on the solid bedrock of respect and mutual liking learned through the years, love was an indefinable emotion that crept up and took root in the heart, often when you were not looking for it and least expected it.

Love bloomed indiscriminately and for reasons no one understood, often striking two people who were totally unsuited or were in disparate places in their lives — like Caleb and Abby.

It was near impossible to imagine two people less likely to suit, yet despite that, and despite not knowing it at the time, they had each seen something in the other they needed to be whole.

She began to think it was the same with her and Gabe, and yet she had almost let her stubborn pride and resentment blind her to the truth. She would make no excuses for him or herself or their past. The truth was that even back then she'd recognized something in him that she lacked and yearned to possess.

He was interested in almost everything and she was single-minded. He was curious and she was cautious. He was spontaneous; she was structured.

Yet she'd been drawn to something else about him. She sensed there was a hunger gnawing at him, but she had not been able to pinpoint what it was. Only in the past few weeks had she realized that his happy-go-lucky persona was nothing but a veneer to hide his loneliness, and his years of defying convention had been a quest for some indefinable something to fill the void in his life and his heart.

An emptiness left by a dearth of love.

Lying immobile, trying to keep the noise of her crying as quiet as possible, her aching heart threatened to break as she tried to imagine what it must have been like to grow up with Lucas Gentry as a father in a house that was not a home. With no one to comfort, to encourage, to love. She could not reconcile the image with her own loving upbringing.

She imagined what it must have been like to grow to young adulthood with Lucas setting the standard. There had been no one to teach Gabe and Caleb decent values, respect for women or the difference between love and desire. That he would grow up to be a scoundrel was not so surprising. The surprise was that he'd grown up to be decent in spite of his upbringing . . . or lack of it. Libby's goodness and integrity surely ran through his veins.

Rachel could almost imagine Gabe's thoughts as he wandered aimlessly over the country seeking the next city, the next amusement, the next woman. Maybe *here* would be the place, *this* would be the diversion, *she* would be the woman, only to realize that they were not.

She was positive of one thing now. He was not the same man she'd fallen for nine years ago. She couldn't imagine that Gabe throwing himself between a bullet and a woman who had wronged him so badly. This Gabe had made great strides in becoming a different person. This Gabe was a man she could love and trust, and yet it had taken the prospect of losing him to make her realize it.

If he did die — and that still was not outside the realm of possibility — he would never know she loved him or that she would say yes if he did ask her to marry him. Faced with the possibility of losing him, she was certain she wanted nothing more than to spend the rest of her life with him, teaching and showing him all about the love he'd never known.

She would let him teach her about the things she lacked and so desperately needed — like spontaneity and seeing the unexpected humor in the commonplace and what it was that made him so fascinated with so many areas of life. She wanted to wade in the creek, to fly kites, to go off for a weekend without a plan. . . .

She prayed, asking God to spare Gabe, for her sake and Danny's. Prayed for another chance to get things right. Even knowing that her requests might not be answered in the way she wished, when she whispered "Amen" she was at peace.

She had done everything in her power to restore him to health. He was fine for the moment. It was enough. Like Libby, Rachel believed that God indeed had had a plan when He brought them all together again. They would just have to wait to see what it was.

The following morning dawned sunny and full of promise. Gabe had slept soundly through the night. If he was able, she would have him sit up today.

After a quick breakfast and a single cup of coffee, she left her father in charge of the patient and headed across town to see how Sarah was doing. She hoped the woman was enough recovered to tell her exactly what had happened.

She found Sheriff Garrett there with the same goal in mind. They exchanged smiles and greetings.

Sarah was propped up in bed and was having a light breakfast, though she said she wasn't the least bit hungry. She was still groggy from the laudanum and had trouble keeping her thoughts corralled, but she managed to give a reasonable account of

344

what had happened on the Antoine road.

"I'd gone out to the Allen place to take Nita some supplies. She's been having a hard time of it since Yancy was killed."

Nita was an Indian who, to the consternation of many in town, had married an Irish logger some thirty-three years before. Not only had they held it against her, they'd looked down on her son, until he'd left to make his own way in the world.

"The boy is back from prison now, you know," Sarah said. "Though someone well over thirty isn't a boy, is he? He's quite a menacing-looking individual," she said with a shudder. "Big and mean looking. He never said a word or cracked a smile while I was there. Nita said he —"

"Begging your pardon, Sarah, but can you tell us what happened to you and Gabe yesterday evening?" Colt asked, sensing that a gossip session was about to begin. "You said you'd taken them some supplies."

"Yes, just basic things. It's our Christian duty to help others, you know, even if they are savages."

Colt's mouth tightened. "Right. So what happened on your way home?"

"These two masked ruffians ambushed me! They came riding out of the woods and forced me to pull over. Then one of them

345

dragged me from the buggy and ripped off my earrings. Thank the good Lord my ears aren't pierced," she exclaimed. "Ears bleed a lot, don't they, Rachel?"

Not waiting for her to answer, Sarah forged ahead. "About the time they demanded my reticule and other valuables, Gabe came along and told me to give them what they wanted. Well, I told him, told the others, too, that I had no intention of handing anything over. I like my jewelry, and Randolph worked hard to buy it for me. You understand, don't you, Rachel? How a woman feels about her pretties?"

"Of course," she replied, eager for Sarah to move along with the story. She was more than a bit amazed by Sarah's tenacity and willingness to fight.

"Gabe and the other man wrestled around and his bandanna fell down, but I didn't recognize him. I was trying to scratch out the other hooligan's eyes, and he lost his mask, too. You can't imagine how shocked I was to see that it was that no-good Thomerson scoundrel."

"So it *was* Meg's husband?" Rachel asked, forgetting that she was not the one asking the questions.

"I told you that last night," Sarah complained. "You should pay better attention.

At any rate, one of them said that we'd seen their faces. The other one pulled his gun, and I could see by the cold meanness in his eyes that he had every intention of using it. He swung it toward me and told Gabe to stay back. I flung myself into the gully, figuring any harm that might come of it would be better than being shot. As I was going over the edge, Gabe threw himself between me and Thomerson.

"He could have been killed," she said, dabbing at her eyes with a snowy-white napkin, "but he stepped between me and those bullets."

The sheriff and Rachel looked at each other, shocked by the display of emotion. Maybe Sarah had a heart after all.

Colt asked her a few more questions and said if he needed to know anything more, he'd come back when she was feeling better.

After he left, Rachel examined Sarah from head to toe. Satisfied that she, too, was doing well and cautioning her to stay in bed for the remainder of the day, Rachel promised to be back before supper and headed to Ellie's.

She stepped into the cozy café with its cheerful yellow gingham curtains and blue crockery displayed on the shelves. The air was redolent with the mingled scents of frying ham and fresh-brewed coffee, teasing her taste buds even though she'd eaten with her father.

She was surprised to see Win sitting at a table near the window. Ellie was nowhere to be seen, probably in the kitchen. Bethany was standing at the pass-through to the kitchen, waiting for an order. Her hair, strawberry blond instead of dark auburn like her mother's, rippled down her back in loose waves. She turned and recognized Rachel. The smile that bloomed on her face shone in her slanted brown eyes.

"Coffee, Miss Doctor Rachel?"

Her words were not enunciated clearly because of the extra length of her tongue, but you could still understand what she was saying.

"That's right, Beth. And will you add some of that condensed milk if you have it?"

"Yes, ma'am."

Rachel took the seat across from Win. "Eating alone?"

"Everyone else was still asleep, and I needed my coffee," he told her with that easy smile of his. "Of course, the ham smelled so good I decided on breakfast, too. May I buy you some?"

"Thank you, but I ate with Dad."

"How's Gabe?"

"He had a good night. Everything seems fine this morning. I don't suppose you know if your mother rested or not."

"No. Have you found out anything else?"

"Sheriff Garrett was at Sarah's when I went to check on her."

Bethany arrived with the coffee and set it down carefully. "Thank you," Rachel said, smiling at the young girl. "You look very pretty in that blue dress."

"Thank you, Miss Doctor Rachel." She turned to go back to wait for the order.

"What a shame," Win said, watching her go. "If it weren't for the Mongolism, she'd be a beautiful child."

Rachel speared him with a disapproving look. "She's a beautiful child just as she is," she informed him in a tart tone. "And actually very smart in her own way."

"Forgive me," he said, seeing that he had ruffled Rachel's feathers. "I mean no disrespect, merely that it is a sadness."

"I'm sure you didn't, but please don't waste any time on pity. Neither Bethany nor Ellie would appreciate it, I can assure you."

Ellie chose that moment to step through the swinging door, Win's breakfast in her hands. His relief was palpable. Instead of handing it to her daughter, she said, "Will you please bring that little bowl with Mr. Granville's gravy, Beth?"

"Yes, Mama."

The smile Ellie bestowed on her daughter lingered as she turned back to Win. "Here you go," she said, setting down the plate filled with fried ham, biscuits and three eggs over easy.

Win looked at the spread with combined pleasure and dismay. "You wouldn't want to marry me, would you?" he asked, his tawny-brown eyes gleaming with that wicked, teasing twinkle.

Ellie's face flooded with color, and Rachel thought she saw a bit of panic in her brown eyes. Though she could hold her own with the old-timers who often tormented her about one ridiculous thing or another, she was unaccustomed to casual banter from handsome strangers. Certainly the upright sheriff didn't tease this way. He was far too serious.

Quick to recognize that he'd overstepped some invisible boundary, Win held up a hand to stay whatever she was about to say. "Forget I asked," he quipped with another of those ready grins. "You'd be the death of me."

"I beg your pardon," Ellie said with a frown.

"I'd weigh a ton if I ate like this every day," he told her with a rueful smile. "Die of a heart attack."

The tension in Ellie's shoulders eased, and she turned her attention to Rachel in an attempt to take the conversation another direction. "What did you find out from Sarah? I know Colt went out with a posse, but no one has heard who they're looking for yet."

"Elton Thomerson," Rachel said and proceeded to recount Sarah's tale.

"Too bad Colt didn't get the information last night. He might have been able to arrest him before he left the country," Ellie said.

She was right, but there was no way Sarah would have been coherent enough to tell her story the night before. "Whether he's picked up and tossed into prison or took off for parts unknown, Meg will be left to fend for herself," Rachel said.

They discussed Meg's situation for a few more minutes. Rachel told them that Nita Allen's son, Ace, was out of prison, and Win informed them that they planned to stay in Wolf Creek at least another week to monitor Gabe's progress. Eventually, the conversation returned to the robbery and Sarah's tearful championing of Gabe.

"So Gabe took a bullet for her," Win said, spearing up another bite of ham.

"That's what she said."

Three more customers came in, taking Ellie away from their benign gossip session. Rachel left Win to finish his breakfast and went back home to see about Gabe and tell her father what she'd learned about the robbery.

Consciousness returned with a stomach-churning wave of pain. Gabe gave a groan and tried to sit up, which only cranked up the anguish a notch. His hands went to his head, though it seemed as if he were moving them through molasses.

Immediately, he felt cool fingers wrap around his wrists to force them back to his sides. He opened his eyes and saw Rachel standing there. She placed the back of her hand against his forehead and then his cheek.

"Do you know who I am?"

He frowned. "What kind of stupid question is that?" he asked, feeling as if he were speaking around a mouth full of cotton wool.

Her lips twitched as she fought to suppress a smile.

"Do you know who you are?"

He squinted in irritation and pain. "A better question might be who are you and what did you do with the mother of my son?" he mumbled somewhat testily.

Joy bubbled through her. Thank God there didn't seem to be any damage to the brain. He would be fine if they could keep the infection and fever away. She did laugh then. His dry sense of humor was one of the things she loved about him.

"What's so funny?"

"You are."

He scowled. "May I have some water, please? My mouth feels like I've walked ten miles through the desert."

"Just a little," she said, pouring an inch into a cup. "If you think your head hurts now, you don't want to find out how it would feel if you start vomiting."

"What's wrong with me this time?" he asked.

She explained his injuries as she slipped her arm beneath his shoulders and eased him upright while he pushed against the mattress. She held the cup to his lips and he sipped slowly, savoring every drop. "Thank you."

"Do you feel like being propped up

awhile? I'm going to give you something for the pain."

"Maybe for a while," he said. "But no pain medication."

"We've been through this before, Gabriel," she said in a firm tone as she placed a couple more pillows behind his upper torso. He groaned and grumbled the whole time she eased him to a sitting position.

She crossed her arms over her chest. "I rest my case. Just let me give you enough to take off the edge during the day and help you sleep through the night. Please."

"You're a tyrant."

"And you're a hardhead. You'll heal better if we can stay on top of the pain," she wheedled.

"Fine," he said, his face gray with agony. "I do feel like I've been rowed up Salt River."

She measured a small amount of laudanum. "Well, you *were* in a fistfight, besides being shot. Can you tell me what happened?"

"Rachel. Is there any possibility that you've been in Pete Chalmers's hard cider?"

"Humor me."

"Sarah was being robbed. I went to help. The guy, someone I should know but don't remember, was going to shoot her, and I tried to stop him, so it seems I was the one who got shot."

"Very good," she said, giving him an irritating, patronizing pat on the hand. She wet a cloth with cool water and began to bathe the perspiration from his face.

"Is Sarah all right?" he asked.

"It seems she bailed off into the ravine while you took the bullets. She has a sprained ankle."

"She's lucky she didn't break her neck. I remember her trying to help me stand up and us leaning against each other as we hobbled to the surrey. She was crying and saying that I would *not* die. That she might have been responsible for my misery, but she absolutely refused to be responsible for my death."

"That sounds like Sarah," Rachel said, putting the washcloth back into the basin of water. "Now go to sleep."

"Are you going to be this bossy when we get married?" he grumbled.

"Probably."

At the end of a week, Gabe was still suffering from headaches, but he was feeling well enough to sit out on the front porch with her father or Danny and enjoy the late-spring breeze. Thankfully, there had been

355

no sign of infection. Rachel credited it to her thorough cleaning of the wounds.

Sunday afternoon found him sitting with his eyes closed, and his head leaned against the tall back of a rocking chair while Danny played a game of checkers with Ben. Caleb and his family and all the Granvilles were there. They had shared a final meal together before Pip and the others headed back to Boston. Rachel knew his interaction with the company had tired him, but he refused to rest since it was their last time together for several months.

A desultory breeze tickled the leaves of the rosebushes and sent the yellow heads of the coreopsis bouncing to an unheard rhythm. Stomachs filled, eyelids heavy, the conversation was as aimless as the gentle wind drifting over them.

Rachel couldn't recall when she'd felt so at peace. After she had foolishly replied to Gabe's question about marriage with a facetious answer that could only be construed as a "yes," she'd been waiting for him to bring up the subject again. So far, he'd said nothing. She wasn't certain whether to be disappointed or relieved.

Though it was almost every woman's dream to find the right man and marry, the thought of committing to a lifetime with someone raised all sorts of worrisome questions for a woman set in her ways. She wondered where they would live and if Gabe would tire of her racing off into the night at the beck and call of the people in town. Would he really be happy in Wolf Creek, and perhaps most importantly, would he want to have more children? He doted on Danny, but what would he be like as they traveled through the ups and downs of a pregnancy together?

Wonderful.

Somehow she knew that as well as she knew her own name. She was lost in thoughts of a little girl who looked a lot like Danny when she saw a surrey headed toward them, trailing a cloud of dust.

"That's Sarah's rig," Edward said. And indeed it was. Her husband, Randolph, who everyone thought deserved far better than what he had for a wife, was driving.

"What on earth can she possibly want?" Libby said. "Hasn't she caused enough trouble?"

They didn't have to wait long to find out. Randolph pulled to a stop near the rose-laden arch, helped his wife down from the buggy and handed her a set of crutches.

"Hello there, Randolph," Edward said. "Come and join us. We have a couple of

357

extra chairs."

So far, Sarah had not said a word or made eye contact with anyone. All her attention was focused on maneuvering the stone pathway.

"Thank you, Edward," Randolph said. "It's a lovely afternoon, isn't it?"

"Indeed it is."

Sensing that the adults might not want children present, Blythe took it upon herself to herd them into the house for a lemonade while Sarah hobbled up the steps and sat down next to Rachel.

"I'll wait in the buggy," Randolph said.

"Thank you, my dear," she replied with a smile of genuine gratitude. "And thank you for understanding."

He nodded and strode out toward the road.

"I'm so glad you're all here," she said. "It will make this easier."

Her gaze moved around the group, all people whose lives she had complicated with her unbridled tongue. "That ordeal last week opened my eyes to a lot of things," she said, jumping right into the subject. "Staring down the barrel of a Colt puts things into perspective really fast. I realized in that moment that I have been a Christian in name only. Oh, I've spouted scripture with the best of them and helped the needy, but it was all more something to do than something I really felt in my heart. It will take some time, but I mean to change that."

She inhaled deeply, as if she were fortifying herself for a battle. "The first thing I wanted to do was to come and thank you, Gabriel." Her voice quavered with emotion, and there was no hint of her usual smug superiority. "If you hadn't come along when you did, I might have been found in that ravine dead."

"No need to thank me, Sarah," Gabe told her. "Anyone would have done the same."

"If you believe that, you're more naive than I've been led to believe," she said with a touch of asperity. Again, she let her gaze rove around the gathering. Her eyes were overbright.

"I have hurt all of you deeply by spreading rumors and gossiping and stirring up all sorts of trouble. A lot of folks in this town who'd been treated like that would have just driven by without so much as a fare-thee-well. And I honestly can't say I'd blame them."

"Maybe you aren't giving the people in town enough credit," Abby said. "Yes, you have hurt all of us, but everything has come to rights, and I feel that I speak for us all when I say that we've forgiven you." She gave Caleb a sharp look.

He nodded.

"Gabe? Edward? Rachel?" Sarah queried and received three nods in tandem.

"Well, Elisabeth," Sarah said, pinning Libby with a pointed look. "What about you? Can you forgive me for . . . Lucas?

Libby was silent for long moments. Finally, she looked at Sarah. "Knowing you weren't the only one, Sarah, makes it easier. Certainly I can. While no one wants a marriage to break up for any reason, and I was devastated when mine did, I'm certain I was much happier with Sam than I ever could have been with Lucas. Forgiving you for your part in my losing my boys will be harder, but with God's help, I'll manage that, too, in time."

"Thank you. I don't deserve it, but thank you all." Tears spilled down Sarah's cheeks. She grabbed her crutches and heaved herself to her feet.

Rachel's eyes felt prickly, as well. As furious as she'd been at the woman, as much as she had detested Sarah's behavior, she felt a sudden sorrow and even pity. She hoped that Sarah had truly repented for her wrongs and would turn her life around.

At the bottom of the steps, she turned and

looked from Gabe to Rachel and back to Gabe. When she spoke, there was a hint of the old Sarah in her tone. "No doubt you'll think me pushy when I say this, Gabriel, but you really should marry Rachel. That boy of yours needs the security of knowing both his parents are together."

Gabe turned to look at Rachel, but his words were directed to Sarah. "For once, I think you're exactly right, Sarah." One corner of his mouth lifted in a teasing half smile. "In fact, she's already said yes — more or less."

"I don't recall your asking me to marry you," Rachel denied. "I believe you asked me if I would be so bossy when we were married."

"And you said 'yes.' "

"I said 'probably,' " she countered. "I didn't think you knew what you were saying since you were under the influence of a painkiller at the time."

"I knew, and I meant it."

Smiling, Rachel leaned toward him and whispered, "So did I."

And then she kissed him, the imperfect man who had stolen her heart. Danny's prodigal father, finally come to a place filled with love. Home.

QUESTIONS FOR DISCUSSION

1. Have you ever known anyone like Sarah VanSickle? Why do you think she got so much pleasure from seeing other people miserable?

2. When people in Wolf Creek found out Rachel had a child out of wedlock, many were quick to judge and condemn her. Christians should hate sin, but how should they treat the sinner?

3. Lucas Gentry's treatment of his sons and the belief that their mother abandoned them played a major role in the kind of men Caleb and Gabe became. Do you believe the influence we have on our children is important to their social, emotional and spiritual welfare? Should we be more aware of that influence?

4. Lucas refused to let Libby take the boys

with her when he forced her to leave Wolf Creek. Do you know divorced people who use the children to hurt and punish the other? Why? Who is really hurt in the end?

5. Rachel blamed Gabe for what happened between them in St. Louis. Have you ever done something wrong and tried to justify your actions by saying it wasn't really your fault and placing the blame elsewhere? Did you truly believe it, or were you trying to ease your own guilt?

6. Rachel was very bitter after Gabe left her. Were her feelings justified?

7. Rachel harbored ill feelings toward Gabe, but she didn't try to poison Danny's mind with name-calling and blame-placing. Was this the right thing to do?

8. Being robbed helped Sarah to see the error of her ways. Have you ever known it to take a major disaster to make someone realize the sin in their life?

9. Gabe left Wolf Creek seeking new experiences, many of them bad, hoping to fill the emptiness in his heart. Have you known people who have tried to fill their

emptiness with getting ahead, seeking power, becoming shopaholics or worse — alcoholics and druggies? What would it take to fill that empty place?

10. Gabe had never known any woman like Rachel. Have you ever known a person whose life was changed because of the love and concern of another?

ABOUT THE AUTHOR

Penny Richards has been writing and selling contemporary romance since 1983. Confronted with burnout, she took several years off to pursue other things she loved, like editing a local oral history project and coauthoring a stage play about a dead man (known fondly as Old Mike) who was found in the city park in 1911, got a double dose of embalming and remained on display until the seventies. Really. She also spent ten years renovating her 1902 Queen Anne home and getting it onto the National Register of Historic Places. At the "big house" she ran and operated Garden Getaways, a bed-and-breakfast and catering business that did everything from receptions, bridal lunches, fancy private dinners and "tastings" to dress-up tea parties (with makeup and all the trimmings) for little girls who liked to pretend to be grand ladies while receiving manners lessons. What fun!

Though she had a wonderful time and hosted people from every walk of life, writing was still in her blood, and her love of all things historical led her to historical fiction, more specifically historical mystery and inspirational romances. She is thrilled to be back writing and, God willing, hopes to continue to do so for many years.